Urban Limit

By Steve Zell

Tales From Zell, Inc. ™
Portland, Oregon

ISBN-10: 0-9847468-4-6

ISBN-13: 978-0-9847468-4-2

Second edition: June 2017

10 9 8 7 6 5 4 3 2

Edited by: Leigh Anne Beresford
Artwork: Urban Limit© 2016 by Steven J. Pitzel

Acknowledgements

Thank you to my wife, Nina, and to our daughter Victoria. In some ways writing a novel is like bringing a new baby into the family, one way or another every family member plays a part.

Very special thanks to my cousin, Leigh Anne. It's a lucky man who has both a great family and truly great friends; and in LAB (my internal acronym for her edits) I am blessed to have both rolled up into one! Thanks for being steadfast in showing me my goof-ups and possible pitfalls while editing this book – and for still being my good friend and family when I went ahead and ran with some of that stuff anyway...

Urban Limit

Chapter 1

How the hell did I get here?

Ken Carroll pressed his back into the ergo dynamic leather chair in his glass-walled 5th floor office and pushed himself back from the walnut desk, also ergo dynamic with 50-some touch-adjustable levels. The brass bar on that desk read "Solutions Marketing Director." *Solutions marketing director with a sure shot at VP.*

Solutions marketing director heading out to a well-deserved four month sabbatical. Beyond the glass wall, the oak and ash of Portland had just begun their turn toward fall.

You got here by running away. That was the irony.

Five days before his last semester in Eugene had ended, Ken Carroll collected his books, papers, and brushes, and walked out of class. It had been a gesture, no more than that. Ken would graduate with honors nevertheless.

At that point, he'd already been six years at the University of Oregon. The extra two years had nothing to do with his work ethic; the one thing Ken Carroll had never been able to do was choose *that one thing* he *should* do. He enjoyed engineering; he enjoyed creating art. *He loved making music.*

That had forced him to change majors twice. Those changes had cost him two extra years. And five days before his last term ended, Ken's patience had ended as well. Post-graduate work wasn't in the cards.

Two years on the road and five rock bands later, Ken Carroll came to realize making a living in music wasn't in the cards either.   If he wanted to play, he'd have to pay.

So, BFA degree in hand he'd taken the first well-paying, halfway interesting job that came his way - junior technical marketing engineer for Portland Micro, a booming computer chip maker. One year later, he married.

Seventeen years later, here he was.

Portland Micro provided three weeks of paid vacation every year, four after ten. That sounded fair enough at the time, but what he eventually came to realize was what his new job *didn't* provide was an actual opportunity to take those vacations; but he was already on that treadmill. He slaved his way up the chain to director, and VP was in sight. Seventeen years straight, a long, wide, river of press releases, PowerPoint presentations, and tradeshows interrupted by nothing more than his daughter's weekend sporting events, and an occasional day-trip to the mountains.

Until now.

After seventeen years of service you not only earned a sabbatical at Portland Micro, you were *forced* to take it; no ifs, ands, or buts. Four months paid vacation - the company's grudging admission that even the most dedicated employees burned out eventually, and an incentive against early retirement, which could come as early as fifteen years.

With sixteen weeks of free-time ahead of him and seventeen years of hard work behind him, Ken Carroll had indeed paid enough to play.

The long, concrete span of the Fremont Bridge curved just north of the office. From here he could see a smoking stall backing traffic miles back on the I-5.

He wouldn't miss the city traffic, he wouldn't miss any of this, just like he hadn't missed sitting through those final sessions in Eugene.

"Hey, short-timer." Tom Driscoll, current VP and Ken's direct report, let a thin smile slice his broad, eternally red face. Thirty years at Portland Micro, the writing was on the wall; Driscoll would not be hanging around for his second sabbatical. Not for the first time over the past year, Ken felt that sinking in his gut that only terrible timing brings.

You're gone for four months...and Driscoll's last day could be tomorrow.

But there was nothing he could do.

Two offices down, the shades were shut tight in Mickey DiMario's office. They had been all morning. The software marketing director wasn't in this morning. Likely a bender last night. More than likely, he had little desire to wish his "good friend" and biggest competition for VP a happy sabbatical.

"Ken?"

"Mickey has everything he needs from MicroTools, right? It's his deal."

"Whaddayou care? You're outta here."

"You know me, Tom – I'm all about caring."

"If you really like the place that much – I might be able to slide your sabbatical out a year. You could stick around and hold his hand."

Ken slid his laptop into its case. He zipped the case crisply as he stood and shook his boss's hand.

"Not a chance."

-=-.=-.=-.=-.=-.=-.=-.=-.=-.=-.=-.=-

Ken whistled as he wove the black Yukon Denali down Macadam Boulevard toward Lake Oswego. Whistling was one thing he wasn't particularly good at - especially through the wide grin that hadn't left his face since he'd left the building.

Hell, he could *learn* how to whistle. *He could learn anything he wanted. Plenty of free time ahead. Free time? What was that even like?*

Maybe he'd work on his skiing skills - give Kristi a run for her money.

Fat chance of that.

His daughter was so damn good at skiing, so utterly fearless she was scary. Scary good at everything. If Ken had the "jack-of-all-trades" gene whatever it was that spliced in from Mandy's DNA had shot it full of steroids. Kristi was Master of All.

Right on cue, Kristi's theme - the opening percussive salvo from a song he didn't know, from a band he didn't know blasted over the Denali's speakers. Not for the first time, it struck him just how passé, just how far behind he'd fallen in one of the greatest pursuits of his life.

"Hi Kiss-Kiss," he answered, her childhood nickname slipping out before he could stop himself. The hands free unit automatically dropped the discouraging traffic reports to the background; brought Kristi's constant, no-nonsense voice into crystal focus.

"Hi Daddy – I'm glad *you're* in a good mood."

"What's up?"

"Home-school packets aren't here. Mom's freaking out."

"Tell her its okay."

"She says she doesn't trust the postal workers in Cedar."

"Tell her I talked to the school Superintendent this morning, she said it's not a big deal." From somewhere in the background, Mandy's voice, *"tell your father…"*

"Kiss – put your Mom on."

"Mom!"

The metallic cacophony of frantic movement in the background; a crash of metal - most likely a drawer of silverware.

"What's going on over there?"

"I'm not freaking out."

"Hi, Hon."

"We need those school packets. We have to sign off -
"

"Mandy, we're all set. I talked to the Superintendent today. We're signed. We're good. Anything we might've missed is online."

"You're sure?"

"Come on, Hon. Everything's online these days."

"I'd rather have the hard copies here in my hands."

"It's a paperless world, hon."

"I feel like we've missed something."

"We haven't missed anything. It's all covered, trust me. "

"Have you passed TJ's? We could use a few things."

He hadn't moved fifty feet in the last five minutes. Trader Joe's market was six blocks away.

"Not yet. I'm sort of treading water here. What do we need?"

"French Roast. That creamer you like. A case of Bare Foot – the cab, not the pinot. And five rib-eye steaks."

"Steaks? They even have those at TJ's? Geez - anything else?"

One hour later, Ken pulled onto their cul-de-sac six blocks from the shores of Lake Oswego. They had wanted a house on the water more than anything. Seventeen years and several promotions later, six blocks was as close as they'd gotten to get to that prized lakefront.

The Lake just kept getting more expensive. The entire Portland Metro area was that way now. And it wasn't that their house was small, it was the land it was built on. Their backyard was essentially a cedar deck with a hot tub. Urban Growth Limits. Portland wanted to keep the forest and farmland free of pesky humans. The result was certainly less urban sprawl, but the population density was fast approaching unbearable. Developers snapped up five-acre lots to shoehorn in dozens of tall-skinny townhouses or buzzing low-rent apartment hives. Parking was non-existent, roads were crowded, and city planners and road crews moved like molasses. Widening a street was like adding a new bust to Rushmore.

The result: in the last ten years a small-town paradise peopled by decent folk with Mayberry-like manners, had turned into a mean little territorial battleground. Etiquette on the packed surface streets had taken that inevitable slide toward the nasty, middle-fingered meanness of Los Angeles.

You had to move out of cities, *way out*, to find a respectable piece of acreage and breathing space these days.

But they'd found everything they needed on Cedar Mountain, their own five acres of pristine forest bordered by even more pristine forest. A wide, trout-filled creek ran right through the property. And sitting high on a bluff overlooking the mountainside was their dream house, a beautiful, technological marvel, filled with everything Portland Micro built and more.

Sure there were drawbacks. The nearest town was a harrowing trek over five miles of winding logging road. But that's what the restaurant-sized Viking freezer was for, the walk-in pantry big as their Lake Oswego master bedroom. The power and water hookups had cost a small fortune – and they'd be on septic tanks for at least a year, but the reception from their satellite dish was clear as a bell, complete with high-speed, high-definition broadband and every channel known to man. A nearby cell tower ensured dropout-free wireless service.

They were set.

More cars than ever were sardined inside their cul-de-sac tonight. Ken shook his head as he squeezed his over-sized car up his undersized driveway.

No. I will not miss this. Not at all.

Ken piled two bags of groceries on top of the case of wine and hefted it most of the way through the kitchen door before it struck him things were way too quiet in the Carroll household.

"Happy Sabbatical!"

"Sweet Jesus!" He nearly dropped the load. The back slaps didn't help.

Half the neighborhood, an accumulation of fencing/softball/volleyball/ski mom and dad friends made through years of Kristi's sports, and the four coworkers Ken really cared about – they were *all* there.

Okay, so maybe there were some things he *might* miss.

Two hours later, Ken was sitting on his deck under the stars, feeling fat, dumb and happy with rich food and wine from a party at his house he didn't even have to host. He gazed through the bare windows at walls stripped of photos, books, and nick-knacks, and wondered if this house had ever truly been theirs.

Amanda was still making the rounds. Her lithe silhouette resembled the Femlin's from those Playboy magazines Ken had secreted under his bed as a kid. She'd had the boobs enhanced after the twins were born – all other enhancements she owed strictly to Ashtanga Yoga. Tough to believe she was the mother of two teens. Thirty-eight and folks still confused her with Kristi.

He could see Kristi, sitting tall and confident on the living room floor, sport-sculpted face framed in thick, sun-bleached gold as she held court with sad-eyed admirers from Lake Oswego High. She would be sorely missed by the Laker athletic department this winter, and judging by the number of males in attendance, it looked like more than a few hearts had already been broken in the student body.

"Did her trophies fill an extra truck?" Mahesh had switched from Cabernet to scotch. This was his "only night of the week Hindus can drink alcohol" night. That was a standing joke – his "only night" magically changed to any night they chose to party. And the truth was he was Catholic.

"Just about. She's something else."

And she was. Where Ken had hopped impatiently from one field of study to another, in a very real way avoiding the one field he loved most, Kristi threw herself completely into everything she did. She'd lettered in four sports by the end of her sophomore year. And every one of her coaches had given her the same advice, *"quit all those other sports and focus on this one."*

He'd heard similar advice from his own professors. When it came down to it, it seemed some people were only comfortable with limitations.

"What should I do?" she'd asked him one day.

He didn't even hesitate.

"Don't give anything up. Do it all until you have a reason not to."

And when the usual girl sports; soccer, softball, volleyball, began to bore her, she'd set her sights on cross-country skiing, marksmanship, fencing - at sixteen, she was already a world-class competitor in two multi-discipline sports, the Modern Pentathlon and Winter Biathlon. The big question now was whether or not she'd choose one firmly over the other.

And then there was her twin brother...

Reed's window was lit only by the sickly blue glow from his computer display. Reed had made a perfunctory, Boo Radley-like appearance earlier in the evening before retiring to his room, most likely into his computer-generated fantasy-land - *Mythykal.*

"She is an amazing girl." Mahesh shook his head, "Amazing. And every bit as pretty as her mom."

"Yes, she is. By the way - quit looking at my wife and daughter." Ken grinned.

Mahesh raised his glass, "To beauty!" Tumblers clicked, and Mahesh swallowed deeply. "So Mickey DiMario will be guarding the hen-house now."

"Mickey's not so bad...his *reputation* is." Ken's voice didn't even convince himself. "Out of my hands."

Ken! Ken! Ken! Voices had been steadily rising from the hot tub. The loudest voice belonged to Frank Bennett, their next-door neighbor, his snow-white, tree-trunk legs pouring shapelessly from Hawaiian print shorts, disappearing into the steam and bubbles below.

Ken wiped his lips with the back of his hand; raised his glass to his waterlogged friends.

"Keep an eye on him for me, okay?"

"Always, my friend. Whatever you need."

The sliding door opened to the steamy aroma of chlorine, sweat and bourbon.

"What do you think of that Joint Task Force thing? Lot of right-wing hooey right?"

"I have no idea what that is, Frank."

"It's Big Brother looking down on Portland. We said, "No!" to the feds a few years back. But it looks like the Portland cops are caving now. A few pumped-up workplace violence incidents and everybody thinks ISIS is planting IEDs in our driveways."

"That sounds suspiciously like politics. Not interested. *Go Ducks!*" He raised his glass to his alma mater.

"*Go Beavs!*" Frank raised his own glass.

"Now *that* is something worth fighting about."

Ken's parents had stressed that one never talk religion or politics with friends one wanted to keep, and that advice had stuck. Friends were more important than theology and politics. He'd spent most of his life in Oregon and few of his friends knew whether Ken was a Democrat or a Republican. He prided himself in that.

Jesse headed the Neighborhood Watch – a good guy – but probably the king of *Right-Wing Hooey* in these ultra-liberal parts. He had a silver goatee, and the wavy wet hair on his head had twisted up into what looked like horns.

"We have to live in the post-911 world." Jesse said.

"Frank, Jesse says you need to live in the post-911 world," Ken said. "Did that help?"

"You laugh" Jesse held back a belch, "but you hear what's going on now? They're disarming us. You can't have a gun if you collect Social Security. And once they've got our guns - the Feds are going to grade neighborhoods for *whiteness*, for...*w*hat is that crap word? *Diversity.* You don't have the right frickin' *diversity* they're gonna buy up the house next to you with your taxes and move Muslims in. Allah says, d*eath to you, neighbor!*"

"You must hate black people," Frank said. "You were probably happy that PETA killed all those poor black people in New Orleans."

"I think you mean FEMA," Jesse corrected.

"Whatever, FEMA - they knew all about those shitty, crumbling levees – didn't matter to those white boys in Homeland *In*security that all those poor black children died."

Ken nearly took the opportunity to remind Frank and the others of lily-white Lake Oswego's notorious nickname, but in the end he simply raised his glass in a final toast.

"To my nutcase, over-politicized friends. *Love* the absolutely thrilling conversation – but I have a sabbatical to think about. *To sabbaticals! The longer the better!*"

"I'll drink to that," Frank said. *"You lucky bastard."*

-=-.=-.=-.=-.=-.=-.=-.=-.=-

"Phone on. Tom Driscoll."

"Aren't you on sabbatical?" Amanda glared, arms folded.

Ken bit his lip. The road was narrow, winding, beginning that steep climb toward Cedar.

"Phone on," Ken commanded the hands-free unit again. Nora Jones voice dropped, the hands-free unit sputtered, Maria's voice, Tom Driscoll's Admin.

"Ken?"

Static. Then Nora Jones' voice came back in loud and clear.

"Phone on!" Nora Jones slipped quietly away, static came in loud and clear.

"Maria, where's Tom?"

"Sabbatical," Amanda reminded him, firmly.

Driscoll's text had been short, only two words: *MicroTools situation?*

Situation? What situation? The deal was done. It wasn't even Ken's deal.

"Phone off!" Kristi commanded firmly from the middle seats.

She replaced her iPod's ear bud, her smile wide in the rearview mirror. Sitting behind her Reed looked more like Andy Warhol's spawn than Ken's. His newly bleached white hair hung slack over black sunglasses as he stared out the window. His sallow cheeks weren't far in hue from the new hair color. Reed hadn't said a word since they'd turned onto the Interstate. *He could be car sick* – Ken was sure he wouldn't last five minutes in that cramped back seat himself.

Situation?

"Phone on, Tom Driscoll" Ken said. "This might be important."

"Not to you, not now," Amanda said. "It's Portland Micro's problem."

"Phone on! The phone should work better than this. I know there's a cell-tower not too far from here."

Ken craned his neck, eyes straining through the darkly tinted windshield to pick metal from forest, as though he really might see the cell tower through the thick stand of cedar, through the sheer rock walls of the mountain.

"Try your iPhone, Hon."

"What – to call your work?"

"Call anyone. Call your Mom. I just want to see if it works."

Amanda sighed, dug through the recesses of her Louis Vuitton.

Finally, she said. "Out of coverage."

-=-.=-.=-.=-.=-.=-.=-.=-.=-

Kristi watched the forest open grudgingly onto the *mighty metropolis of Cedar.*

The first real clue a town was approaching was a broken down service station with one of those ancient gas pumps, the kind with the big round top and the narrow, slope-shouldered frame, the nozzle holstered like some cartoon-cowboy sidearm.

Then, one by one, log cabins appeared through the evergreen, then a hotel built from dovetailed cedar logs held together by some sort of yellowish goo. The Bait Shop was next. It sported so much moss and lichen on its roof it seemed the forest had reclaimed the shack outright.

This berg was what had uprooted her from school and friends, homecoming – maybe even the senior prom. It wasn't like she'd been queen of the scene at school. She knew she was popular, she was pretty and her Olympic aspirations had already made her a home-town hero; but those same aspirations had mostly eclipsed her social life.

The chalet-style *Shoe and Ski* revealed the main attraction of these parts – certainly the main attraction for Kristi – weaving through thick stands of trees, mere needle-strewn paths now, but very soon snow-carpeted roads to heaven - some of the sweetest cross-country skiing trails in Oregon.

"Now we're talking."

Outside of fencing, Cross-Country was Kristi's favorite, though not nearly her best, event. The move to Cedar was her opportunity to hone that particular skill to razor sharpness – free from coaches, free from catty schoolgirl games, and best of all - free from the shallow (if not entirely unwelcome) attentions of boys.

Just past the Shoe and Ski stood the *primo* eatery and watering hole of Cedar – the rustic Cedar Creek Tavern.

Dad eased the big SUV onto the narrow patch of gravel and cinders that made up the Tavern's parking lot.

Kristi stretched her long legs – and, immediately behind her, Reed did the same – kicking her seat-back with purpose as he did.

"Why do we have to stop at this bunghole?"

The comment didn't require an answer, so Kristi didn't offer one as she hopped out, just happy to breathe the sweet mountain air and feel the crunch of cinders and gravel beneath her feet.

Dad seemed to have finally (if only temporarily) given into his total loss of connection with work. The smile on his face was a stark contrast to the scowling wooden Indian

standing guard at the Tavern door beside him. Kristi
wondered that such a thing as a wooden Indian could even
exist in Politically Correct Oregon. *Certainly not in Lake Oswego
or Portland.*

On the other hand, Mom's face was unreadable. She'd
donned her sunglasses the second the car stopped; she would
remove them moments later, once seated comfortably inside.
It was one of those bizarre rituals Mom had.

Reed slouched along beside Kristi; loudly scuffing his
heavy black boots up the log steps to the door.

The smells of sawdust, beer, and smoked meat inside
the darkened, nearly empty tavern were strong but not
unpleasant. Kristi had suffered through a period of
vegetarianism, partly for humane reasons, but mostly because
red meat had made her feel heavy and slow. She was over
that now. She needed the protein.

Two older boys sat in a booth at the far end of the
room; three fossils with beer bellies pressed the counter.
Every male eye was on her thin Hollister sweater as she
focused her own eyes on a buck's head mounted on the far
wall. The fat young waitress was sizing her up too.

"Anywhere you like," the girl said.

Mom found a booth by the window. Kristi knew
Mom would slide next to that window for the view, quickly
determine the draft from it was too cold, and then ask Dad to

change places with her. Dad would oblige her. Dad was a saint.

Kristi slid in on the *kids'* side. Reed dropped like a sack of overripe tomatoes beside her, legs turned into the aisle so the server would have to avoid his big feet. Dad would scold him.

"Honey," Mom said on cue, "it's a little drafty here."

"No problem."

They followed their established protocol. Dad gazed out the window as he slid over, that goofy smile still on his face. Kristi didn't mind it one bit, good to see Dad this happy. It had been a particularly tough year for him at work. Building the house, even with all the trouble that had been – made it bearable for him– that and her sports. He never missed a match when he wasn't traveling for work. She loved him for that – even if he did cheer with the stupid *Crack*berry plastered to his ear.

Dad wasn't an athlete – the truth was he was sort of a klutz. But that made his being there even more special somehow – a lot of her teammates' folks never showed up at all. Mom wasn't into sports, only Yoga, but she'd get there when she could.

And then there was Reed...

Kristi examined his wan face – the only real color was the red from zit clusters. She hated his badly bleached hair

with the bushy split ends, his sunken chest, and slumped
shoulders. What she wouldn't do to put him on a
conditioning program, change his diet… Reed showed up for
her events – but he usually sat high up in the stands by
himself and brooded. Half her teammates thought he was a
stalker.

Their server tripped over Reed's feet. Reed didn't
move.

"Reed?" Dad said.

Reed moved his feet in.

Kristi ordered a salad and water – the males in the
room seemed keenly interested in that order. One boy,
probably a college guy and not bad looking except for the
stupid beard, *seriously dude? Are you storing breakfast in that thing?*
– was sheepishly checking her out while feigning a deep
interest in his raised coffee mug. Kristi decided she wouldn't
be spending much time in town.

Once lunch was over and the bill was paid, she
dropped behind her family just long enough to look the other
away, smooth down her sweater and capris, and leave no
doubt that she was, in fact, ignoring the good-looking older
boy with the disgusting beard.

-=-=-=-=-=-=-=-=-

Five minutes past Cedar the mountain switchbacks went from scary to brutal; the climb so steep and the turns so sharp it seemed the road fell completely away beneath them, and nothing but thin air remained between the Denali and the rock-strewn valley floor far below.

Kristi's stomach rolled with every turn, she'd have felt so much safer on her skis. She turned up the volume on her I-Pod, Mozart helped. She closed her eyes.

When she opened them a few minutes later the sheer rock had been replaced by a deep green forest of Douglas-fir and vine maple, broken only here and there by leaf-strewn, sunlit meadows.

They reached a small wooden bridge over Cedar Creek. Deep crystal pools, and gurgling falls led up the mountain through a lush tangle of autumn color all the way through their property and beyond. Dad stopped the car halfway over the bridge, rolled the windows down, and turned the DVD player off. Kristi removed the buds from her ears.

No sound but the creak of timber beneath them; the soft babble of water. Here and there red and gold leaves fell silently to the water, floating quietly beneath them over an endless stairway of sparkling stones. Framed by the rear-view mirror even Reed's face held what Kristi could only describe as awe, and this wasn't his first time up here either. She knew what her twin was thinking.

We actually live here now. This is real.

Mom took a deep breath of sweet mountain air; her grin matched Dad's as she turned back to him, and for a moment it seemed like they would kiss - which would have been gross - their parents weren't prone to PDA – Public Displays of Affection. Thankfully, they both just chuckled softly. That was awkward, Kristi thought. But *almost* romantic.

"We did it," they said at once.

"Yeah, we actually did." And with that, her dad seemed, suddenly, ten years younger. The squint lines, the tight set of his lips and brow, had vanished.

The not-so-well-hidden truth was out, at least to Kristi. They'd rented the Lake Oswego house temporarily to a family new to Oregon, supposedly to return in four months. But that wasn't the real story behind this. The rush of the city, the constant, day-to-day pressure and politics of the job. Dad had reached his limit, Mom had finally acquiesced and quit goading him to do more, to acquire more. Dad meant to escape. And they were all with him now.

She wondered if Reed had any idea.

Nearly half an hour more of mountain road passed by before their new home, or at least portions of its forest green roof, shiny gold solar panels and three chimneys, appeared between the trees. The road dipped precipitously down, dropped them below the view of their property, and once again she saw only the forest and gray rock until they came, at last, to the wide gate and grand stone columns that guarded their ridiculously long new driveway.

The gate opened when it sensed their car – but it stopped suddenly not halfway through, recycled and tried again. So much for error-free technology.

"That's weird."

Her dad tried overriding it with a button on his console, but that didn't work either. He turned off the car's engine,

"Stay inside."

Kristi pressed her face to the window.

"What's wrong?" Mom said.

"I don't know, hold on."

Ken shut the door behind him. In the silent forest, the sound of his boots crunching the gravel was like someone coughing in church as he made his way to the gate.

At first it looked as though a large boulder had come to rest at the bottom of the drive, until a breeze lifted its fur. A trickle of ice water seemed to speed through his veins.

The big wolf snarled silently into the sky; eyes long dead and flat as coins.

Ken climbed back into the cab, relieved but dizzy.

"Well, the electric fence works…maybe a little too well," Ken said. He successfully overrode the sensor this time. The gate opened fully, sweeping the carcass to the side in a cloud of dust.

"*Oh…*" Kristi moaned as they passed it.

Reed pressed his face to the glass as his father drove past the body.

"*Wow!*" Reed said.

Chapter 2

"Park Service?" Amanda suggested. "Fish and Game?"

How *did* one have a large dead animal removed from ones property in Cedar? This wasn't a car-struck raccoon on the sidewalks of Lake Oswego, or a starved possum in your crawlspace.

In the end, Ken didn't call the Park Service or anyone else, he and Reed simply drove the spanking new green Gator loaded with shovels and plastic tarp, down their driveway to deal with it. Reed, who volunteered for nothing, had volunteered for this – the idea of hanging a real wolf skull on his wall was apparently a "hot" one. He came along despite his mother's assurances that no such thing would ever make its way into her house.

As they neared the fence Ken was sure Reed would reconsider. The gate had manhandled and mangled the already badly decomposed animal, broken it wide open. A brownish trail of noxious fluids lay over the gravel and dust. Some ten yards away the stench was overwhelming.

Sure enough, Reed hopped off the Gator, his hand covering his nose and mouth.

"God – let's just leave it for the crows."

"They had their chance at it," Ken said. Not one winged garbage man circled the skies above them. Not a vulture, not a crow.

Ken passed the broken animal and switched off the Gator. He tossed a pair of work gloves to his son and pulled on a pair himself; wishing his tool collection included gas masks.

They unrolled the tarp, hooked the eyelets to the Gator's tow chains, and the two of them set about the nasty work of shoveling and rolling chunks of a once proud beast onto it.

"This is like *Goodfellas*," Reed muttered, referring to a grisly scene from one of their all-time favorite movies.

Reed was right, here they were, spending their first afternoon in some of the most scenic country Oregon had to offer, performing an act gruesome as a Mafia disinterment. Maybe even worse than the act was the idea kids these days only had *movies* for a frame of reference. *Don't kids read anymore?*

"Any Poe in those school packets?"

"Huh?"

"The Premature Burial – Fall of the House of Usher? Anything like that?"

"Usher? You listen to Usher?"

Now it was Ken's turn to go blank. Finally, he said, "Edgar Allen Poe. *The author."*

"Oh. That guy."

Reed coughed as they tied the tarp around the putrid remains. Once the deed was done he stood straight, his back resting against the stone column. He looked to the sky, and closed his eyes. Ken thought the boy was about to be sick. Instead, Reed recited softly:

> *"We grew in age – and love – together,*
> *Roaming the forest, and the wild;*
> *My breast her shield in wintry weather –*
> *And when the friendly sunshine smiled,*
> *And she would mark the opening skies,*
> *I saw no Heaven – but in her eyes."*

Ken stared at his son, utterly floored.

"Tamerlane." Reed said, climbing into the driver's seat this time.

Ken nodded, taking the passenger's position without protest.

"And no…" Reed added, "It *wasn't* in the home-school packets."

"I'm impressed. A little shocked. But impressed."

Reed started up the Gator, "You know, I don't just play video games all day."

That was news to Ken. Good news.

"Where do we want to put him?"

Ken pointed his chin down the road.

"A few hundred yards out in the forest."

The Gator tugged, hitched, then dragged the load, scraping the gravel loudly behind them.

"I've never seen you with a book," Ken shouted over the din.

Reed nodded.

"It's online."

-=-=-=-=-=-=-=-=-

Their shadows flitted from tree to tree, stretching and shrinking with the flames, up the walls of the darkened house to the huge boulders beyond; a tribe of dancing giants – or the ghostly remnants of such a tribe.

Outside the ring of fire in the pit the night air was biting cold. Even the cold seemed different here, deeper somehow. *What would it be like when it snowed?* Reed wondered.

It was Dad's idea to make this first supper at the new house a BBQ. Meals at the fire-pit to celebrate special events would be a new family tradition and that was cool. It was like he was at Scout camp, but now they actually *lived* at Scout camp, they lived where most people only came to fish and ski. That was awesome…in a way. At least for now.

But man, it's wicked cold.

And the move couldn't have come at a worse time.

There was a girl. Nobody, not even Kristi, knew about her. She'd come out of nowhere one day at school while Reed was slouching his way between Algebra and English, late as usual. Hunched under the stairwell; snow white hair with blue tips, a blue sapphire stud in her nose, a silver ring flashed from her lower lip. A spray of morning glories tattooed across her bare shoulder.

She lit up a cigarette right there in the hall.

As Reed passed, she glanced his way, startled at first; anyone strolling outside the classrooms this late had to be faculty, or security. But it was obvious Reed wasn't faculty – he was just some stupid slouching kid - so she blew smoke his way and grinned...

"Out in the wild," Kristi said.

"Huh?"

"What planet you on, dawg?" His sister motioned to half a s'more on the log1` bench beside him. "You gonna eat that?"

"Naw, go for it."

She took it lustily.

Their parents huddled in a blanket across the wide pit, faces upturned to the stars.

"They're kind of cute like that," he said.

"Gross."

"You're a major prude."

"You didn't eat much."

"You're not my mommy."

"You pissed off or something?"

The BBQ idea was okay - or it would have been any other time. Ribs were the only meat they had that wasn't frozen though. Not exactly the most appetizing thing after what he'd been through this afternoon. Even now Reed couldn't help looking in the direction of that wolf's final resting-place, couldn't help seeing all that...*stuff* oozing out of it.

He'd probably go vegan tomorrow.

But that wasn't the biggest thing on his mind anyway.

"Do you think everybody's the same? I mean, you know, inside?"

"Wow, little bro's going deep."

He shook his head.

"You know, the "little brother" thing's not exactly accurate. I'm pretty sure it was a C-section."

Kristi grinned, wiping the chocolate from her face with an outstretched index finger and thumb, giving him the classic *Loser* sign.

He ignored it, "Whatever. Anyway…someone can look totally *out there*, right? But still be, you know, the same as anyone else. You know – they *want* the same thing everyone else does?"

She shook her head, washing down the chocolate, Graham cracker, and marshmallow with more chocolate and marshmallow from a mug of hot cocoa. Reed figured this had to be more sugar than Kristi's body processed in the course of a normal year. Her eyes were saucers. He wouldn't get a straight answer from her tonight.

But, as usual, she surprised him.

"Look, we're twins, right? Two buns in the oven at exactly the same time - even came out more or less the same time."

He nodded.

"Okay. Do you know *any* two people more different than you and me?"

It was a straight answer all right; even though it was exactly the one he didn't want to hear. As usual, shallow sissy the snow queen who didn't spend time with anyone unless she was thoroughly dominating them at something, had it all figured.

She licked the fingers of her glove like a cat cleaning its paw.

"You haven't like – *discovered girls* or something?" she said, "Because…that *would be truly gross.*"

"Kristi. You know that one of these days I'm seriously going to kick your ass."

"Bring it, sister. Don't sing it."

Oh yes, he would. One day he would totally kick her ass. Sure he would. He glared at his sister.

She grinned – knowing *exactly* what he was thinking. She'd whip his ass any day. No question.

Reed's new room was huge, all the rooms in this house were.

Not that Reed needed a particularly big room. He had his Mythykal posters, and a collection of medieval weapon replicas. Outside of that stuff all he needed was a desk, a chair, and place big enough to hold his custom Alienware PC with its massive water-cooling system – a system he'd proudly installed and then disassembled for the move himself. He rarely even used his surround-sound speaker system anymore, preferring his wireless 3D-sound headset. Pulling on those big ear cups was like donning a helmet for battle – a ritual that only helped immerse him in the game.

Just a couple more boxes of clothes and magazines to deal with and those could wait.

He re-attached the intestinal-looking hoses of the cooling system, carefully refilled the PC-life-sustaining glowing fluid with a sense of ceremony and exactness bordering on sacrament. Soon the gurgling of escaping gasses stopped, the blue lights swam once again through his bionic creation's innards, the eyes of the alien symbol lit and the machine once again pulsed with life.

With all hoses, cords and dongles attached, Reed logged on for the first time in his new home. His fingers drummed as he waited for the satellite connection to take hold. He was sure he'd miss the throughput of their land-line in Lake Oswego; *wireless here has to suck...*

But sure enough, his favorite server appeared quickly in the list. Moments later Reed was gone and *DeerSlayr Wolfyn* had taken his place. The warlock dwarf, level 58, his minions at his side. DeerSlayr even sported an avatar version of Reed's newly bleached locks.

Here with the cold, blue-gray tones of *Roland's Ice-Forest* dancing in his eyes, flying his Griffon over the treetops, Reed was truly alive. Tonight he would do battle, he would kill and steal and gather plunder from the corpses of the vanquished, and he wouldn't even *think* of sleeping until he reached level 60.

Behind Reed, beyond the double-paned, acoustically treated window sheltering his new bedroom, lay another forest entirely; one filled not with CG avatars and objects, but with very real, and very hard, sharp rocks, massive trees, and dangerous animals.

In that forest near the electrified boundary that marked-off the Carroll's piece of Mount Cedar, another sort of wolf surveyed this new situation, this new intrusion. This wolf stared with envious green eyes that saw through deep night as easily as day.

Once this mountain had been remote, secret; a safe hideaway. But as they destroyed their cities, more wealthy Americans brought the stink and decay of Western urban life here with them. Their coming was only a trickle now, not yet a tide.

But a tide was surely coming.

Chapter 3

The wide-stance Warrior Pose, now bending down, one hand touching the black *Manduka yoga mat near her ankle, the other raised straight to the sky in a picture-perfect Triangle Pose.

Ken sipped his fresh-ground Summatra coffee and leaned against the polished cedar banister. He listened to the gentle babble of water beneath their staircase, the sweet and gentle voice of Deva Premal softly repeating mantras in crystal clear high-definition 11.1 surround sound through the wide open den. He watched his wife move swiftly in silky silhouette through the first series of Ashtanga Yoga poses. These were her "easy" poses, a gentle warm-up before the much more demanding, gymnastic-like moves of *second series*.

Ken had tried Yoga for a while. He didn't have the time, he didn't have the patience – couldn't stop his own nagging mantra, *"if you've stolen these precious moments away from work – why the hell aren't you writing music?"*

He wasn't sure which series Amanda was up to these days, he just knew she was good – and fun to watch. Especially here with nothing but mountain, forest, and sky behind her.

Their first morning in the new house.

He of course had already pushed every "power-on" button in his studio, called up Cakewalk's Sonar, and even laid down a couple scratch piano tracks. The tracks themselves were crap, just a test of the system. It all worked. He'd also gone through all the house systems – a program called Pro-Tek from one of Portland Micro's software partners controlled it all from another computer sitting next to his Digital Audio Workstation in the studio. It controlled the security cameras – localized power and heating, the retracting indoor blinds and outdoor shutters, the pumps and heaters for the windows and the walkways outside, and *the shaker* - the snow shedding system for the roof. He loved that system - it was basically the same technology used to clean dust from the mirrors in high-tech digital cameras. They weren't only skinned with a slippery anti-fungal, anti-stick Teflon-like material – they actually shook on demand – the same "technology" dogs used to flick water off their coats; amazing how even the most advanced technology often came down to something stupidly simple.

Judging by the temperature drop they'd had last night, it wouldn't be long before he had a chance to test that system.

The *bang* of the front door swinging into the mudroom wall broke the peace before Kristi could stop it.

"Whew! Sorry! Daddy, what's for *breakie?*"

Ken watched his daughter tug off her jacket, jump out of her neon orange cross-trainers, and hang up her holster in almost one continuous movement.

"I don't know – what are you making?"

"What are we having?"

"What are you making?"

"What are we having?"

"What are you making?"

"Enough!" Amanda, didn't even break her Sun Salutation, "You two are so annoying."

Ken grinned as Kristi pecked his cheek, still steaming from her morning run.

"How's your 'hill of pain'?"

They'd spent several months of weekends clearing rocks and saplings from a slope adjacent to the south face of the house, marking out her own private ski run, complete with a tow line that stretched all the way to the gate. For now it would be her conditioning track. Not that she was out shape.

"Great – can't wait till it snows."

"That reminds me. I've got to get the snow bikes ready."

"Lazarus rises…" Kristi announced.

Reed appeared at the top of the stairs, his white hair rumpled, a new patch of redness on his forehead – probably from resting on his desk, the same clothes he'd worn yesterday creased and wrinkled from one more night in his desk chair. Ken wished he'd never introduced his son to computers.

"Everybody – quick shower, pull on some fresh clothes, we're going into town for breakfast."

"Fresh clothes?" Reed yawned, "To go to *Cedar?*"

"Where are we going for breakfast?" Amanda toweled her neck and forehead. "Not that awful Tavern?"

Ken shrugged.

"Why don't I just whip up an egg-scramble here?"

"No eggs. We forgot to pick them up yesterday."

"Uggh," Amanda said. "It's not like we're back in Lake Oswego – we can't just drive to the market every time we forget something."

"There are a couple other things I need to pick up at the General Store anyway."

"God. I'll make a list. *We've got to change our habits,*" she shook her head. "Gas is expensive."

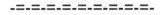

The restaurants, Amanda thought as they left the Cedar Creek Tavern for the second time in less than twenty-four hours, feeling the full weight of an-over-buttered Cedar Tavern spinach omelet and over-buttered white-bread toast wallowing at the bottom of her innards. She would miss the restaurants of Portland Metro; breakfast in Sellwood and Hawthorne, and of course, she would miss her yoga shala in the Pearl. Yes, she could move through her entire practice herself, do it anywhere, but she looked forward to traveling to Mysore, India next summer to practice with the gurus.

She'd been over all this of course, weighed the benefits and drawbacks. The move from the city had been Ken's certainly, though one she supported if only to save his sanity – but once that great wheel had been set in motion Ken had set the dial to whip speed. It wasn't until the basement had been dug, the foundation poured, that she truly understood this was real. At that point there was nothing to do but spin with it.

She had done that and covered most of the bases. She had her own tech head-hunting business. But for the occasional lunch with HR reps, she could conduct that business from anywhere on the planet. She had already home-schooled the twins through eighth grade – private schools had their own problems and the Portland public school system was abysmal. Tales of rampant sex and drugs in Middle School made the idea of raising your kids like veal in cages a more attractive option. They'd given Lake Oswego High School two years. The school had been great for Kristi on the athletic side for a while – but her real interests lay in non-sanctioned sports like fencing and cross-country skiing.

Then there was Reed...

Maybe home schooling in the early years had left both kids lacking somewhat in social skills. Kristi could be a team player but she was obviously more comfortable taking things into her own hands. Her teammates looked up to her, and with her looks boys loved her. But she was a loner too.

Reed didn't even have sports – all he had was the Internet.

And as for her own social needs, and Ken's, Amanda wasn't much for throwing parties. Ken wasn't subtle in letting her know she *killed the fun with over-planning and second-guessing.* What he didn't understand was that good parties didn't just happen. You had to plan, organize, and coordinate.

He had been extremely thorough with the house plans though. He was such a "know it all" she'd always called him, "Mister Smarty Pants," but even she was surprised to see him sweat details the way he had with this house. Every contractor, electrician, plumber, mason, consulted with him every step of the way – and he seemed to know exactly what they knew, what they could do and how to get around what they couldn't.

The result wasn't only a beautiful home – and it truly was beautiful – it was a high-tech fortress.

Ken walked right past the Cedar Creek Market to the General Store.

"Kids, go ahead and buy what you want." Ken said, "Your mom's right. We won't be making this trip often."

Thank you for nothing. They couldn't sustain this.

It hit her then as she hadn't let it before.

This is real. The long-planned escape from the city, the sale of their house. It wasn't just a pipe dream. It had actually happened. It was here – they were here. Last night wasn't a stay in some beautiful suite in some far away land – it was their first night in their new life.

She tried to summon the "stick it to the man" attitude she'd felt when she first quit Portland Micro to go into business for herself, the same attitude that had set all this in motion. But instead of a deep well of bravado inside, she suddenly found a hollow pit in her stomach.

Finding a dead wolf just outside their gate yesterday didn't help.

She looked back down the road that first brought them from Portland. Only a short distance down that road the forest completely enveloped it, swallowed it completely.

The General Store was either a converted barn, or a warehouse made to look like one, with three floors of goods spread from basement to loft, all joined by a split-log staircase running up the store's center. The front of the store sparkled and bristled with touristy frills, woodcraft, blown glass, painted birdhouses and seed; home and auto hardware crowded the shelves at the back; a large camouflage-painted slab of cedar hung from motorcycle chains beneath the rafters declaring in bold white letters that "Hunt and Ski" was the loft's domain. The basement was packed with thick winter clothing. No fashionable lululemon yoga garb here – although Ken had kidded Amanda that Marynia the General Store proprietor would be happy to order *that stuff* for her if she couldn't find it on the Internet.

Of course he was on a first-name basis with Marynia. He'd been here weekends supervising their little home project for two years - everyone knew Ken. The Cedar General was a family-run affair, like most concerns in town. Robert and Marynia Warner had a daughter, roughly the twins' age, whose name escaped Amanda.

Among other things, Marynia ran the order desk in the hardware section. She was an attractive, though somewhat hardened woman from the Ukraine. Drywall, nails, and chainsaw parts, not yoga-wear, made up the bulk of her business. Their daughter manned the cash register at the front; husband Robert mostly dealt with the hunters and skiers.

But right now he was dealing with Kristi, *and it wasn't a new pair of skis he was showing her baby.* Not one of those small-caliber competition rifles, but a hunting rifle. She watched in horror as Kristi took it with ease, balanced it in her arms then sighted-in a deer head mounted high on the wall behind the counter. Amanda saw herself launching up the staircase, yanking the thing away and bludgeoning Robert with it. Instead, she bit her lip and kept her distance.

There was no stopping Kristi. Words of caution only emboldened her. Amanda found herself doing what she often did when confronted with Kristi's flirtations with deadly things, she turned around and walked the other way.

There was *nothing* for Amanda in this store.

She found their short list in her purse. The market was two doors up the street. Two weeks ago she'd taken care to stock their new home's medicine cabinets with enough drugs, anti-oxidants and homeopathic remedies to keep the entire population of a third-world nation vital and strong. The freezer and pantry were stuffed to the gills; the Denali had been packed with snacks and fresh fruit.

But they had forgotten eggs.

Jesus, we're citified homeowners, not survivalists. Cedar was only a few miles from their dream house, and barely 90 minutes from Portland. She took a long deep breath. It wasn't like they'd taken up residence in the Arctic. *Why was she making such a big deal out of this?* Things would settle down. Ken would quit spending. Normal life would return.

She found Ken at the back of the store. He had apparently cracked a joke even Marynia got – low and behold - Marynia was actually laughing.

"Hello, Missus Carroll."

"Hello, Marynia."

"We're getting a dog!" Ken announced as joyfully as a little boy.

-=.-=.-=.-=.-=.-=.-=.-=.-

On the road some fifteen minutes later, eggs in the back and greasy breakfast roiling in their innards, they were still arguing about Ken's purchase.

Amanda worked hard not to grind her teeth as Ken pulled between the two spruce saplings that marked their turnoff from the main road. He'd planted the two Colorado Blue's himself a year ago. It was hard enough finding this place in the summer – and snow would be falling soon enough. They passed only two other gates along the way. There's wasn't the only house on the mountain by any means – but neighbors were few and a long way apart.

"Hardwood floors – we have hardwood floors in the den and living room. She's going to scratch them to ribbons. There's going to be mud everywhere!"

"Granite floor in the kitchen – tile in the mudroom. We've got plenty of places to clean paws and trim nails."

"And dogs are so cool, Mom!" Kristi said, *"They just love you!* Unconditional love."

"She'll chew everything. And a Chocolate Lab – they're huge! Who's going to clean up after a big dog like that?"

"I will," Reed said from the back.

Ken checked the rear-view mirror; *had he picked up someone else's boy by mistake?* He glanced over at his wife, who was shaking her head, "no."

"Reed will."

"God," she muttered.

"See it'll all work out."

They'd only been on the mountain two weeks when Reed woke to see actual snow mixing with the rain beyond his window.

It wasn't like they never got snow in Lake Oswego. It made everything look cool for a while, but it never stayed more than a day or two. Snow on the mountain would be a whole new animal. Just seeing it out there sort of made him want to plug in the old PlayStation and play Winter XTreme, do some gnarly 520s.

Almost. *Naw, he was long past those stupid kid games.*

Like most nights, he'd spent the last one playing Mythykal. He was stuck in the tar at level 59. It was frustrating as hell. He had friends who were level 80 and above. He'd gotten to level 40 mostly with their help – summoning them when his quests led him to trouble, letting them do the damage and share the plunder. That was cool for a while and then it wasn't since he couldn't do the same for them. It was like he'd found this fantastic new world online only to be the lame *little brother* again.

He'd toughed it out on his own and fought all the way up to the high fifties, but that had taken *forever*; it was taking a *whole other* forever to move forward.

Far off in the cavernous house he heard the endless repetition of the mantras his mother played while she moved through her yoga poses. To Reed, it sounded like terrorist brainwashing, like commands from Al Qaeda or ISIS:

Put on the belt, put on the belt, put on the belt, walk into the café, walk into the café, walk into the café, press the button, press the button...

Kristi was out running early as usual. Bad weather meant nothing to her. Nothing affected her at all. What was that big word: unencumbered? It wasn't his word – he'd heard one of her coaches say it about her – along with the usual ones: fearless, unstoppable... Yeah, Kristi was *unencumbered*. Things like fear and pain didn't matter. Boys didn't seem to matter either. It was so weird. He'd give his right nut for a girlfriend – even though losing that particular piece of his anatomy could further gum up the works so to speak.

But nothing affected Kristi.

When she wasn't running up and down the steep trail on the front side of the house, he'd see her running down to the gate and back up the hill again. Freezing rain didn't bother her. Nothing bothered her. She was the Energizer Bunny. She was *frickin' nuts*.

He didn't see her in the yard now, but *the yard* was five acres of forest these days. She could be anywhere, doing anything. She was probably climbing the boulders on the north face of the mountain or skittering over treetops like a monkey.

Waste of time.

Back on the wide-screen Ultra High Definition TV, which served as Reed's computer display, DeerSlayr Wolfyn stood expectantly in the courtyard of the village where Reed had left him, white hair flowing from his horned helmet, his limbs always moving, chest heaving with each programmed breath. The Mythykal guys did a great job keeping the avatars in perpetual motion even at rest – they always looked alive and ready for a new quest. DeerSlayr held his favorite battle-axe now; as a Dwarf Warlock he could use a vast array of weapons, could cast any number of spells, and access the most-used weapons and spells from ribbons within easy reach along the perimeter of the Mythykal view port.

But Reed, who reluctantly had to admit he lived in this world, couldn't handle another quest right now.

He should be doing his Algebra. But that didn't exactly appeal to him either.

He logged out, shut the computer off and headed downstairs.

The third world chanting of ISIS' secret commands was only a little louder from the stairway. There were speakers everywhere; you could send any audio you liked around the house in high-definition surround. Movies, and music were all packed on terabytes of drive space on the servers in Dad's studio – you could play the same movie – or different ones on every display in the house – and adjust the audio accordingly. Yeah, it was sweet.

The living room and den were wide and open and built from a lot of the same materials you saw outside. The whole purpose was to make the house an extension of the forest - there was even a stream running under the flagstone stairway. The huge window showed nothing but forest and wide expanse of sky – gray and dramatic now, heavy with sleet.

Mom was sitting in lotus on her mat; candles flickering, ribbons of incense twirling up into the rafters.

A rhythmic *pok! pok! pok!* had started up in the recreation room downstairs, and that meant Kristi had returned.

He found her in her fencing knickers and jacket, knees bent, pouncing, the flattened tip of her epee striking the exact center of the small foam target on the wall with each and every lunge.

"You know, even God rested on the seventh day."

"Yeah? How many Gold's did he win?" she said without breaking her rhythm.

"Blasphemer."

"Wimp."

"KYA," He gave the chat room acronym for *Kick Your Ass.*

"IYD" She returned with the chat room acronym for *In Your Dreams.*

"You know, it's not like you're ever going to have a real sword fight with anyone."

"It's not like you're ever going to fight giants and trolls, video boy."

"Video games build hand-eye coordination."

"BS"

"The Army uses video games to train recruits."

"No. The Army uses video games to recruit losers like you."

"I'm serious. I get a lot of coordination from video games."

"Show me."

The big fencing mask was spinning toward him before she'd even pulled herself back into position for the next lunge. He barely caught it in time to save his nose.

"I know you're a big shot fencer. BFD." He set the mask on the floor.

She handed him the epee and stood to one side.

"So show me how coordinated video games have made you. Hit the target even once and I'll worship you like a God."

It wasn't like he'd never held the epee before. The leather grip felt strong and alive somehow in his palm, even though the warmth and dampness of her sweat on it was a little gross. He liked the balance of the blade with the big bell that enveloped his hand – the loud ring it made whenever another blade struck it. It was nothing like his heavy medieval replica swords - but those at least mimicked something real, something that could actually hurt someone. This was supposed to be like the rapiers of Renaissance time, but it wasn't really. It was really just a toy.

"Any day now."

He'd done it before – just not often. He stood more or less the way he thought she had.

"Bend your knees. Sit into it."

"Give me a break, I know how you do it."

"So do it."

Dropping down into that awkward pose actually hurt. He'd been sitting way too long in his cushy wheeled chair, his knees, butt and thighs not having to do much of anything.

"Keep your leading foot straight, knee bent straight over your toe or you'll blow it out and I'll have to push you around in a wheelchair the rest of my life."

"Give me a break."

"Do it right or don't do it."

She was so annoying. Still, he aligned his foot and knee, wobbling a bit. He straightened his arm, took a bead on the center of the target. Hell, the bulls-eye was at least twenty times bigger than the stupid flat tip on the epee. No problem. He pounced at it –

And missed not only the bulls-eye but the entire target by two feet. The blade scraped along the wall as he lost his balance and stumbled forward.

"Yeah – those games are really good for you, keep playing 'em, champ."

"I just have to get the feel of it. I'm not used to it."

"Obviously."

God, she was a pain.

He lunged again, his thigh shaking from overstretching his hamstring on the first one – and missed again, but less than a foot this time.

"See, I'm getting better."

He was sure he'd hit it on the next one. But he wasn't sure he could lunge again – there was that telltale pulling sensation in his groin. He would really feel it tomorrow; crap he was feeling it *now*.

"Nice job, video boy."

He whipped the sword toward her; she caught the mid-blade with her gloved hand easy as a frog snatching a fly from the air, and held it fast.

"Don't *ever* do that again. *I'm not wearing a mask!*"

"Lighten up."

"No. This isn't one of your stupid video games – *you don't spawn another eyeball when you lose one.*"

What a bitch.

She took the epee from him, moved back into position, and began another series of lunges.

She was done. Reed had been dismissed.

He moved over to their vintage Missile Command console, rolled the track ball, intercepted bomb after bomb, noisily blasting them to bits. Missiles streaked, flying saucers exploded. None of this commotion distracted Kristi.

Man he wished she would try Mythykal just once, he'd tear her a new one all right; he'd whack her to pieces.

Even in his *own* head that sounded lame. Reed shut down the big console and slouched back upstairs.

-=.=.=.=.=.=.=.=.=.=-

A commotion of fast paws, excited whines, and the happy, oily smell of puppy fur.

"Here she is, Mister Carroll. She's a sweetie."

Kalyna's sad brown eyes nearly matched the pup's as she nuzzled her. A large and bulky kid, like so many kids these days Ken thought, on the fast track to becoming a large and bulky adult. She'd inherited a bad start from her father, Bob. The two of them looked almost like siblings as he joined her at the counter.

"Aren't you? Aren't you a sweetie?" Bob said.

Ken put his face down to the puppy's darting, wet snout, letting himself be sniffed, licked and therefore, properly introduced. That done, the pup turned her attention to her brand new collar and leash, gnawing whatever parts she could reach.

"She *is* a sweetie." Ken said, "She's beautiful."

"I've got her crate at the front of the store, mister Carroll. She's used to it."

"So you think that wolf had been dead for a while?" Bob asked.

"At least a week, maybe two."

"Birds and critters should have gotten to him way before that."

"I didn't see so much as a crow in the sky."

"Well, that's odd is all I can say. Usually doesn't take too long for dead things to show their bones around here." He let the dog work its sharp baby teeth over his huge calloused hand, and shook his head. "Good to know the Gray Wolves are back in Oregon though. They pretty much disappeared a few years back."

That wasn't the best news Ken could have heard. They'd need to keep the dog close by during the day and not let her out at all at night. Amanda wouldn't exactly be thrilled with that.

Getting the pup through the store was a challenge –
she'd wet herself, his jacket, and a good section of the back
counter when he'd first scooped her up. By the time they'd
made it outside she'd gathered a small crowd of kids looking
for whatever there was to do in Cedar; a cute, chocolate lab
puppy had quickly turned into that *thing to do.*

No use fighting puppy love. He gave the leash to one
of the older girls, and let the pup love them up while he and
Kalyna loaded the crate and enough chows and dog treats to
winter an entire team of sled dogs.

He left the kids waving and cooing as he drove out of
town. Great that there were kids close to the twins' age
around town. Maybe Reed would break out his shell and
make some real friends.

A couple hundred yards from their gate, the scars the Gator
had left dragging its cargo into the forest had started to blend
in, but were unmistakably there.

That there were wolves at all in these parts was reason
for concern. He knew there were cougars out here and they
were no less deadly. But there was something cunning, even
sinister about a wolf, at least our lore had certainly painted
them that way.

But there was a dignity there too and he felt, as Ken
passed the ugly scar they'd made on the landscape, a sense of

sadness. He craned his neck for a look beyond the treetops. Still no birds circling overhead - of course the wolf was likely just a few scattered bones by now.

He hadn't gone more than twenty feet past that hole in the forest when curiosity got the better of him. Ken slowed the truck, backed up to the Gator's trail and stopped. Their new pup, asleep soon after they'd left town, was on her feet now. Excited little whines from the crate in back of the SUV.

Wouldn't hurt to take her for a poop walk before he brought her inside the house anyway.

He fixed her leash as she lightly gnawed the back of his hand.

"How 'bout a walk, huh? Sure, you'd like that."

So quiet out here. And cold - it had to be a good ten degrees colder up here than it was in town and clouds were rolling in.

She was bounding away before he'd even set her paws on the ground – an indignant and surprised yelp when she hit the limit of the leash.

"Slow up, little one. No hurries, no worries."

How had a wolf died next to their gate in the first place? Was it really the electrified fence? The voltage was rated to startle, certainly not to kill. Could have been struck by a car or some off-road vehicle of course, hard to believe a wolf wouldn't have heard something like that coming a mile away though. Maybe it was just sick or old.

Maybe a hunter shot it.

Maybe. Hadn't seen any bullet holes though. Of course the gate had done a job on the carcass before he'd really gotten a good look –

This time it was Ken who reached the leash's limit. Less than a hundred feet into the forest, not halfway to the rocks where he and Reed had unloaded the beast, the puppy had stopped cold in her tracks.

"Come on, girl –"

He tugged the leash. She wouldn't budge.

"What's –"

A breeze pulled at the hair behind his neck, set his skin tingling.

Nothing but trees and rocks around them.

No. That wasn't quite true.

A sound, a whine, almost a mewing from the puppy, then silence. Her eyes were wide.

Ken took one step back, then another; eyes locked straight on the forest ahead of them. There was a sensation, like a message tuning in he couldn't quite parse, a warning sign spoken low in some long forgotten language.

Something was out there. No. Some *things* were out there. Watching them. The feeling was unmistakable.

He carefully lifted the pup in his arms, slowly backed his way toward the road, eyes still struggling to penetrate the deep forest ahead.

The smell of fresh rain through the branches, freezing drops splashed his face and hands. White pebbles began to pepper the forest floor. Lightning flashed with a sound like waves crashing overhead, and Ken turned and ran for the truck with everything he had before the next flash hit. A barrage of hail rained down on them, ripping through the boughs like machine-gun fire. In an instant, the forest floor was white with bouncing pebbles.

Ken didn't bother with the crate, he jumped into the cab puppy crooked in his arm, and floored it to their gate, hail beating the roof, exploding over the windshield.

It wasn't until he saw the garage door rolling up that Ken's heart quit pounding. By then the hail had quit.

Snowflakes were falling.

Home.

He actually laughed as he pulled up beside the snow bikes, stopping just short of the generator. What had they both heard? Wind? The coming hail?

Whatever it had been was gone now. The pup was a barking tornado of paws, tongue and floppy wetness in his arms.

"Okay, hold on! Hold on!"

He let her explore the concrete confines of the garage as he hefted her crate into the mudroom, half-expecting a Brady Bunch onrush of happy family to greet him.

But it wasn't like that in a big house like this. In a house this size, everyone had their own space and plenty of it.

"Just you and me, dog."

She barked, looked happily up at him, then squatted and peed on his boot.

Now he was really laughing, "Oh yeah, Mandy's *gonna love you.*"

-=-=-=-=-=-=-=-=-=-

His life sucked.

Kristi was right. None of the stuff Reed was good at made him better at anything else. *She* was good at everything she tried, and every sport she played – no matter how stupid or obscure – seemed to make her better at every other sport. It wasn't fair.

His *sister*. Why didn't he have a brother? It wouldn't have been such a big deal that Reed was the "nonathletic" one.

He wished he'd had more time at Lake Oswego High. If he had a girlfriend things would be different. The girl with the blue-tipped hair must have been a transfer. He didn't know anything about her – but she'd smiled at him...just before she'd blown smoke at him. She had wide, almond-shaped eyes outlined in black like a cat. She wore a low-cut chemise and even though their whole exchange had lasted a few seconds at best, he had gotten a good sense of the treasures that lay just beyond his sight. Thinking about that now started a flush of warmth through him.

He didn't know her name, he'd only seen her initials scrawled in blue Sharpie on two of her books. Actually, they hadn't look like initials so much as chemical symbols: Wy Chy. He tried the Periodic Table of Elements in vain. He'd tried the school directory too in case they really were initials, no one at Lake Oswego High with names starting with either Wy or Chy. "Wy Chy" could have been a screen name too, a shorthand way of saying "Witchy." Maybe that was it, maybe she thought she was a witch or something. He'd tried Facebook and found a lot of witch-like screen names there, but none of the pics were even close to being her.

But what difference did any of that make anyway? He wouldn't be going back to Lake Oswego High, and even if he did go back what chance did he have with a pretty girl like that? The sad truth was pretty girls liked jocks not lame dumb-asses like him.

His own *sister* could beat him up.

He had just about worked his psyche into the point of losing himself once more in the mystic lands of Mythykal when he heard something he was afraid he'd never hear in "his mom's house."

A puppy barking!

He dashed down the stairs and through the den, stockinged feet flying over flagstone, hardwood, and granite and when they finally skidded over the Mexican tiles of the mudroom floor.

It was like the pup *knew him*, had expected him all along! She jumped into his arms.

"Wow! Hey, you! What's your name? What's your name?"

He looked up at his grinning dad, who shrugged.

"No name yet - but she's a chocolate lab – maybe do something with that."

"Geez, I don't want to give her some candy-" he stopped himself just short of *candyass* - the word he was going for. "- sounding name, like Hershey…"

"What's wrong with 'Dog'?"

Reed considered it. It was kind of cool. There was a big, over-protective robot in the old *Half-Life2* video game named Dog that acted like one. Yeah, that name would be way cool. He nodded through the licks and tail slaps.

"Yeah, *Dog*. What do you think, Dog – that work for you girl?"

The licking renewed with vigor.

"Yeah, it works for you, sure it does."

"She needs to go outside." His dad said, tossing a balled-up work towel into the trash bin.

"I'll take her."

"Make sure you keep her close. Use the leash."

"Sure," His dad said some things about feeding and watering her; sure Reed would get all that stuff taken care of – right now they had some exploring to do. He pulled his jacket off the peg and had just cracked the back door open when his Mom walked into the mudroom and stood there in her lime green yoga outfit, arms folded and jaw clenched. She shook her head, and the meaning was clear: *no way*.

The puppy looked her square in the eye…and growled.

Dad could be sleeping on one of the couches tonight.

Jeezus it was *hella cold* outside.

Their breath froze, and hung in the air around them. Dog wet the freezing ground as soon as her paws touched it. He was grateful she'd at least waited that long. Then she pooped.

"Dog – you gonna start that already? Man."

There would be that whole poop-on-the-newspaper thing they'd have to go through. That was going to be a major pain.

Hell, he'd get past all that – *he had a dog!*

Reed found a shovel in the garage, happily running his hand over the Polaris Indy snowmobile. And one of the four Ski-Bikes parked there. Yeah, once the real snow hit, they'd be having some real fun.

And judging by the cold – *that would happen soon.*

He made an executive decision and designated one of their three trash barrels the "poop" barrel. He surveyed what he could of their property through the trees. They had a wire fence but that was more like a property boundary than anything else, nothing that would keep a puppy inside – or any predators out for that matter. There was a lot of dangerous stuff he'd have to teach her to stay away from. There was that fifty-foot drop in back of the house. Sure it gave the den window a pretty spectacular view of the forest, but 50 feet would be a Dog-ending drop for sure.

The rules were going to have to be different here than they would be for a pet in Lake Oswego. He'd show her around the property – but she'd have to know the forest around them too in case she got out and had to find her way back.

The first rule.

"Okay, Dog, here's how it is. Poop near the house and I've got to pick it up. Way out there in the trees – you just go for it. I'm just telling you this now – but you'll understand later. If you pinch one off and it gets snowed-over – that's good as gone."

He didn't think ahead to how that might haunt him come spring.

Dog was a handful all right. She wanted to run everywhere, see everything, at once – her backside rushed one way while her front half darted toward something new. And each time the leash tugged her, she'd spin around and chew it – then a squirrel or some other critter would race by and she'd nearly yank the leash right out of his hands.

Reed and Kristi had done some exploring in the forest since they'd moved in, and he'd walked the perimeter a few times while the house was being built. Amazing how different looking at it from a "puppy-safe" view was. He began to understand how parents with a toddler looked at things like power plugs and stairways.

At the same time a place like this *had* to be puppy heaven. Tons of stuff to check out, sniff, and chase. And for someone who spent hours immersed in make-believe medieval worlds, living in a forest was pretty cool for him too.

Then again…it sucked to be home-schooled again. He'd been home-schooled practically his whole life. The two years at LO-Hi had been tough in a lot of ways; but it sure was great to have girls around who *weren't* his jock sister. Not that he ever had the nerve to talk to any of them.

He hadn't said more than "Hi" to WyChy. Man, if he were at school now he knew he'd figure out something cool to say. Sure he would, at some point anyway.

A tug on the leash brought him back. Dog's explorations had taken them to a far corner of the property. There was a little rise here, and then the floor dipped quickly into a deep pocket hidden by trees and thickets of razor-sharp blackberry all the way down to Cedar Creek.

From the hill you could just make out the rooftop of another house maybe a mile away. Smoke poured from the little house's chimney.

Nice to know they weren't completely alone up here.

Dog tugged again, of course she heard the creek below and had to explore it. Reed obliged.

The further down they went, the quieter it got. It was darker, choked with ferns and vines. The tree trunks and roots were mossy and the forest floor thick, spongy with fallen needles and decayed wood. He could easily see himself as his Mythykal alter ego down here, DeerSlayr Wolfyn, battle-axe in hand; his big red Orc minion, what the players referred to jokingly as a *raspberry,* beside him.

Here in the real world, Dog was his minion, he guessed. But neither he nor Dog had any weapons to swing, no spells to hurl at their enemies.

This isn't one of your stupid video games – you don't spawn another eyeball when you lose one.

He buried the thought. The last thing he wanted to do was hear his sister in his head.

Dog made a beeline for the water and Reed had to rein her in just to catch up.

The creek was crystal clear down to the smooth, mossy rocks below. A wide quiet pool had gathered above a stout boulder and a precarious damn of smaller rocks. *That's where the trout would be waiting;* there had to be some big ones hiding behind the short waterfall below it where a smaller pool had formed.

Dog dipped down for a taste of mountain water; she yelped when Reed snapped her quickly back.

"No!"

Yeah, the water was *mostly* clear, except for one syrupy greenish-brown line snaking over the surface from somewhere upstream. The line broke into tiny globules over the rocks, regrouped in the pool below them.

"Hold on, Dog."

Reed tied the leash to an exposed root and snapped off a nearby branch. He pushed it across the surface of the pool. The snaky line broke the same way it did over the falls, spread and then regrouped like balls of mercury around the branch, collecting in the thin green needles. As he dragged it back a stench of rot came with it.

Reed dropped the branch on the bank, quickly wiped its sap from his hands onto boulders, a tree trunk, and finally onto his jeans. He sniffed his hand. Only the smell of pine, not that gross, rot smell.

"Dog, let's go."

But Dog sat with her ears pricked up, her head cocked to one side. *Listening.*

A gust far above them swayed the treetops, branches whispering gently over the babble of water. The sound didn't distract her. Dog scanned the opposite bank, looked upstream and locked on something there.

She growled.

Then Reed heard it too, a soft rasp of wood nearly covered by the babble of the creek and the breezy whisper of branches above them…it came from the shadows in the woods just across the creek.

Wolves!

Crap, what was he thinking coming down here? They'd already found one dead wolf. Wolves hunted in packs. What the Hell was he thinking?

Reed saw nothing but darkness past the tree trunks and ferns. Only shadows.

One of those shadows moved away from the rest.

"Run!" Sweat broke from his forehead, down his shirt and chest.

"Run!"

He broke for the hill and Dog broke with him, she yelped when the leash yanked her back, still tied firm to the big root.

"Fuck!" Reed dove for the root, yanked the loop and Dog was free.

"Come on, come on!" Dog passed him up the hill, immune to the branches that snatched Reed's arms and legs, the needles that slid out beneath his feet. His sore hamstring sang with pain, his heart and lungs, conditioned only to power a body seated at a computer for hours on end, thumped and burned in his chest.

Not twenty yards past the crest of the hill, Reed collapsed against the trunk of a tree, gasping for breath, wheezing like an old man. Icy rain spitting down through the branches above him, like a taunt.

Dog was already back to normal; exploring, snuffling through the pine needles, snapping at raindrops. Any perceived threat gone and forgotten.

Reed waited to catch his breath, a ridiculously long wait. He looked back toward the creek.

Nothing but trees, ferns, and a few clumps of hail that hadn't yet melted away.

He was scared of his own shadow. He was completely out of shape.

"This is no good, Dog…" A couple more lung-burning breaths before he could finish. "I gotta change this. I'll never keep up with you."

Chapter 4

Dog barked sharply, lunging at the gray-white flakes that swirled around her. She snapped them from the air, ate them.

Her first time in the snow, and just watching her antics made Reed laugh. He remembered acting pretty much the same way when he was a little kid.

Flakes gathered at his feet, in his hair and on the sleeves of his jacket; they floated for a time along the surface of the creek, until the water pulled them one by one, down to the smooth stones below. Even those stones had grown a skin of whitish gray snow.

He opened his palms, watched the flakes settle. It was a warm, dirty snow.

Beside him, the creek was slowly turning to gray sludge. A single line of dark green fluid broke across its surface, thrashed like a snake until it broke over the falls and became many little snakes that twitched with strange life.

"Dog, let's go."

But Dog lay on her side, motionless, her tongue bloated and gray. A dark greenish syrup dripped from her lips and snout, stretching all the way to the middle of the creek. All the way to the tail of the snake.

-=-=-=-=-=-=-=-=-=-

Reed sat up fast. Fully awake now.

His screensaver, a twirling blue battle-axe, flew from corner to corner of his computer display, spinning away as it struck just beneath the bezel, bounced away... His heart thumped, but he was petrified, unable to lay back or swing his legs off the bed. He breathed deeply, let the dream drain completely away.

A thick column of blue-gray moonlight from the window.

Dog slept peacefully in her big house in the corner of his room, breathing easy, a twitching paw betraying her puppy dreams where she was most likely chasing squirrels. Reed first planned to set up Dog's quarters in the mudroom to minimize accidents and cleanup. That didn't work. She started crying the moment Reed left her. Then he pulled his sleeping bag downstairs and lay beside her. That quieted her down. In the end he'd hauled her whole bedroom upstairs to his.

He couldn't let himself go back to that dream.

He pushed his body, aching from the day's unaccustomed exertion, to the side of the bed; he swung his legs over the side like a bundle of old wood and rested his feet on the floor.

Just a dream. A seriously bad dream.

The moonlight revealed nothing more sinister than the meadow that served as front yard, the big silver Viking barbecue, the fire pit and adjacent hot tub.

After that there was nothing but forest.

No. *There was something else.* Something pale moved between the trees. *A ghost.*

Reed held his breath.

The buck stepped from the woods, wide rack of tall antlers bristling over his head. He studied the house, decided nothing there would harm him and strode majestically across the yard to the forest beyond.

Reed's breath escaped. So much for Dad's electrified fence, *so what else didn't work?*

But this was just a deer and deer were cool. *Just a deer. This time.*

Reed plopped down in his familiar desk chair, still too spooked to sleep. He donned his headset and logged on. In moments, he was lost in a brand new quest. This one required him to fly his Griffon steed a good distance, and then walk a good distance, and then ride a ferry across a wide river. *Man, a hyperspace button would be sweet.* Sometimes the *real-time* aspect of Mythykal travel was a real pain, even though it obviously made traversing the imaginary world more realistic than it would be if people just teleported from place to place. Little by little, he began to get sleepy again; so sleepy that a female Elf caught him by surprise with a spell.

DeerSlayr Wolfyn was thrown flat on his stomach. He rolled to his feet, stunned and embarrassed, but with most of his health intact.

The elf wore a mop of white hair spiked with acid blue tips, she was a level 62, and the digital info overhead gave the name: WyldChyld.

Wy Chy!

"Oh, my freakin' god…" he whispered. He froze – and the next bolt she hurled slammed him against a tree trunk. His fingers danced over the keyboard, DeerSlayr and his raspberry swung their weapons, cast spells, but she and her minions were too good, in moments he and his minion were toast.

He re-spawned, rescued his corpse and retrieved what he could – the few things she hadn't stolen.

But which way had she gone?

Her info tag said she was from the Malwor tribe, not a Glokkun like he and his mates. She was the enemy and that meant he couldn't even talk to her – literally. If he even tried his words would come out in some senseless form. There were rules against fraternization in Mythykal.

But there had to be a way to do it. Someone out there had to know how - someone out there had to know *her.*

He consulted his maps, looked for the telltale blue dots that showed his mates' locations and didn't see any highlighted - it was late enough now that even his friends were asleep, their avatars suspended.

The nearest town was Bryn Shyre. He located a tavern there called the One-Eyed Eagle. The taverns were always good places to gain insight, and often where High Level players hung out talking up their exploits or plotting schemes. One of them might have seen her – *maybe WyldChyld was even there!*

Bryn Shyre sat on the far end of the Silver Valley, a disputed territory bordering the Land of the Dead. Another long walk if that was your only mode of travel. But no need to walk when you had the services of a Griffon mount. He dug into his bag for the blue rune stone – the charm that summoned his winged Griffon. The stone was gone.

WyldChyld had stolen it!

Chapter 5

Ken didn't know what kind of birds they were, only that they were much smaller than the hawk they tormented.

But the small birds were organized, relentless.

One snap of the hawk's beak, a piercing squeeze of her talons, would have ended any of them. But the tiny birds gave her no chance to rise above them, to defend herself. They attacked from above and behind, diving in turn, one by one. Striking and striking again.

Relentless.

Ken watched them from his own perch, an arm-less (to facilitate guitar and keyboard work) swivel chair complete with lumbar support, shock-absorbers and silent silicone wheels; an ergonomic throne designed *for the serious pro audio technician* or so they said at the Beaverton Guitar Center.

Essentially it was a stool with a back.

But it definitely fit the bill for his studio – and it really was silent when it rolled or spun, with no tell-tale creaks as he leaned forward or back. He could sit in any position he desired to record vocals.

He'd built his studio lean but solid. There were only two pieces you'd call extravagant - a Mackie mixing board he'd chosen for its *super clean preamps,* and the most expensive Furman power conditioner they made – *to kill the buzz and keep your tracks fresh and sweet.* The Furman sported a back-lit LED on the front that told him where his voltage actually was at any given moment - "just enough info to make you paranoid," they'd warned him. Ken knew the power in their house was already solid and well-grounded. He'd practically held the electricians' hands as they wired this house. He had battery backups, uninterruptible power supplies, and ground rods sunk deep into the foundation. When it came right down to it, he'd really only bought the Furman for the cool blue tube lights that pulled smoothly from the bezel like the radioactive rods in a nuclear reactor.

He'd purchased a tall rack for his outboard effects and synthesizer modules, most of them gathered over time and here now for old times' sake – the rack was topped by a patch-bay with a dozen inputs and cables.

The whole effects rig and mixing board was really little more than an input and control surface for his PC;

outside of his vocals and guitar, the sounds, the effects, came from a Digital Audio Workstation package called Sonar.

Ahh, technology. It was beautiful.

It was all there, right before his eyes.

But at this moment his eyes were mostly on the hawk and her tormentors. The little birds were barely dots now in a sky grown thick with gray clouds. Ken actually left the comfort of his serious audio technician's throne to stand at the window and watch them, the hawk flying lower and lower with each strike. And then they disappeared beneath the treetops.

The view from here was striking – like the den, nothing but sky and forest. The birds had barely left his sight when Kristi broke from the forest far below him.

It couldn't have been much above 30 degrees out there, and still she was dressed in only a light white jacket and gray sweats. Black holster straps crisscrossed her back. Kristi ran headlong down the hill – an effort she attacked like everything else, flat out. He shuddered, the hill was steep, one misstep and his beautiful daughter would flatten against a tree trunk like Wile E. Coyote. But he'd given up telling Kristi to slow down. There *was* no slowing her down.

Once the serious snow hit, and it would any day now, this would be her very own ski run. Not far from that bottom of that run was a dry wash that butted up against an old slide site and dead-fall.. The soft dirt and decaying wood would damp the ricochet and thud from her competition weapons.

Why did she have to pick such dangerous sports…

There were some things he just didn't like thinking about. Ken turned back to his console and punched up the song he'd started yesterday.

In a flash the entire arrangement was there: rhythm tracks, keyboards, even a scratch vocal, the lyrics mostly gibberish at this point; all in neat colorful waveforms stretching across his three wide-screen displays.

Man, he loved this stuff.

In a matter of moments he was lost in the music, fiddling with new sounds, new chord voicings.

Then he had an idea for lyrics – it came from the scene he'd just witnessed – the hawk and her tormentors. The song would describe the way little things could build up and bring you down, break you. He pulled the mic over, hit the phantom power button and armed a new track for record. Finally, he was ready to drink from the creativity well, lost in the moment.

That's when the phone rang. Amanda's cell number flashed across the display.

He sighed, clicked the speakerphone. He disarmed the track.

"Hi, hon."

"Tell Reed he needs to wash the blanket that dog sleeps on. And the food it eats smells awful."

"Okay."

"And he's on that computer now more than ever. Did you notice that? The only time he gets off is to walk that dog. He's gotten just like you and that studio."

"Hon – you know, we don't have to use the phone to talk about this."

"I'm at the market now – is there anything you need?"

Yes, peace. Uninterrupted peace. Do they sell that there?

"No, I'm good. Maybe more Half and Half for the coffee."

"You shouldn't be using that. You know your cholesterol is off the charts. Drink green tea."

A yoga shala in Cedar, that's what he needed. A place where Mandy could hang out on her own...*hang out for a long, long time.*

"Then nothing. I'm good."

"You're not going to spend all day locked in that studio are you?"

"Not all day."

"I'll call you if I see anything else we need."

If you see it buy it, that work for you?

Ken took a deep breath.

"Okay, love you."

"Love you too."

Ken shook his head as he clicked the phone off. He quickly ran through the various menus on it until he found the ring tone controls. He set it to "none." Flash-only would suit him just fine in the studio from now on.

He started the tracks from the beginning. In a little while he was nodding along to it, feeling it again. He pulled the mic boom in, re-armed the scratch vocal track.

The phone light pulsed. He watched it from the corner of his eye, a rudely off-tempo counterpoint to his drum tracks, he looked away, as the intro solo faded off he began to sing.

His Blackberry rang – Mandy's tune.

Ken sighed. He disarmed the vocal track.

"Yes?"

"Have you called Mahesh? He called this morning."

"No, not yet."

"It sounded important."

Of course it did. It always did. It probably was. But I'm finally making music now. The first week of sabbatical Mandy couldn't have been more adamant about him relaxing, forgetting all about Portland Micro. Now...

"I'll call him."

"Is Kristi running with that rifle on her back again?"

"It's a .22 it's not going to explode, okay? She knows what she's doing."

"It's dangerous."

"Yes. It's a dangerous sport. That's our daughter."

At least she hadn't tried strapping the deer rifle on her back…yet.

"Love you."

"Love you too, bye."

He re-armed the track for record. What was that lyric idea?

Had the MicroTools software been delayed? Was that what Mahesh wanted to tell him? Jesus, that wasn't even his deal – it was Mickey's.

Christ! He disarmed the track; hit the speed dial. Then he shut off the call button before it could finish.

He wasn't going there. This time was his – and the weeks were already flying by. Screw MicroTools! Screw his promotion! He wasn't here to work for Portland Micro.

Small things building to bigger things, important things.

That was the idea behind this song. That was the concept. Not exactly inspired. Shit, it was a crappy idea – like singing about the frothy cappuccino you had this morning. Exactly what he hated about a lot of the alternative crap out there passing for music now.

Vapid. Insipid.

He stood up, headed over to the bar. Yeah, he'd had a small wet bar installed in the studio. That was an extravagance. But it was cool. When he finally had friends up here, they'd make music – and they'd have a few drinks while they played.

Ken dropped ice in a crystal tumbler, decanted two fingers of single-malt over it and enjoyed the cold, sweet burn as it traveled down his throat. He poured another, swirled the ice in his glass on his way back to the console.

Better now.

His fingers drummed the padded console.

He started the tracks from the beginning.

Crap, the kick is off. He stopped the tracks, nudged the errant drum back in place and started again.

What the hell was going on with MicroTools? His part was a simple transaction, nothing more than that.

He stopped the tracks, shut down the workstation entirely, and hit the speed dial. He took another drink as Mahesh's phone began to ring.

Outside, the treetops, the mountains beyond, were fading to gray; the dark clouds billowing across the sky were rolling right into them, obliterating them. White flakes, the first real flakes of winter snow, drifted lazily, silently past the double paned, krypton-filled, soundproof window.

Within moments they weren't drifting, they were free falling. A moment later the gray skies themselves were fading – fading into white.

How long had he stood there just staring at it? Where was Mahesh? Why wasn't he picking up?

He killed the call, punched in Amanda's speed-dial number.

She answered on one ring.

"Mandy."

Nothing but static on the line. *Dammit.*

Finally Mandy's voice, but broken.

"...got...but – still - -eed, th-"

"Can you hear me? Wrap it up and come home. A huge storm's coming."

There was a long pause. He imagined Amanda, never one to take his word, checking the store windows for confirmation. The very thought made him angry.

"...Denali is four wheel drive," he heard her explain.

Shit. Why couldn't she just listen to him? *Why couldn't she ever just listen?* He brought up the web browser, queried weather for their zip code. Cute little snowflakes against something not so cute at all, the phrase, *"Severe Weather Warning."*

"Come back now. You're not used to this mountain. You won't be able to see."

"...e ju...need a few more...ings..."

"Listen to me. *Get back here now!*"

Static. A moment of nothing, then her voice, flat.

"...coming back."

He called Kristi.

Kristi was breathing hard when she answered, it took her a moment to answer, and when she did more static came with her voice. *What was going on with that goddamn cell tower?* He glanced out the window mostly by reflex, there was no possible way he could see the tower from here.

"Daddy?"

"Better head back to the house."

"It's just snow — I need to shoot."

It was hereditary. Damn it!

"In two minutes you won't be able to see the deadfall let alone hit it. Your toes will freeze in those shoes. *Get your butt up here!*"

There was silence on the end of the line, then static. Finally...

"I'm coming back."

The view from his window was nothing but white.

There's a blizzard outside my window. A blizzard my wife and daughter could be stuck in.

He went completely blank, standing before a wide picture window that showed him nothing. *Nothing at all.* Precious seconds went by.

And then the truth hit hard: Mandy was safer in town exactly where she was. There was a blizzard and he had just sent his wife into the heart of it. Up a mountain road that was already dangerous, deadly now.

He punched the speed dial. So much static on the line now he could barely hear Mandy on the other end.

"Go back! Drive back to town, go inside the store. Wait it out!"

He couldn't hear her response. Had she heard him at all? He cursed the phone, cursed the fucking cell tower.

"Wait it out! Can you hear me? Mandy! Wait it out!!!"

At least he knew where his son was – *sitting in front of that damn computer.* But if he wasn't... He almost dialed Reed's mobile. Instead, he ran to Reed's room.

Reed and Dog weren't there, the display showed nothing but a spinning ax bouncing from corner to corner like the ball in the old Pong game.

-=-=-=-=-=-=-=-=-

A ribbon of smoke swirling up from a chimney. Why did that just *feel* good?

Reed was plenty warm. These days he didn't move out of the house without his black North Face jacket, a wool hat and his black Lug boots.

Dog had done her business – now she was off the leash, having a grand old time snapping snowflakes from the air.

There was a Holy silence that seemed to fall with snow, a perfect peace broken only by the crunch of his boots and Dog's play. This was the way things should be.

And there was the neighbors' roof far off in the distance, with its warm, gray smoke curling from the chimney. He imagined the logs, snapping and glowing in that fireplace, images of Christmas, of hot cocoa in mugs.

Mom and Dad didn't like using actual logs all that much, the fireplace in the master bedroom used little wood pellets – the one in the living room was gas. The other one in the den could supposedly *handle* logs, but it was gas too – and gas was basically what they used in there. No matches – you lit it with a remote.

At least the pellet fireplace smelled like real wood burning – but you only got the aroma outside the house – the unit was glassed in and airtight. Sometimes technology sucked.

He and Dog hadn't been all the way down to the creek since that first day she'd arrived. The hillock where he stood now was as close as they'd gotten. The branches here were so thick barely a snowflake had reached the ground. It made the entire area look darker than ever.

Could a pack of wolves be waiting in those shadows?

Did wolves have a home or did they move from place to place? He'd heard the term "wolves' den." But with all the heavy construction going on to build their house – all the noise, machinery and men – would wolves really have stayed put if they lived here? There had to be a million better places for them to hide in this forest.

Reed still carried a lingering unease about this part of the creek from his dream, though the details of that dream had long since faded. Even so, there was a part of him that wanted to go down there and face his fears - the *DeerSlayr Wolfyn* part of him.

But he wouldn't be facing those fears today. The whole make-up of the snow was changing now. The flakes were smaller but falling wicked fast, and they were sticking now – really sticking. It would be a long, slow hike back to the house.

"Okay, Dog – playtime's over."

She bounded back to him, snow glued to her fur now. He stuck the leash between his teeth and roughed up her shoulders. But before he could snap the carabiner on her collar, she barked and pulled away from him.

"Hey!"

She loped over the bank toward the creek.

"Dog!"

And then he heard what she had – down in that dark place – *another dog was barking.*

"Damn it!"

Do wolves bark?

He wished he had a weapon – Kristi's .22 rifle, or even one of her stupid pellet guns. Anything. But he had nothing, nothing at all.

"Dog!"

There was no real trail and no time to pick his way through. Branches slapped, poked and sliced into him with every step. Reed slipped, slid three or four feet, stopping just short of a shin-busting boulder.

The barks he heard now were welcoming not aggressive. The dogs had found each other. And then something else.

Was that another voice?

A whispered command nearly lost under the dogs' chatter and the babble of the creek.

Dog had indeed found another pup. Small, tan and stocky, a blunt head with a big white dot over the snout. A Pit Bull. He was a boy, so butt-ugly he was cute. The dogs were sniffing other, getting acquainted. No sign of an owner. He must have imagined the voice.

Reed squatted, snapped the leash securely onto Dog's collar. The other pup stood erect on his stocky legs, eyeing Reed with that squinty mug.

"Come here, boy. Come on!"

The pup stepped forward, hesitated, then licked Reed's hand. Reed took the liberty of roughing up the muscular little frame. The guy was like a ten-pound block of bicep.

"Where you from, Homey? Huh? Where you from? You the neighbor's dog? You're a long way from home aren't you, boy?"

The snow snaked its way through the thick boughs, flakes settled on the rocks, frosted the carpet of needles around them and melted into the water. Some of them began to float...

Something about that sent a chill through Reed that had nothing to do with the weather.

He remembered his dream now; *gray-white flakes floating on the creek, then sinking...sticking to the rocks below. Flakes that weren't really snow at all. Ashes...wave after wave of ashes falling like snow.*

The green effluence that had snaked over the surface their first time here was gone now – but the pine bough he'd held out to it... that same branch lay right there on the bank where he'd dropped it. It had been a young, needle-covered branch freshly snapped from the tree, the sort of bough that stays green on your mantle from Christmas right through New Year's if you're the kind that likes to keep the season going forever...

But two feet from the tip he'd dragged over the water, only the twig skeleton remained. Beyond that, the needles were the burnt orange of old rust.

A branch snapped on the other side of the creek. That sound was unmistakable, even over the soft babble of the water.

"Hey? Who's there?"

He stared into the shadows across the bank.

Nothing.

More snow swirled around them now, drifting against the rocks. The cold was really biting into him now.

"Hey, is this your dog?"

Still nothing.

"I'm not hurting him. He's okay here. I'm not mad you're in our yard or anything. I think the fence is stupid anyway, okay?"

Wind sawed the branches together high above him. Armloads of snow dropped from the branches as they shifted overhead; there was a muted *"whump!"* and an explosion of white where the clods struck the ground nearby.

"Come and get him, okay? I can't just leave him out here. It's too cold. I can't take him with me…" the next part was lame but it was true. He almost didn't say it at all, but finally he did.

"I can't bring him home 'cause my Mom would kill us both."

Was that a giggle he heard? Sure it was. A girl.

"Look, if you don't want to walk over the rocks, I'll bring him over to you."

He tied Dog's leash around a big rock – making sure she couldn't get to the dead branch and chew on it. He scooped the stout little fellow up. Warm, smelly puppy licks on his face.

Actually, he wasn't so sure he could negotiate the rickety rock dam without getting wet – he didn't know how the pit bull had gotten across dry.

Sure enough, the rocks were as slippery and unstable as they looked.

Dog barked a warning from the creek bed, and the pit bull squirmed like a Boa five times its length and size.

"*Crap.* Hold on boy I'll get us across. Come on. Help me out here."

He was almost there; the thick treads on his trusty Lug boots finding purchase, rocks settling in under his weight. The water looked anything but inviting, more like ice that just hadn't quite figured out it was time to settle down and stiffen up yet.

What the hell was he doing? The last time he'd been here, he was sure there were wolves watching him from exactly where he was headed right now. Here he was, picking his way toward that same spot over skull-cracking, ice-covered craggy stones and water so cold it would yank his last breath away if the fall didn't kill him.

And for what? For whom?

Someone who didn't even want to be seen.

Who did he think he was? Batman?

Damn, he was thinking too much. *Have to concentrate.*

The anaconda chunk in his arms twisted hard, Reed over compensated – *and slipped.* He lashed out with his foot, found a lucky rock, and jumped.

"*Oh!*" A female voice moaned from the other side.

He *almost* made it. Reed let the dog go just before his butt hit the bank; his boots dragged through the freezing water, filled to his ankles.

"*Crapshit that's cold!*"

The girl stepped quickly into the open, the little dog in her arms now.

Instantly the biting cold, the pain in his hamstring disappeared.

He'd never seen anyone - *anything* so beautiful. She was a Hispanic girl about his age, with wide eyes so dark you couldn't tell where the pupils ended and the color began.

She stood there like a startled deer – then bolted back into the shadows of the forest.

"No – it's okay!" He pulled himself up, his right hamstring sang. He dropped back on his butt.

"Crap! Come back!"

The rustling in the undergrowth stopped. Just out of site, he knew she was watching him now.

He gathered himself slowly, painfully, to a stooped but more-or-less standing position. His boots were waterproof – but he wore them loose like all the other cool guys – now he knew why his dad said that was dumb. His feet were wet, freezing. *He had a real problem here.*

Dog whined, threw sharp little barks at him from across the water. She was worried, she was cold, and now she was tied up, helpless – if there really were any wolves, or cougars, or coyotes – or any of a number of nasty things out here…how the hell would he get back to her?

He looked where he was pretty sure the girl was still hiding, *watching.*

Dog barked. Reed couldn't leave her there much longer.

Music, Dad's ring-tone: a musical riff from an old movie, *Our Man Flint*. The riff was far off though, barely audible.

From the other side of the creek, Dog barked at Reed's red cell phone as it vibrated now, pushing the snow around it. It was right where Reed had first bent down to pet the pit bull.

Crap. Double-crap!

The snow drifted as it pleased now, a thick blanket of white spreading over the creek bed. The water looked like an ice slushy, more flakes floating on top, and just the sight of that made the vague dread from Reed's dream potent and real.

He had to get back across it soon. If the snow looked this bad down here with the thick evergreen roof above him — *it had to be a blizzard everywhere else.*

Another ringtone: Goyte's *Somebody that I Used to Know*. Kristi was calling him. A half delirious smile from that; Reed had used *I Like Big Butts,* for Kristi's ringtone, but once again she'd stolen his phone and re-programmed it.

One of the stepping-stones he'd used to get over here had tumbled over with his fall. It was one he really needed to get back over there. Right now that rock was just part of the big whitewater slushy lazily overflowing it's banks beside him.

He'd have to get wet and cold – *really wet and cold* – to get out of this. Hell, *what difference does it make at this point?* He'd already lost the feeling in his toes.

Reed took one last look at the spot where the girl had been; sure she was long gone at this point. Not even a trace of her footprints remained where she'd stood. Snow covered everything now.

He laced his boots tight, wrapped the extra length around the hooks and tied them twice.

He found the shallowest point he could find and stepped in. The water ran up over his calf like iced-lightning.

"Sweet baby Jesus!" His teeth chattered. He'd always thought that was a joke. He pushed forward.

The water was deeper and the current was stronger than he'd imagined, and he was much slower than he imagined. The ice water splashed his crotch. Expletives exploded between his chattering teeth.

Just move forward. Keep moving forward.

He commanded his brain to swing the numb muscle sticks carrying him toward the bank, but the commands to actually pick up his feet were completely lost in the translation, and his right leg was mostly dragging, uselessly, behind him.

Dog barked from across the creek, urging him on.

"Ye-ye-yeah, D-D-Dog…"

Something flashed under the slushy water in the pool above the damn.

Yup, I was right, he thought, dully. *The big fish are hiding out right there. If I live through this – I'll come right back and fish those bad boys out. If.*

Dog barked.

Not far now, not far. Come on legs, just move. You can do this.

The ice-water wicked up his jacket, found purchase there, inched higher. And then, as if by magic, the water wasn't so cold anymore…in fact, *it was sort of warm.*

Reed realized that, at some point, he had stopped dead in the water. How long had he been that way, he wondered.

The water wasn't bad. It was okay once you got used to it. *You just had to get used to it that was all.*

Was Dog still barking? Yes. Seemed to be. Mostly she was shaking off snow. But she seemed to be moving in slow motion now, and she seemed really, really far away.

The snow was sticking to his jacket. He couldn't shake it off. It wasn't even snow so much, it was…more like a skin, a shiny, thick skin. It snapped off in places, fell away like an old shell.

Should tell the dog to quit barking. She'll wake everyone up and everyone in the house is tired.

So tired now.

What the fuck?

He was in the middle of a frozen creek. *Jesus, had he fallen asleep standing up?* Horses did that, didn't they? A burning flow poured out of him. *I'm peeing.* He couldn't even stop it. The heat of it shot pins and needles down his thighs; at the same time it drew the last of his body warmth with it.

The fish flipped just beneath the surface, rippling the snowy slush. Reed's eyes followed the silver flash. He was a big fellow all right. *A really big fellow,* the fish flipped over again –

"Jesus fuck!"

Reed dove across the creek, frozen fingers clawing into the snow for purchase. Icy water splashed his chest, his face; rocks bit into his chest but he didn't care.

"Mo-motherfu –! Sweet Jesus!"

He'd made it. He was across, he was out! He kept digging forward on his elbows anyway, pulling his feet as far from the creek – *from that awful thing in it* – as fast as he could, until Dog was jumping on him, licking his face.

He hugged her with everything he had left.

"Sweet Jesus," he exclaimed again. "Sweet baby Jesus!"

Reed turned slowly back, his brain wanting to see exactly what *It* was in the water, but his heart fighting that urge with all its might. *It was refraction, a trick of light.* The sort of optical nonsense that made things look weird in the water.

That's what it was. That's *all* it was.

He forced himself to look back at the pool.

But it wasn't the pool, or anything in it, that caught his eye now.

The girl had stepped out into the clear again. The most beautiful girl in the world had been watching over him, making sure he was okay.

He tried to smile for her.

The growl of the Polaris Ski Do engine from way up the bank.

The girl bolted into the cover of the other bank, her boots kicking up chunks of snow behind her.

Reed stuttered. *"G-G-Goodbye."*

He couldn't bring himself to look at the pool again. Just a few yards away from his numb legs, the burnt branch was mostly buried, the part he knew that still had needles anyway. But the bare part was still just that, bare.

Not even the snow wanted to settle on it.

"Reed!" His sister's voice sounded muffled, so far away. But he'd never been so glad to hear it.

"D-Down here! ...*the c-creek!*"

His voice broke, it was pitched higher, more like a girl's voice, than Kristi's.

A lump of snow beside him played *"Somebody that I Used to Know"* If he could breathe he'd laugh. Reed dug into the snow; his fingers showing all the coordination and articulation of bratwursts. Finally he recovered his phone, slid the phone icon to answer, and pressed it to his ear, he could barely hear Kristi through the static. *Dad would really be pissed about the coverage down here.*

"Got - GPS—ord-nates – --- hurt?"

"Just – freezing. Pulled my hamstring again."

"How --- get down?"

"Anyway you can," he said. "No trail."

"-kay – keep the cell on."

Another engine roared – the other Polaris. They'd probably started together but Kristi had beaten Dad down here. Frozen as he was, Reed still had to smile at that. *No one beat Kristi at anything.*

Across the creek, the small tufts of snow left by the girl's escape into the forest were already filling in, turning to shapeless mounds.

He was careful not to look at the wide pool in the creek.

-=.=.=.=.=.=.=.=.=-

"Phone on!"

Static. Nothing but static.

The map showed nothing. Of *course* it showed nothing. There was nothing up here but logging roads.

You are nowhere.

She'd chided Ken for over-reacting about the poor cell coverage. Now Amanda craned her neck the same way Ken always did, futilely searching the impenetrable forest for that great and powerful cell tower.

The forest itself was disappearing before her eyes, the trees and rocks blanching to white. The road ahead was barely discernible.

She was quite a ways from town now - but her trail was still visible, she was certain she could make her way back if she could just find a safe place to turn around.

No. Stay put. Stay here. The heater works. The gas tank is full. You've got a load of food and water in the back.

With a rush of panic she realized what she had just done – prepared an inventory for survival.

She blinked. *Come on, it's not that bad. We're not the only ones on this mountain.*

"*Phone on!*"

Nothing but crackle and hiss.

"*Damn it!*"

Nothing she could see ahead but thin road, mountain to the right and canyon to the left. She pulled the Denali as close to the mountain as she could, and set the brake.

Okay, okay. Just breathe. Pranayama breathing. She closed her eyes and mouth, began the slow, even draw of breath through her nostrils that had always calmed her before moving through her most difficult poses.

"MP3 - Krishna Das. Number 3."

In moments the cab began filling with the calming twang of a sitar, the warm rumblings of the melodeon, and the deep mellow chanting of Krishna Das, the calming mantras of Kirtan.

She powered the seat back down, folded her legs before her in lotus, and closed her eyes.

Outside the warm serenity of the cab, snow fell and drifted, blanketing the narrow road, blurring its boundaries.

A few hundred feet from Amanda's pocket of warmth lay another sanctuary.

The she wolf lay alone in her den. Ears pricked, nostrils twitching, head cocked to favor her one good eye. *The intruders were here.*

She stretched, rising in a series of downward, back and finally upward motions that would have been eerily familiar to Amanda; roughly the same *up and downward dog* poses Amanda had practiced six days a week for five years now.

The wolf kept her head low as she peered from the entrance of her den, ever aware of the dangers these men presented as she tested the bitter cold air.

Her mate was gone, fallen victim of the sickness that had affected so many. There would be no other mate. The pack had thinned and there had been few vital male pups *since the intruders had fouled the water.*

Her pack assembled as if from nowhere; like her, little more than gray shadows through the gauze of snowfall. Satisfied her own kind outnumbered any others here, she moved out.

Head held high, her tongue tasted the air, ears pricked for the telltale sounds. *Yes, they were the calls of the intruders.*

The others locked with her gaze. The she wolf's lips had formed what Amanda might have mistaken for a human expression, perhaps a smile; but there was no smile in it, only hunger.

The teeth of men are small, useless things. What they carry makes them dangerous. Separate them from what they carry, and they are prey.

The pack closed ranks and marched toward their prey as one, fluid as water flowing downhill.

-=.=.=.=.=.=.=.=.=-

"The Sheriff has a Sno-Cat moving up the road. They'll find her if she just stays put," Ken said.

"What if she doesn't?" Reed was still wrapped in towels; he'd sat for nearly an hour in a tub of tepid water, yelping from the sting of his own blood as it fought its way through the constricted channels of his extremities again. His fingers and toes were okay, just tingling now. No sign of frostbite.

But they could have lost him. Just that easy, they could have lost him.

But Amanda was still somewhere on a dangerous mountain logging road trapped in a blizzard that hadn't let up for hours.

Get back here. Now! That's what Ken had told his wife. His own words stung him. The last thing he knew she'd heard from him on that *fucking* phone. *For once he'd been forceful, for once he'd taken charge. Because of that, because of him, she was lost out there.*

Peace. Uninterrupted peace. That's all he'd really wanted for nearly twenty years, the reason he had dragged them all from their home - his own childish quest for uninterrupted peace. Why? So he could write music no one would ever listen to anyway.

He was only vaguely aware his son had spoken.

"What?"

"What if she made a wrong turn or something?"

"We've got her GPS coordinates," Kristi said. "The Denali isn't moving."

"Yeah – but what does that mean? It could be halfway down the side of the mountain. *We can get on the snow bikes and find her like you found me!*"

"It wasn't half this bad when we found you. We wouldn't get a half-mile in this – they'd just be looking for us too."

"This is crap. All we have to do is go straight down the road until we find Mom! This is bullshit."

They'd just rescued Reed – now Ken wanted to knock his lights out. He fought the urge; barely able to keep his voice even. *But the truth was he was fighting an even bigger battle with himself not to take a Polaris and look for Amanda on his own.* But as soon as he left, he knew they would follow. His whole family would be at risk. It was a treacherous passage to town in the best of conditions, with sheer drops of five hundred feet or more in places. In this weather, he'd accomplish nothing and his kids would have no one to look after them.

But they would have peace, uninterrupted peace.

Chapter 6

"So what's it like being a Narc, Mark Dark?"

"I'm not a Narc, Danny-boy." And his last name was two-syllables, pronounced *Dee Ark,* not dark. Not that Danny cared.

Mark D'Arc shoved his elbow into his best friend's forehead as he adjusted the big mirror between them. He was almost sorry he'd let Danny hitch. And the Sheriff would be pissed as hell if he found out.

"Oww – that *almost* hurt."

"Read me those coordinates again. Be useful for once."

Danny obliged him.

"She's just off a logging road."

"Good call, Sherlock." They were on a logging road themselves. Every road on this mountain was a logging road.

"You know the one. That gash in the hill before we turn north."

Mark nodded.

"Okay."

He'd made these runs with the Sno-Cat too many times. Tourists were always trying *"that little dashed shortcut right there on the map."* Even Oregonians who should know better – *Portlandians* mostly - underestimated the Oregon wilds and just how dangerous it was out here; they thought the wilderness was a Cub Scout camp.

But Californians were the worst.

Usually they were pretty much okay once he found them – just hungry, thirsty and stinky, but glad as hell to see him. But sometimes, they weren't okay at all.

He was thirteen, helping his dad on Search and Rescue the first time he'd seen a dead person. He'd gotten the full treatment his first time out: an entire family of California tourists frozen inside their big SUV. You might have thought they were just huddled up sleeping. But their faces were blue, and the kids' eyes were open. He'd never get that image out of his head; that first look inside after he and dad had scraped the snow and ice from the windshield. It was as if someone had painted the nightmare version of that old auto billboard: the American family's road tour. *See the USA in your Chevrolet.*

"Careful, cowboy."

A moment of eerie weightlessness before the treads caught.

"Got it. I'm good."

He hadn't been out in weather like this often, not even with the Cat. Even the halogen lights had trouble cutting through the milky soup out there. In all his twenty-two years, he'd only ever seen it this bad once, and that hadn't turned out well.

He should have waited. The woman would be fine sitting this storm out in that big old Yukon Denali all gassed up and full of food, as long as she didn't let the snow build up over the tailpipe... *Of course, what were the odds she'd think of that?*

Who was he kidding? He wouldn't leave *anyone* out in weather like this.

Danny was eyeballing him.

"What?"

"I say this as your best friend: You have to shave that thing off."

Mark ran his fingers through his long beard.

"Babes love beards."

"Yeah, the babes who live in trailer parks."

"You see those babes on Duck Dynasty? Hell. Screw you."

He moved away from the mountain to make the oncoming curve; he could feel the treads slide.

Oh, shit. This is not good.

The treads caught, the Cat lurched forward again, sweat was breaking over his brow now, but they had passed the worst turn. They were okay, he knew his way around this mountain better than anyone – with the exception of Sheriff Hicks, of course. And it wasn't like he could have waited anyway, this storm system had stalled over the coastal range, it wasn't moving anytime soon.

The acid burn of Tequila ripped through the air like jet fuel.

"You *really* are a dick, you know that?"

"Come on – this is the *good* stuff. *Jalisco Blanco,* baby. I ripped it off some illegals."

Mark shot Danny a glance more frigid than the outside air.

"Do you have any idea where we are, and what we're doing? We're on a mountain driving a road one *"C"*- hair wider than this can's treads in the middle of the *frickin' Perfect Storm.*"

Danny slipped the flask back into his jacket – but not before he took one quick swig.

"Spoilsport."

"Dick-wad."

Mark D'Arc shook his head, he knew it was so wrong he'd have laughed if he wasn't scared half to death. They'd been friends since kindergarten, lived on this mountain their entire lives. If nothing else, Danny tried to keep things light.

"So you think that stuck up jail-bait's gonna jump in your arms when you bring her mommy back?" Danny said.

"Dude, she's like eighteen or something," he said by way of an answer, but the truth was, yes, he *was* hoping to meet Kristi Carroll. "You have no idea who she is do you?"

Danny shrugged. "I know she's jail bait."

"Kristi Carroll? *Lady of the Lakers? She's an Olympic contender.* She'll medal too. I'll put money on it."

"Yeah, yeah. Big whoop. She's just a nice piece of San Quentin *Tail* if you ask me."

"Shit – why do I even hang out with an illiterate butt-hole like you? It's San Quentin *Quail* – not tail. You can't even *read* a frickin' sports page – hell, you can't read the comics."

"Oh yeah, you're Einstein."

"You're a complete idiot."

"New subject…" Danny said. "When that faggot, Chuck Speers, and those shit-heads from Medford got busted - you had *nothing* to do with that, right?"

"You just keep proving my point."

"It *was* you. I knew it."

"Oh yeah, I'm a regular G-man."

"Elliot Nest."

"Yeah. Whatever. That's me. We're here."

He pulled the Cat as far up the side of the mountain as he could without tipping. A moment's peace in the storm, only a few flakes slip-sliding to the floor now. But all the swath of Halogen light showed him were snow-covered trees in a snow-covered forest; a small, blue-white gash of a road slicing away into the side of the big, blue-white mountain. He swept the searchlight in a wide arc around the Sno-Cat. Nothing. He turned off the engine, popped the door open and listened to the forest.

The cold came in with claws. The cab shook with a gust, then silence.

In every direction, nothing but snow. Beautiful but eerie, quiet as a cemetery.

He'd lived on this mountain his entire life; it still amazed him how fast things could change up here.

"Yeah," Danny said. "We're here. *So where is she?*"

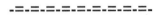

DeerSlayr Wolfyn, the crusty, powerful dwarf warlock, walked through the Land of the Dead. He hadn't summoned Raspberry or Syndee. He

wandered alone, looking for a fight in the snow-covered forest. He didn't care if he died.

There was nothing Reed could do. His hamstrings ached so bad his legs had barely carried him upstairs to his room. His Dad didn't even have the balls to try and find his mom. Kristi wouldn't do it either, and he had no chance of finding her himself.

I'm a worthless piece of shit who can't help his Mom when she needs me most.

He couldn't even save *himself* today. His sister had.

So in the end, Reed had done what he always did when faced with the truth - that he was just a pathetic loser - he retreated to his room, logged onto his computer, and became DeerSlayr once again.

So where were the Malwor thugs now? Where were the hordes of computer-generated dinosaurs and ogres and orcs when he needed them? There had to be someone to fight. He was a lone traveler in the frickin' Land of the Dead – certain death to Glokkun and Malwor alike.

Before him, a wide creek cut through a snow-covered riverbed. If he wasn't feeling like crap, he probably would have laughed. Reed had lost himself in Mythykal to escape his real life – and now DeerSlayr was reliving his day, every bit as useless as his real-life counterpart.

Where had that girl come from today? She was *so* pretty.

She'd run away – but she'd come back when he'd gone into the water. She waited to make sure he was okay.

So why was she so scared of him?

The stream at DeerSlayr's feet was clear, there were even fish in it.

Reed shuddered; DeerSlayr backed away.

Exactly what had he seen today? *That thing in the water.* It couldn't have been real; the light playing with his eyes – refracted images in the water. He didn't see what he *thought* he had. *He couldn't have.*

Snorts and hissing behind DeerSlayr. A group of raptors had him cornered, the river blocked his escape. *Fine, he had them right where he wanted them.*

They snapped their toothy jaws, swung their tails, DeerSlayr wielded his ax like the warrior he was, left hand, right, both hands, undercuts. Blood and scales flew, flecking the snow around him, painting it. Their blood. *His blood.* What did it matter?

His health subsided. Theirs emptied completely.

In the end, DeerSlayr stood alone once again; hacked bits of the vanquished reptiles seeping into the snow around him. His ax ran with blood. He hadn't even needed to hurl a spell.

But he'd lost quite a bit of health in the fight. He lifted his shoulders in a sigh, turned back to the water.

A bolt of energy struck him squarely between the shoulders, knocked him clean across the stream. Another blow would finish him. Well, that was fine. What did he care?

He raised his head wearily, and turned to face his cowardly opponent.

WyldChyld stood across the river, hands raised summoning another spell to hurl, another bolt of lightning, her white hair tipped with blue flame, writhing like snakes about her face.

And then she too was struck by a spell.

She corkscrewed into the air, then landed neatly on her feet - ready to fight.

DeerSlayr planted his ax in the ground, and used it to pull himself to his knees. In the gray forest beyond WyldChyld a tree broke into hundreds of tiny gray squares, collected itself into a tree shape again, it broke apart just as quickly. A small gray shadow flickered across the trunk. DeerSlayr yanked his ax free and flung it toward the tree in one fluid motion. It spun right past WyldChyld's hips and struck the trunk right where the shadow had settled. The shadow burst and faded away.

WyldChyld spun away and hurled another curse – *at him.*

So much for being nice.

From another world he watched DeerSlayr's body, *his body*, sink into the snow.

As the Land of the Dead faded before his eyes, he saw WyldChyld recoil, then fall to the ground, rolling, struck from all sides. Just before he blipped-out entirely, he saw her body sink into the snow too.

He'd asked the barkeep in Bryn Shyre about her. Apparently, the message had been relayed.

Reed tapped furiously at the keyboard.

Re-spawn! Damn it. Re-spawn!

DeerSlayr did re-spawn, finally, or his ghost did, but all the way back in Bryn Shyre again. Now he'd have to make that ridiculously long journey back to the Land of the Dead to retrieve his body.

Damn it.

He floated over the serpentine streets, wondering if there might be any chance at all WyldChyld had spawned back here too.

He was becoming familiar with Bryn Shyre now, the shops, the alleyways. By now it should be like home, he guessed. He'd come back every night since his first visit to the One-Eyed Eagle, and he found himself heading toward the tavern now, even though his first order of business should have been getting his body back.

He crossed onto the street where the tavern was located only to find it blocked by five guards.

What's up with that?

As a ghost, the guards wouldn't make any difference anyway. He passed right through them. Two hunters were stupidly trying to negotiate with them.

"We have business at the Eagle. Five silver if you let us pass."

"No business there today. And if we want silver…we'll make it."

"Was that a ghost?" One of the guards said.

"Crap…" The other said.

The One-Eyed Eagle was gone. In fact, that entire section of the street was gone. In its place, a series of gray cubes and flickering squares like the ones he'd seen earlier. Small yellow hash-marks outlined the areas where windows, doors and other bits of architecture had once been.

"What the fuck?"

"Nothing to see here." *A ghost guard.* He'd never seen one of those. The Mythykal programmers were fast as hell.

"What's going on?"

"Nothing our magic cannot set right. Retrieve your body and re-spawn."

"I keep getting attacked by things I can't see."

Now the ghost guard seemed interested.

"Is that why you're dead?"

"Yes."

The guard took a tired breath. He shook his head wearily, then checked a readout that was only gibberish to DeerSlayr.

"Surely, I shall return you to your body. You traveled in the Land of the Dead, where you were set upon by thieves near the Pyrian Spring."

"Yeah - I saw something weird first – a bunch of little square pixels like the ones across the street there -"

The guard held up his hand.

"Please, speak the language of this world."

"Yea, 'twas witchery. Before my very eyes the bark of a tree vanished in a – *come on, it was a bunch of gray pixels, the texture blipped out for a second, okay?* Just before *whatever it was hit me with a bolt.* Is that what happened to the Eagle? Is that why it's just a bunch of untextured polygons now?"

The guard winced.

And, like that, the ghost of DeerSlayr Wolfyn floated over his body in the snow-covered Pyrian Spring in the Land of the Dead.

Yay, teleportation! If they can do it why not just make it part of the damn game?

Across the creek, WyldChyld's body.

He floated across the creek to it. WyldChyld had obviously taken plenty of time and care building her avatar. She was a comely one all-right.

This was perfect. The teleport had bought him the time he needed.

Instead of collecting his body, he hid behind a tree and waited for her to respawn.

It seemed an eternity before he saw her floating across the river toward him; DeerSlayr moved further under cover of the trees.

She stopped over his body.

She's checking me out, he thought, proud and happy behind his trees.

She moved back to her body, reclaimed it then and crossed the river to his again.

She started looting his body.

"Hey! Stop that!" He hollered, floated out from behind the tree.

But she couldn't hear a ghost, and she was Malwor – anything he said would have been gibberish to her anyway.

He floated over his body, quickly reclaimed it before she could do more damage. She raised her sword ready for him to rise – so she could quickly kill him again and gain a few more points.

She's ruthless!

DeerSlayr caught her down stroke with the hilt of his ax – knocking her backwards with the force.

He held up one hand *hold-on* – half-prepared for her to cut it off with the next swing of her blade.

She backed away, circled. Prepared a curse.

What could he do? He couldn't speak to her directly. Couldn't make her understand. *It was useless to try.*

But she was six levels higher than he was. That didn't mean he *couldn't* best her in battle, he was a crusty, hard fighter himself – dirty when he had to be – but...

Back at the keyboard, Reed typed the one thing he and WyldChyld had in common. He typed it over and over again.

"LOHi LOHi LOHi LOHi"

She stepped back. Had she recognized the slang acronym for Lake Oswego High? Or had she seen it as mindless gibberish, or worse yet, a war cry of some sort. Would she even see a pattern or were the letters truly scrambled? He had no idea, really. His typing had been a desperate gesture.

To his amazement and delight, she said,

"LOHi>"

He nodded. Wait... *what did the right angle bracket mean?*

Reed scanned his keyboard. The right angle bracket was the next key left of the question mark. *Oh man – had she typed a question mark on her keyboard?* Sure she had. *LOHi* had come back to him the same way, LOHi, only because she'd just typed the letters back to him the same way she'd seen them on her screen. But now she was repeating those letters as a question, only her "?" came out like a ">" on his screen.

Now he had it - *everything he typed came out one as the letter one key to the right on her screen!* The letters weren't scrambled at all for Malwor, they were only off by one key.

Okay. Okay. Just don't kill me while I try this out. He began to sweat.

He typed, "KIGu"

Her answer came back slowly…but oh, so surely. He laughed.

A crooked smile on WyldChyld's face now.

"LOHi" She said, then, "LOL" Laughing Out Loud.

":P:" he typed, ":P:", which, on her screen, would return, "LOL."

DeerSlayr Wolfyn *did* laugh out loud now.

"We broke the code. We can talk!"

"But we're not supposed to. You're *Glokkun rot!*"

"And you're *Malwor scum!* So what?"

"I think they can kick us out for talking to each other."

But what did he care now. He was actually talking to the girl he'd seen under the stairs at school, or chatting with her at least...at least he *thought* he was.

"You *ARE* the girl from under the stairwell, right?"

"Hah – are YOU the guy with the Lugs, the guy who'd rather hang out in the hall than class."

"That's me."

"Why haven't you been at school?"

"I'm out of there now – home-schooled."

"Lucky boy. Where do you live?"

"In Cedar."

"Where the F is that?"

"Up in the mountains. Cascades."

"That's gotta hella' suck."

"Hella' – except –"

A bolt of lightning knocked the wind right out of him. The forest canopy above them pixilated as an eerie gray shadow raced across the branches.

"The thing's in that tree!"

WyldChyld's curse and DeerSlayr's ax struck the tree with one explosive flash. The gray shadow shattered; the fading bits of it sank to the ground and vanished. The tree looked normal once more. DeerSlayr climbed the trunk; retrieved his ax.

"What *are* those things?"

"Hackers," WyldChyld said. "They've messed with the servers for a couple months now. The Mythykal coders say they've got it handled. But they don't."

A team of guards appeared from nowhere.

"Breach!" One of them yelled.

DeerSlayr fell back, hurling a curse toward WyldChyld– a tree behind her turned to salt and crumbled. She sliced the air with her sword, missing his head by a good two feet, pirouetted, then flung a curse of her own, an unlucky crow perched innocently on a nearby boulder dropped to the snow-covered ground, stone dead.

The guards watched the Glokkun and the Malwor hurl ineffective curses, wildly wield their weapons – apparently incapable of actually landing a blow.

"Pathetic!" one guard spat in disgust just before the entire security team blipped out of sight.

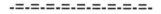

Fucking cold. Danny clapped his gloves together. Hopped in place. *What was he fucking doing out in this?*

He'd gone along for the ride. Now he was freezing his face and tootsies off looking for some latte-sodden bee-yotch who'd probably never driven that big SUV anywhere but Starbucks before she tweetered her tight ass up here.

Stupid fucking bee-yotch.

Jesus it was cold – and quiet. Until the walkie talkie hissed.

"Don't wander off too far, bud."

He clicked to speak.

"Maybe you should, you know, call in some backup or something and have a shot."

"Sorry, bud, we're it. They can't send anyone else. Storm's not going anywhere. Walk south another five minutes, then head back to the Cat."

F'n Boy Scout. Mark was such a straight-arrow. Always was.

"Make yourself useful," Mark had said when he handed over the walkie talkie.

Then he'd taken the Sno-Cat up the road Mom Carroll should have taken. Danny was walking back the way they'd come, looking for any trail into the woods they might have missed – or any sign she went over the cliff. Wouldn't be tough to do here.

Boy Scout. Damn Boy Scout.

Man it was quiet up here; no wind now but the snow was coming down hard again. Danny couldn't remember seeing this much snow drop this fast. *Global fucking warming.*

He figured he'd gone nearly half a mile from the northern cut-off, checking any break in the forest and rock a big SUV might be able to fit itself through if Mrs. Starbucks had the bright idea of leaving the road to find a shortcut through a snow-choked forest in a blizzard.

Nothing. Nada.

Crap, he hadn't dressed to hang out in this. Didn't bring his good gloves and the damn snow boots were just an old pair that happened to be in the Sno-Cat; they were way too big. He pulled the moth-eaten gloves off with his teeth, breathed some life into his frozen fingers. He stomped his feet.

Well heck now, while the gloves were off - why not indulge?

Danny slapped his pockets until he found the right Velcro flap and ripped that up, yanked the zipper beneath, and soon his icy fingers found the leather-covered flask. He eagerly twirled off the cap, then paused long enough to take an appreciative whiff – *ahhh, the sweet burn of Tequila in a snowstorm.* He sucked a shot into his ample cheeks, rolled the sweetness there for a moment then swallowed it all down.

"Oh yeah! Thank you, Ernesto Gonzales-Gonzales!"
Such a sweet burn!
That was better. Warmer now.

He'd already taken three or four such indulgences on his way down the road, and now the lightness of the flask - a gift from his ol' favorite *muchacho* Ernesto – made him sad.

Sad to think how closed-minded folks were too. Folks acted like the *illegals* up here were some kind of disease or something.

It was almost like they were frickin' second class citizens or something.

Mark was squarely in that camp. Mark didn't want the illegals here.

"Mark – you just don't like Mexicans!" Danny shouted into the wind and snow.

But the Mexicans, legal or not, were Danny's friends. Especially his ol' favorite muchacho, Ernesto-Ernesto Gonzales. No, it was Ernesto *Gonzales-Gonzales,* wasn't it? Damn, those double names were a bitch. Ernesto had not only provided him this fine Agave nectar – but some damn serious smoke too.

Danny knew better than Mark. The country would be nowhere without the illegals working all those crops – doin' all that agro shit they did. Americans wouldn't do that work.

"Where's the *agro* they work on up here?" Mark always said, "agro" being his short slang for agriculture. "What crops they growing in the mountains, dude? Pine-cones? Deadfalls everywhere. Nobody even chops timber up here anymore."

Hell, Mark was a *narc.* Danny would never call him a snitch – he loved the dumb idiot too much to ever say that.

But he was definitely a narc. Nobody but Danny really knew that for sure, and nobody but his best friend Danny would ever say it to his face – but it was pretty obvious. If you partied *and Mark saw you* – eventually you got busted. Wasn't hard to figure out. So you kept things on the down-low with him.

Mark Dark the Narc. *Such a frickin' boy scout.*

Sure the Mexicans worked pot farms up here, maybe they even had a crystal meth lab or two. So what? People had to party.

"Racist pig! You hate Mexicans, Mark Dark the Narc!"

Almost scary how fast the sound was swallowed in the silence of endless snow, so cold now it fell dry, shin-deep powder he wasn't walking through so much as pushing into drifts now. Even the Sno-Cat's wide trail was fading. You only even knew there was a road here 'cause of the break in the trees. If that lady turned off somewhere, and she must have – she sure as hell wasn't here - there was no way to tell where she did it anymore.

Hell, Missus Starbucks is already home, warming her tootsies in front of a nice log fire with a big, hot paper cup full of latte.

Bitchfuck it's cold!

The idea of a hot drink right now sounded real good - *a nice Mexican coffee with chocolate and a double-shot of Tequila.*

His flask was empty. *Crap.* He shook it.

"Now that is a shame." Damn thing practically emptied itself.

He pulled off his gloves again, opened the cap and upended the little leatherette container over his upturned mouth, his tongue flicking for any last drops. Man, that endless gray above him didn't look good. It was just endless gray goop hanging right on top of the mountains. The gray and the snowflakes twirled overhead. *Crap he was dizzy.* Bad idea to look up real fast like that.

He brought his eyes down, *and liked what he saw even less.*

One big silver eye stared at him from the forest. He sobered quickly.

A wolf, a huge one. She had only one eye – a*nd that eye wasn't anywhere near where it should be.* Halfway over her snout, like a frickin' cyclops. What might have been her right eye was barely a lid-covered wart.

"Jesus, fuck..."

She moved slowly forward.

Danny had a pistol, didn't ever come up here without one, but it was in another Velcro'd and zippered pocket inside his jacket. He could feel the weight of it there – *he just had to remember how to get to it...*

He took a slow step backwards trying to put a little more distance between them, buy a few more seconds while he found his gun. He took another slow, easy, backwards step, and another, rolling the zipper a little further down his chest as he backed away, his fingertips searching the Velcro flaps. She matched his steps one for one. A dark stream followed her, flecking the snow.

Three dark blotches in her side. A *wounded* wolf. *Shit.*

The wolf's lips drew into a snarl that was almost a smile. *And suddenly, she wasn't alone. Gray shadows sprang from the tree line.*

The walkie talkie squawked loudly, just as *he found the pistol grip.*

"Danny! Where are you?"

Danny dropped the flask, drew the gun and pulled as the wolf sprang and – nothing.

Fucking safety.

He smelled the gaminess of their fur, the hot bodies springing over him as he tripped and slid.

Clicking the safety off was the last thing Danny's hand did before it was torn from his wrist like soft bread. A wolf choked it hungrily down. The gun discharged, but Danny barely noticed the 9mm round tear through his thigh. By then, Danny's throat had already spilled his life's blood into the snow.

-=.-=.-=.-=.-=.-=.-=.-=.-=-

"Come on, Danny. Pick up."

Mark had already driven a good distance past the point where they'd parted ways.

All Danny had to do was head back the way they'd come, look for broken branches, dirt clods in the snow – anything they might have missed on the drive up.

Walk a little ways down the road and come back, that's all Danny had to do.

Danny was a good guy, but he was a *fuck-up* sometimes. *Damn it, he could be a fuck-up.*

Where are you now, buddy? Where are you?

Boot tracks wavered off the road, straight toward what Mark knew was a shear drop of two hundred feet on the south side of the road. *Danny knows better - no way he'd gone over the side.*

What if he'd gone over to take a quick look, to make sure the SUV hadn't gone over? You had a good look at the side of the mountain from there. Danny could have leaned too far, just lost his balance and slipped over. *He had that damn flask with him. The Tequila.*

Why didn't I just take that damn thing away from him – just till we got back?

A little further down the road, Mark found Danny's tracks again. They turned away from the cliff, back up onto

what little there was of the Cat's original trail, nearly
obliterated by fresh powder now. The storm's second wave
had hit hard.

The boot tracks wavered off the Cat's trail again, back
toward the side of the road. Mark swung the halogen that
way, the light picked up yellow rims of ice in the snow; pee
tubes that formed the word "D A N N Y."

God, you're a dimwit. But, for the first time since Danny
had left his sight Mark was smiling.

Yup, that was Danny all right. Probably drank down
the whole damn flask before he let loose with that.

The first good laugh he'd had today died in his throat
as he fishtailed into a bend in the road.

*The wolves turned their bloodied faces into the spot light, but
only one of them fled. The others turned their attention back to the
tattered scarecrow in the snow, shaking it like mean kids fighting over a
broken doll.*

Mark floored the Cat, struck the side of the mountain
and nearly caught air. He pulled the brake, snapped the AR15
off its mount, rammed a clip in its belly and threw the cab
door open with his shoulder.

The first bullet whined through the wind and snow,
glanced off the road behind the wolves. Deep in the forest a
branch exploded in a cloud of snow and splintered wood.

The pack gave him their full attention, now.

The second shot was a hot hammer against Mark's ear, but little more than a tennis-ball *"pok!"* in the storm. One wolf spun a quarter turn in the air, dropped face first in the snow.

The pack scattered.

Mark ran, stumbled, caught himself and fired three more shots. Bullets ripped through the nearest wolf's hind quarters kicking his legs out beneath it, the wolf skidded sideways through the snow.

But Mark barely saw any of that. All he saw now was a *thing;* a scarlet ruin of meat and bone in the snow, the thing wore Danny's shredded blue coat and the boots Danny had found in the cab, two sizes too big.

Chapter 7

When people go missing in the mountains of Oregon, they become a story, a media event.

The story of Amanda Carroll, mother of two – most notably Oregon's very own Olympic hopeful, Kristi Carroll -

combined with the heroism and tragic death of a volunteer searcher during those first hours, was tailor made for the news. Like many stories of the missing, Amanda's was told first with pragmatic optimism; Amanda Carroll had plenty of food and water. If she remained in that large, black vehicle she would be easily spotted from the air once the storm broke and the search planes could fly.

As days went by and the planes and choppers flew and the searchers fanned out to find nothing, the tone changed quickly to urgency, and then to desperation with an almost macabre mix of preventive information. There were sidebars and insets on the dangers of car heaters and carbon monoxide poisoning, the disorienting effects of hypothermia. As two weeks went by and the chances of wilderness survival dwindled to none, desperation became cruel speculation. Amanda Carroll's marriage was dissected, her state of mind questioned. Within three weeks Amanda was the despondent mother of two who had deserted her children and escaped marriage to a workaholic husband. Amanda's tragic disappearance had been downgraded to an elaborate hoax.

With all their tried and true methods for keeping *missing persons* stories newsworthy exhausted, the news media left. The event was over. Amanda Carroll's story had played out.

-=-=-=-=-=-=-=-=-

How do you tell a man that the body of the woman he loves may not be found till the spring thaw, if ever?

Sheriff Billy Hicks was faced with exactly that question now. It wasn't the first time he'd told a family their loved one wouldn't be coming home. Cedar Mountain was *Billy's* mountain, the search and rescue efforts coordinated by Billy himself, often from the cockpit of his own plane, an aging Piper Cherokee that was his pride and joy.

It was personal with him. Over the years he'd helped a lot of families. He'd let a few down.

The man who sat in his office today wasn't the same one he'd met only three weeks earlier. Ken Carroll had lost fifteen pounds easy. His face was drawn, bearded, and that beard was sprinkled through with gray. Three weeks ago a young man had stood in his office, shocked and disoriented - even angry at times – but vital and young.

His kids weren't with him today. They hadn't been for a few days now.

How would he handle this without his family beside him?

In the end Ken Carroll took the news with a simple nod.

-=-=-=-=-=-=-=-=-

Kristi had beaten her best today. Down the hill in twenty-eight point zero three seconds. The ten shots she'd fired had clustered within two centimeters.

She was stronger, faster, better than ever. She'd double-timed it back up the hill in her snowshoes, with her skis, poles, and boots harnessed to her back. She dropped them, snapped into her boots and skis, and shushed across the yard to the house without skipping a beat. Once inside she ripped Velcro, unzipped her ski clothing away, placed her entire kit and weapons neatly on the mudroom racks and headed for the basement, huffing maybe, but not slowing.

The unmistakable *pok-pok-pok* of epee –versus-wall-target met her before she reached the stairway.

Reed was at it again.

She moved downstairs quietly, inspecting his form, the power of the push-off from his back foot, the angle of his forward knee and toes, the timing between thrust and lunge, and the length and depth and accuracy of that lunge.

He'd been down here for hours at a time lately. Lifting weights, really working out, and actually hitting the wall target with his thrusts.

She was glad to see the darker hair roots making a comeback on his head. Maybe there was hope for him after all.

Maybe there really *was* something to playing video games. For someone as new to Fencing as Reed was, his accuracy was pretty good. But even accuracy was secondary at this point. Technique was everything.

"You can take those lunges wider now."

He continued, winded, and a little wobbly. Strength and stamina had to be built – and that took time. But you couldn't fence without a base.

"What?"

"Move a half step back, don't be afraid to go lower."

He did, but then his body moved forward too, and his forward knee dropped. He nearly fell.

"Don't collapse. Keep your body straight over your hips. Don't fold over your knee."

"You're a pain."

"Are you just playing or do you want to do it right? You'll get hurt if you're playing. I won't help you do that."

"I don't need help."

Yes, you do. *More than you know. We all need help right now.*

But just this once she said nothing.

Instead she waited.

His next lunge was more of an angry lurch. He nearly lost his balance and the epee.

She was careful not to react.

Reed was careful not to look angrily back at her. He stared at the floor instead. Finally, he asked the question she was hoping for.

"What am I doing wrong?"

She pulled another epee from the stand.

"Watch me. Watch where my head and shoulders are during the lunge."

She lunged twice, she remained in place on the second one.

"Am I leaning forward?"

"No."

"Where is my head in my stance?"

"Right in the middle."

"Your *legs* carry you to your target – *not your shoulders.* Men have a tough time with that – a lot of your strength is up there. But you can't afford to lose your balance in this sport, and your *real* strength is in your abdomen and your legs."

"But I have a longer reach when I lean forward."

"Have you missed the target even once today?"

"Well, duh."

"If you miss your target you *become* a target. If you're off-balance on your lunge your legs won't carry you back to safety fast enough. Your opponent will have your back and win the touch."

Reed took his place and started again.

The effect on his lunges was immediate; they were balanced and smooth. He was a fast learner when he didn't fight her.

"Tres bien! Very good."

He actually grinned.

"Let's bout."

"I said your *lunges* were good. You're not ready to bout."

"Just for the heck of it. I want to see how fast you really are."

"No. You only want to see how *slow* you really are. You don't even know how to parry."

"What's that?"

"Give me a break. You've been to every tournament."

"I'm busting your balls. I know what a parry is."

"Let me see a parry four."

He swung his arm and blade across his body, the tip pointed nearly straight up.

"That...was really awful. What are you protecting – the ceiling? Try a six."

He pulled the blade back and across– the bell ending up two feet past his body in the other direction. Blade straight up again.

"That…I don't even know what *that* was. Sort of a spastic eight."

"Come on – you couldn't get past that."

She pulled a mask from the rack and tossed it to him.

"Okay D'Artagnan, show me what you've got. You know how to put the mask on, right?"

"We don't need the stupid masks."

"Yes, we *do* need the stupid masks. And put down the epee – we're using foils."

"Those are toys."

"They are *practice weapons*. You want to do this?"

She tossed him a foil, chose one for herself, pulled on her glove and stepped onto the strip.

He grudgingly put the epee away and pulled on the mask.

"Uh–uh – mask off until we salute."

"Jesus."

She waited until he stood in place across from her. She brought the bell even with her lips then swooshed the blade down and away. Reed mimicked the move.

"Wait a second."

She took his mask from him, turned it around in his arm then stepped back.

"Okay – put it on now. Bib under the chin then pull up and back. All right. You got it."

"I feel like a frickin' bee farmer."

She took her place. "En' garde!"

He stood there.

"Alle'"

He did nothing.

"That basically means start –"

"I know – I've seen you –"

"Okay then. Let's see what else you've learned."

They stepped forward.

"You're holding it wrong – and way too tight."

"No I'm not."

She lunged, caught the mid-blade of his foil with the thick forte of hers and quickly twisted her wrist – his foil sprang into the air, the guard bell rang brightly against the steel uprights of the leg press machine and the tip of her foil pressed the center of his chest before the foil hit the floor.

"Yes, you were."

Without so much as bending her waste, she slid her blade beneath his foil, and, with a flick snapped it straight up, catching the blade in her hand. She place it in his, turned his wrist up and, bent it in.

"Ow!"

"Baby! You need to supinate your wrist, that will point the blade toward your opponent's chest, and it won't slide off target. Don't squeeze the handle so hard – just use these two fingers and the ball of your thumb – and make sure the pommel – the silver weight on the end – doesn't get stuck against your wrist – that's why I was able to bind your blade and disarm you so easily."

"You could see that from there?"

"You will too one day if you stick with it."

"This isn't easy."

"Nope. But it's fun when you do it right. Work on the parries. Just try four and six for now." She took his wrist, "Keep the blade on target. Think of rolling the guard bell over a tabletop – roll in for parry four, roll out for parry six – – keep it level."

"Okay – but if I keep the blade down – you'll just come over it."

"Try it your way. En garde. Alle'"

She lunged, he whipped his blade high; she slipped neatly underneath and caught him square in the sternum – right where she'd hit him before.

"Ow! That hurts!"

"Yes, it does. We should be wearing the jackets too – and pads – but even then you get welts, it *always* hurts. The pain is motivation for learning your parries."

"What if I just do the same thing with my hand a little lower?"

"Try it. Alle'"

He brought the blade across his chest, point straight in the air as she lunged. This time she double lunged, ending up so close to him he couldn't bring his blade down to touch her. Her point, on the other hand, caught him in exactly the same place.

"Ow!"

"Learn to parry the right way – and you'll never feel that pain again."

He jumped back, lunged at her, she slapped his blade away, hit him in the same place again.

"Stop that! Aim somewhere else!"

"Learn to parry. Keep your blade down. Don't commit so soon."

She lunged, he covered his chest. This time she went low, striking him square in the balls. He doubled over.

"*God – fu-*"

"Learn parry two for that one – *or* we can keep working on six and four until you learn them correctly. Your choice."

He slapped her blade away, lunged; she leapt back, parried and countered, striking his clavicle this time.

"Ow! Quit showing off! I'm trying!"

He lunged until he could barely move, each time with similar results. Finally, he caught her blade, countered, and nearly hit her.

"Good! Good! Now – forward, now back, counter my moves – if you keep lunging you'll just wear yourself out. It's like boxing – back and forth, don't commit until you're sure. Keep your distance until you see an opening. Then strike."

They slapped each others' blades. Suddenly she yelled and stomped her foot twice on the strip.

"Stop! Stomping your foot *means stop!*"

Her blade had been moving so fast he didn't even notice the tip had broken off. Now the jagged steel edge glistened like a glass shard inches in front of his mask

A ball of nausea swelled in the pit of his stomach. If he hadn't stopped, he'd have lost his right eye.

"*That,* little brother," Kristi said, "is why we *always* wear a mask when we fence."

-=-=-=-=-=-=-=-=-

Channel 8 Local News, the lone film crew on site was setting up for what would be Sheriff Hicks' last press conference on the subject of Amanda Carroll. Only one news outlet still carrying the story; a sad blessing there.

Cammie Wilson, correspondent at large and aspiring news anchor, Ken supposed, with her bobbed blonde hair and flawless makeup, was receiving last minute touch-ups before the news conference. Cammie at least, had been one of the more polite reporters.

Two experienced mountaineers had been found frozen on Mount Hood this week. Four fishermen died crossing the sandbar in Coos Bay the week before. Two teen girls drowned in their car when an ice jam broke in Sandy and flooded a crossing near their home. The day Amanda disappeared a young man looking for her was attacked and killed by wolves.

This morning, Amanda had officially brought this winter's death toll to ten.

Oregon Wilderness 10, Oregonians 0. Oregon Wilderness wins this season in a laugher.

This final press conference would announce the score to those few still listening out there, but most folks were sure Amanda had just run off anyway.

When it came down to it, no one out there really cared.

Amanda Carroll wasn't his wife anymore. She was just a story people had grown tired of.

The reporters had been his best hope – keeping the searches going, the attention focused. But once hope had turned to hoax in the news, Ken had had enough of the media. He gave curt, one-word answers. He made himself boring – the best protection against the press he could muster - and it finally worked. These days Ken left unhindered through the back door of the Sheriff's office.

He climbed onto the Ski Doo, but just before he floored it out of there, someone called his name.

Cammie Wilson. She waved off her cameraman, left her microphone in the hands of an assistant and hurried over to him.

Part of him wanted to leave her flattened beneath a trail of cinders and snow. Instead, he took a deep breath and let her speak.

"If you hear anything I can follow up on, please let me help," she said. "I'm so sorry."

Another story is what you want, he wanted to say, *you're not sorry, you're not sorry at all.* But truthfully she was one of the few who had been square with him. He nodded, *yes, he would follow up, eventually,* unable to manage speaking the actual words just now. He didn't bother taking her card again. He had her number.

.=.=.=.=.=.=.=.=.=.

Yellow bits of torn police tape still flapped from some of the trees.

Some *crime scene.*

We won't rest until the wolves who perpetrated this foul murder are punished to the full extent of the law.

The real crime here had been Mark's. He should never have let his friend out of the Sno-Cat with that flask. The wolves were just being wolves. Killing was what they did.

Mark swung the snowmobile away from the middle of the road, away from the packed snow that still held Danny's blood beneath it.

He shouldn't have brought Danny in the first place. Well, that was obvious.

"Dickwad." He said.

In his head, Danny upped that description by calling Mark an *asswipe* - and that made Mark smile.

They'd autopsied one of the wolves he'd shot. No rabies – but, how the thing was even alive was a mystery. It was a freak, full of congenital defects – the weirdest of which – it had two hearts, the second only more or less functional. Wildlife defects out here were getting more and more common, which made it all the more obvious that some nasty chemicals were being brewed in these mountains — and running off into the streams.

Mark Dark, the hometown Narc.

It wasn't just pot, it was Crystal Meth at the very least. God knew what else.

The other wolf he'd hit had managed to drag itself off somewhere to die and was probably buried under three feet of snow by now.

He could have shot them all. Part of him wished he had.

As it was, the ASPCA, PETA and several other eco-rabid groups — and there were a ton of them in Oregon — had already lodged complaints to Sheriff Hicks and Search and Rescue that Mark had even shot two of them. They'd even picketed the tiny one-bedroom shack Mark called home until the news cameras finally quit coming to cover them. Having run *Shumacher Fur* out of Portland after one hundred years of fair business in town, the animal rights groups apparently had nothing better to do than harass a man whose best friend had been eaten alive by wolves.

He pushed the pedal down and drifted around a bend in the road.

"Jesus!"

A woman skier, the tips of her skis dangerously close to the edge of the very cliff where Danny had last relieved himself, was staring over the precipitous drop.

"Ma'am! Don't move!"

She turned to him, slid her visor up. She was young, much younger than he'd thought - just tall. He swallowed. She was strikingly beautiful, *for a kid.* And he knew exactly who she was.

"I know what I'm doing," Kristi Carroll said.

He pulled the snowmobile between her and the cliff anyway, forcing her to back up several feet.

"Your mom's not down there, Miss Carroll."

She grimaced.

"You don't know that."

"We've been up and down this area. There's no sign any vehicle went over the side."

She glanced toward the gorge, then at the bend in the road.

"He was your friend, wasn't he? The guy who was killed."

Mark tried not to react with anything more than a nod, so many levels to that story, all of them painful. Danny's blood alcohol level had been kept out of the news, so was the fact Danny should never have been in that Sno-Cat in the first place. The news hadn't mentioned Mark and

Danny were best friends either, only that Danny was a volunteer. But Kristi had seen them together at the Tavern. Back then, Mark guessed, they were just a couple older dudes ogling her.

Now they were all part of the same tragedy, linked forever by separate ones.

"I'm sorry," she said. "Your name is Mark, right? I'm *Kristi*. Not Miss Carroll."

He nodded.

She turned back to the gorge, and gave a strange echo of a question he'd asked three weeks ago, *"Where is she?"*

A terrible, sad image for him, a tableau framed by a frozen windshield: The beautiful American family out for a road trip. A short cut taken down a mountain road. *All of them seeming to sleep…*

"She must have turned off the road somewhere, one of the logging spikes. We've searched all the obvious ones…"

"You're still looking?" she said, hopefully, "The news said the search was over."

"You don't know Sheriff Hicks. He never gives up. He's already been searching from his plane this morning. Nothing gets past him. This is *his* mountain."

"She's alive," she said.

He bit his lip. He'd given her the wrong sense of things.

"Look, when I say we're looking…well, I don't know any good way to say this –"

"Then don't say it," she pulled her visor down, pushed off down the road. He watched until she disappeared behind the bend, right over the snow that still held his friend's blood.

That went well, jackass.

In Mark's head, it was Danny's voice chiding him.

"Yeah, that went real well."

Yes, they were still looking – the search went on, but not the rescue part. They were in recovery mode now, looking for a body not a survivor, and even that part of the search had become greatly *diminished*; it was just he and Sheriff Billy Hicks now. The Sheriff would keep going no matter whose body was out there, it was personal with him. With Danny's death it had become personal for Mark too.

But he hadn't meant to get the girl's hopes up.

Jackass was right.

So that was Kristi Carroll. When he'd first seen her at the tavern he wasn't completely sure. He'd been searching for her mom before this officially *became* a "search," and this was the first time they'd actually spoken.

Now that they had finally met he'd said exactly the wrong thing.

Dickwad.

Yeah.

He pulled the snowmobile around, got back to the business he'd come for in the++ this very spot. At that point, they'd been searching for signs of a big SUV - broken branches, deep gouges in the snow and overturned rocks – obvious signs an over-sized vehicle had turned off the main road and rambled into the forest.

Finding no such signs, the search had moved further up and finally back down the mountain. The search area had become a wide circle that eventually collapsed right back to this very spot again. Always looking for a big SUV or the path of destruction one would have made through the undergrowth, and never finding either.

That's when the *runaway mom* talk had begun. When the easy answers weren't there – *hoax* was next. But sometimes the obvious truth was too much for people to grasp. The truth was Cedar Mountain had been hit by one of the biggest snowstorms in decades, answers didn't always come fast and easy – especially in conditions that hadn't existed since most of the people in this area were born. The awful truth was that sometimes those answers didn't come until the spring thaw.

He headed roughly the way the Sno-Cat had faced when he found Danny.

He had to force away the first images that came to him, the ones of Danny.

It was only the wolves he wanted to see now.

He felt the rifle's kick, heard that first hot explosion in his ear, the whine of the bullet striking ice and rock beneath the snow.

Then, the second shot. *A wolf, struck in the shoulder, spins, plants face first.*

Danny –

The wolves scatter.

A third pull of the trigger as Mark ran, another explosion – the bullet sings. A second wolf skids and goes down at the side of the road.

That was the wolf they'd found.

He'd been running toward Danny's body then. And the horror that had been Danny was the only thing he'd seen at that point.

Where was the first wolf he'd shot?

The pack had scattered. Smart. Individually they were more difficult to track.

Mark swung to the north side of the road. A quick check of his bearings, and then he plowed into the forest. Everything had changed since that day. The first storm dropped eighteen inches of snow. Two smaller storms since then. Record snowpack this year.

But he'd hit that wolf square. It couldn't have gone far.

Chapter 8

It wasn't cross-country skiing she was doing now it was slalom, and Kristi Carroll wasn't even skiing so much as *flying* downhill. Her balance and timing were perfect, the gates *so* close as she passed them, she clearly heard the snap of the pennants flapping overhead.

Only the cheers were louder.

She found Mark's clean-shaven face in the crowd gathered at the bottom of the run, cheering with the rest of them; he punched the air with his fist.

She skied right past the crowd and then it was just the two of them, skiing together over fresh powder, catching air on the moguls, soaring like eagles they floated effortlessly from hill to hill.

His smile was sunshine on her face.

"I need to show you something," he said.

Suddenly he was five lengths ahead of her, ten, then so far down the hill and into the forest she could barely catch glimpses of his jacket flashing between the trees.

"Slow down!"

"It's not far — come on! I'll show you."

What could he show her? She grinned, sheepishly. There were many possibilities in that question. Mostly home-schooled, shuttled from one athletic event to another, she'd been sheltered from boys her entire life.

But now she couldn't see him at all, she could only hear him calling her forward, leading her on.

"We're almost there — come on."

The sun sat right over the trees, and everything - the trees, the sky, the snow - it was all so blue, and bright, and quiet.

In a small clearing, something black and shiny sat in the snow. Sunbursts glared from it, strobing as the trees whizzed by.

She tried to dig, to turn and slow herself but she had lost control, as though her skis were on tracks and Kristi was simply along for the ride. And those tracks led somewhere she wasn't sure she wanted to go.

"Have a look at this."

Mark knelt beside a truck buried to its windows in snow; he swiped the frost from the windshield with his forearm. Sunlight flared from the exposed, tinted glass.

She shook her head.

"I don't want to see this."

"She's sleeping," he said. "She's only sleeping...look."

"I don't want to see her like that!"

But the windshield was so close now; through the glare, the shadows, the still form within the cab had already taken shape.

"My mom isn't dead!"

Kristi's own voice woke her. She shook, her sheets were freezing, soaked through with her sweat, shiny in the shaft of blue light from her window.

The screen from her I-pad mocked her with 3:00 AM.

Too early to start her warm-ups. Too early to be awake.

It had to be later. It was so bright *and so blue out there.* She pushed down her sheets, wrapped her comforter around her and stumbled to the window.

Too fogged up to see through – *but it shouldn't be,* the windows were heated, built to avoid condensation, weren't they? Her dad said they were filled with some sort of high-tech, inert gas that would keep them dry and clear. She swept the condensation away with her comforter.

Her mother's face stared back at her, cheeks so a white they were almost blue, a shroud of black linen covering her hair...

She sat bolt upright, struggling to free her arms. It was at least five-thirty, an overcast morning, and Kristi

Carroll was awake now, wide-awake, huddled beneath her window wrapped head-to-toe in her comforter.

-=-=-=-=-=-=-=-=-

A familiar and completely unwelcome throbbing wracked her temples. She'd had alcohol exactly once; a party at the house of one of the football players. She'd never do it again for a lot of reasons. Mainly because it had made her feel just like this.

What was she doing out of bed? That's right. She'd gotten up, hadn't she?

There had been a boy in her dreams. *Well, he wasn't exactly a boy – he was a man, the searcher she'd met yesterday – Mark - the guy she'd seen with his friend that first day in the tavern. And that friend was dead now.*

Nearly everyone was sure her Mom was dead too. Even dad had given up.

Mom *couldn't* be dead.

Kristi stood, slightly off-balance, her head pounded. Had she caught something? A flu?

Something creepy about the window.

She forced herself to look beyond it to an overcast day. No wind this morning, only the silent fall of snow. *Once it started, did it ever stop snowing up here?*

Mom is alive.

Tears welled, then fell freely. Her brain swelled against the walls of her skull, and then contracted suddenly; it seemed to drop like a walnut to the bony floor of her head.

The vertigo nearly floored her. She crouched, put her head between her knees. *Sick, you are definitely sick.* She'd been out in the cold, in the snow all day yesterday.

Cold and snow don't cause the flu.

She was healthy, young, as active as you get. She *shouldn't* be sick.

And then as if reason and will-power alone could cure a flu – the sickness was gone. The sadness too, had broken. She was fine, ready to stretch, to warm-up, to start her regimen.

Food poisoning. Had to have been. What had she eaten yesterday? Eggs, salad, cottage cheese. She'd make sure to check the cottage cheese this morning, make sure she washed the vegetables twice today.

Just some bad cottage cheese. I'm fine. *I'm fine and Mom is alive.*

-=.=.=.=.=.=.=.=.=-

They'd been keeping mostly to the contested lands. But even here, they knew they were being watched.

DeerSlayr Wolfyn and WyldChyld, Glokkun and Malwor, together at last. She'd helped him level-up, fighting the dread Orc warriors and leaving him the spoils – then they'd helped each other. Deadly enemies joined in a common purpose; they were both level 75 now, just about as high as you could get. You'd think it *should* be that way – but that wasn't the game. The game required two warring factions. *You couldn't break the rules.*

But they *had* broken the rules and continued to break them, more or less secretly.

"There are no secrets in Mythykal." Syndee, his succubus, stretched her long and shapely blue legs, wiggled her toes. Smooth muscles undulated beneath her scant armor as she moved through a series of aggressive attack moves. Sexy in those moves, even as she prepared to kill.

Was she jealous, of WyldChyld? Sure she was. And she could read his every thought.

"Hah."

"You are!"

"You…are foolish…as you are handsome," she purred, ever seductive and compliant as she chided him. "They track our every move – *and hers."*

"It's true, boss." But for an occasional grunt or groan of exertion, Raspberry had remained silent as he worked, testing his huge muscles against the roots of a gigantic

Banyan tree, leaving the more persuasive Syndee to break the ice of this conversation, as Raspberry often did.

"You summon us to the Frozen River, WyldChyld summons her minions to the Frozen River. We travel to Bryn Shyre; they travel to Bryn Shyre. We complete the same quests at the same time," Syndee whispered in DeerSlayr's ear, her fingers tickling his chin beneath his beard.

"You've enjoyed the spoils," he said.

Syndee acquiesced, kissing the Ebony Bracelet of Isis that lately adorned her wrist; with it she could inflict *Instant Sleep* – a sort of suspended animation - on her enemies. She pulled her knees to her chest then flicked the jeweled winged *Anklets of Antara*, causing them to ring. These gave her a limited power of flight - *and looked pretty hot too* - which was probably even more important to a succubus.

"We fight her minions without landing a blow. No one loses health," Raspberry said.

"I get that. Our fights could be a little more convincing."

With the arrival of Porsche Nytmar, Raspberry and Syndee went silent. Outside of battle, it wasn't their place to interact with other players. They were DeerSlayr's minions. Porsche was a Glokkun Hunter, a good friend, but lately DeerSlayr hadn't been hanging so much with his Glokkun friends. He'd be on a quest with WyldChyld right now if she'd just wake up and join the game. He really had no interest in the "Great Council" meeting – the notice for which had blipped across his screen every five minutes since he'd logged on. But Porsche was available and he was going, they may as well go together. It was something to do. Still, quests without WyldChyld weren't nearly as much fun.

In the *Outer World,* Porsche was a fifteen year old living in Dorchester, England. At least, as far as Reed knew – there was no way to be certain of what anyone was out there really.

"Who were you talking to?" Porsche asked.

Raspberry and Syndee had resumed their exercises, programmed movements with which every player was familiar.

DeerSlayr ignored the question. Porsche had two minions as well, an Orc like Raspberry and a Wood Nymph. The nymph was green and cute in her outfit of strategically placed leaves – but other than that, Porsche's minions had no personality whatsoever.

"So do we fly to this thing or what?"

"Check your inventory – you should have the Mauve Rune Stone, with a...I don't know, some sort of gold ring."

DeerSlayr did.

"Okay, now we just hold them up – and the *magic* takes us."

"Teleporting. *They finally put teleporting in!*"

"Only for the council meeting –"

A flash of purplish light across the screen. A milky way of bright stars swirled around them.

And then they stood, minus their minions (for only players could participate in the Great Council), high up in the balcony of a circular theater. They stood over a great crowd gathered on the floor below; the theater was a great, open stovepipe of a building that resembled London's Globe theatre from Reed's Shakespeare studies – only much grander. Glokkun and Malwor alike were here. But no weapons, no minions. No fighting allowed.

Those standing on the ground floor, the *cheap* seats if there had been seats, were the lower level players, the Groundlings and Pennilings, to put it back in Shakespearean perspective. It was a nice view from up here, nice to be one of the highest level players. Porsche had been playing almost a year longer than DeerSlayr.

An avatar wearing the purple robes of royalty stood silently onstage, his chest heaving with make-believe breath, fingers drumming without purpose; an empty shell not yet inhabited by its owner. Guards were everywhere. Clearly hooliganism would not be tolerated.

"Serious," Porsche said.

"Indeed."

A warlock waved from the balcony across from them. He pushed his way through the crowd, working his way toward them. It took a moment for them to recognize their old friend, Wyz BarnakL. Like DeerSlayr, Wyz had tried a few hairstyles lately. This one was a writhing thatch of violet snakes. The snakehead was a controversial Add-On. The snakes had powers themselves – so, was it a hairstyle or a weapon – or even a minion since the thing was living? Should you have to earn it? Should you have to remove it before entering a tavern or a council chamber? Big questions.

DeerSlayr had recently changed out his recently acquired snow-white locks for his old-school orange dreadlocks. Things being what they were, the more dissimilar he and WyldChyld were, the better.

As far as the Add-Ons went, they were getting pretty obtrusive if you asked DeerSlayr. PureArtz, the game-publisher for Mythykal, had open-sourced the game engine – a huge mistake. Now anybody with a C# coding handbook could make an Add-On. Not just clothing and armor anymore. Entire levels were popping up; weapons with no counter defense, characters with godlike powers – including that whole group of invisible jerks trying to start up their own war party. Lately, it seemed the Mythykal programmers had less and less control of their own game.

Suddenly, tom-toms thudded. Flames shot brightly from sconces lining the edge of the stage. The purple-robed avatar opened his eyes, his name flashed on a gilded scroll above his head, Sygfryd.

"Bugger," Porche said. "He's the CEO of PureArtz. This *IS* serious."

A curtain behind him revealed the seven kings. The rulers of each realm.

The crowd thundered with a cheer, the groundlings stomped and hooted.

"That cheering's enhanced..." Wyz said under his breath, "Greetings, brothers!"

"Ever the skeptic." Porche said.

"No, you can hear it. Echo – delay and chorus. They've fattened up the sound. Nobody's all that happy with PureArtz these days."

"Glokkun and Malwor friends. Players of all levels. Greetings!"

Now DeerSlayr heard it too. A synthetic doubling of the cheering, and Sygfryd's voice itself was deeper, more resonant, it echoed up the walls of the theater. Reed had seen him interviewed online, in reality he was a slight man with a high, almost effeminate voice. *But Jesus, this entire world is synthetic,* and it was pretty damn cool just the same.

"Thank you for joining us. I've brought you and the Great Council together today to discuss some very serious matters."

"The Guardians..." Wyz muttered.

"Who?"

"Those invisible freaks. They call themselves *The Guardians.*"

"Wanks. What do they think they're guarding?"

"The Children," Wyz spat. *"It's always the children."*

"Huh?"

"Us. You know – teens - deliver *us* from evil, save *us* from the horror of sex and violence."

"What – a bunch of *Jesus Freak code-monkeys?*"

A gnome shushed them. Porsche shot him an icy glance.

"Wank."

"I guess so, who else would it be?"

DeerSlayr knew of at least three Baptist kids, and a whole slew of Mormons who were all upper level players. They *loved* the game. It didn't make sense.

"You mean – a bunch of parents?"

"Hah! Like that would happen. What parents know how to code video games?"

Good point.

Several guards had moved close to them.

"Guess we're being loud," Wyz said directly to them.

"As you know," Sygfryd said, "several months ago, we at PureArtz made a decision to open-source the Mythykal engine. To allow creative people with new ideas to freely add to our world here."

"You gave our world away!" Someone yelled. A swell of agreement began, but fell back as quickly as it rose as the number of guards instantly doubled.

"This has greatly enriched the Mythykal world." Sygfryd went on. "I see some of you wearing the wonderful armor our new friends have provided. Many of you have traveled to the new territories and experienced much of the amazing innovation taking place there."

"Bunch of berk hackers. I've been to some of those so-called territories – rotten work." Porsche said, "Pure schlock."

"But, as with all bold new ideas, there have been a few bumps along the way. We expected this, we planned for it."

"Sure ya' did."

"And I've come here in person today to assure you we have the problem under control."

"Sure ya' do."

"What about *The Guardians!*" the shout came from one of the lower balconies. "What are you doing about them?"

A gilded banner appeared over the crowd explaining there would be a Q&A period after Sygfryd spoke, a *subtle* admonishment against interruptions.

"Now, I'd like to introduce two men who I know need no introductions. Architect and Lead Programmer, King Evanrud, ruler of the Glokkun territories, and Art Director, King Edvard, ruler of the Malwor."

Two of the robed council members stood, nodded to Sygfryd and walked together to the podium. Reaching it, they quickly faced-off in mock battle poses. The crowd roared. Then they both turned on Sygfryd who stepped back, cringing in mock terror. The crowd went wild – at least the enhanced ambient noise made it *sound* like they had.

"This is so much shite." Porsche said. "First the grand poohbah of PureArtz, now Malwor scum."

"Dude, they're the guys who actually built the game."

"Well, they shouldn't have sold out to PureArtz, should they have?"

The Moore brothers, Ed and Evan, had created Mythykal in their parents' Mill Valley garage. They'd sold the game to mega game conglomerate PureArtz two years ago but had remained on to oversee production. It was no secret they weren't happy with PureArtz' decision to basically give the game engine away. PureArtz plainly wanted to outsize Electronic Arts' MMPG with the move. All those crazy-eyed teen coders and artists hopped up on taurine-laced soft drinks were slave labor on steroids - and that meant more territories, more levels, more characters, more *everything*, at no cost to PureArtz. It was a stroke of greedy genius.

But it had definitely hurt the game. What did PureArtz care? Their real money came from sports games based on the latest pro baller thug, and car-theft games. Reed was pretty sure All-Pro Dog Fighting would be their next big title.

"Greetings, citizens." King Edvard began. "We are grateful for your support and allegiance."

"But we are not all brothers," King Evanrud said. "Even though Edvard and I share a common bloodline, *we are sworn enemies.*"

DeerSlayr couldn't help feel a bit uncomfortable with that, he found himself trying *not* to search for WyldChyld, but his eyes were shifting, scanning the crowd despite himself. Was she finally awake? He checked his map.

Sure enough, the map showed she was in the theater. But where exactly?

"Although our laws are simple in this matter – *no fraternization between Malwor and Glokkun* – a few have chosen another path, betraying their factions. Their true brothers."

DeerSlayr didn't like where this conversation was leading.

Someone cried out, *"Who?"*

"Burn them!" That from Porsche. That cry was picked up and carried by others.

No, this wasn't good at all.

Where was she? The map didn't drill down further than the building.

No, better for both he didn't see her now.

And just as that thought passed, he saw her in the midst of the Malwor horde and *she was looking straight at him.*

Guards began shoving their way through the crowd. Several converged on a nearby Glokkun Archer, weaponless as the entire crowd was. He saw them, but they had him before feather could have touched bow anyway. In seconds he was hacked to pieces.

The same scene played out on the Malwor side, players now joining the guards in apprehending and dismembering the accused. *And now guards were coming his way.*

When a Glokkun Hunter was attacked only a few feet from where he stood, DeerSlayr recognized his chance. He pushed himself in with a group of attackers, then slipped behind a guard and disarmed him, ripping the sword from his gauntlet, and crushing his skull with the iron of his helmet when the guard turned, shocked.

He killed the two nearest guards without effort. Thanks to WyldChyld, he was a higher level than the guards now.

So THAT's why they don't want fraternization...

The guards hesitated, they had expected unarmed warriors, a slaughter not a fight.

The panicking crowd was forcing its way to the exits now, creating a circle of space around DeerSlayr that WyldChyld somersaulted into, breaking a guard's neck and taking his sword in the same smooth movement.

Wiz and Porsche gave them a stunned look – then they too ran for the exits.

Back to back, DeerSlayr and WyldChyld circled, their weapons aloft. The guards charged and the two warriors cleaved them like butter. Guards poured in from all sides. Spawning back to life faster than DeerSlayr and WyldChyld could kill them.

This would be their last stand.

"Well, it's a good fight anyway," he said.

"Yeah, a good fight."

Then the entire balcony shifted, rose up and dropped beneath them with an explosive roar of fire that sent guards and players alike tumbling over the rails, crushing the trapped crowd below.

On stage, Sygfryd and King Evanrud were openly shouting each other down. King Edvard stood, his fingers mindlessly drumming, as he watched the carnage unfold before him with slack jawed horror.

No, DeerSlayr realized, as the velvet curtains broke into tiny red squares around him; Edvard's fingers weren't mindlessly drumming – *he was typing, trying to code his way out of this.*

The guards blipped out. The theater itself blipped out. Semitransparent cubes bordered by yellow perforations appeared in their place, and the invisible ones, *The Guardians,* were everywhere at once.

The kings themselves became a series of cubes, cones and control vectors.

WyldChyld had fallen when the first explosion had hit.

He was helping her to her feet as Reed's computer display went black.

"WTF!"

Reed nearly tipped his chair. The alien eyes on his black mini-tower blinked, then stared brightly as his system rebooted.

That is *not* supposed to happen. The system load paused, inquired if he'd rather load the Operating System in *"safe"* mode.

"No, no, no. Keep going." He cursored to *resume normally.*

It did, but when he logged on – the cursor spun and stopped dead.

"No…this is *not* happening!"

Not a *catastrophe* – he could restore the system back to its state before the crash. But *Mythykal – his escape, the one thing that had kept him going right now – had become a virus.* WyldChyld, DeerSlayr, his minions, his *friends* were gone.

His entire world was gone.

Chapter 9

"It is very nice in here."

It was a corridor of dirt walls and exposed roots, a roughly carved tunnel that turned away sharply in the distance. Water shimmered along the walls, pooled on the floor. *What was this place?*

"It is warm here, safe. *Very nice in here."* He said again, as if the repetition would make it so.

The man speaking to her was horribly deformed, a large head that would have been more handsome on a wolf. It occurred to Amanda that the man's smile may not have been a smile at all, only an upward curve of the lips, like a dog venting itself. She noted these things without fear. There was no fear now. There was only a promise of comfort that came from this small, misshapen man with the huge canine face.

He waited for her.

Yes, it was warm in here, surprisingly so for a cave. She tried to run her hands along the mud walls, to feel what must be a cold wetness there, but she couldn't. She couldn't raise her arms.

She walked with him, joined by another now, a large, bald man, his head covered with angry red scars, who crouched low to avoid the ceiling. The man was smiling.

"What do they do here?" She asked him.

"They *collect*. And they provide medicine."

She nodded. She was sure she needed medical care. Her temples throbbed; she saw terrible things, so many they no longer frightened her. She shivered; freezing to the bone now, but sometimes her skin burned so hot it seemed her veins ran with molten lava.

Yes, she needed medical attention. She was certain of that.

They collect.

The doorway ahead emitted a strong, medicinal smell as they approached. Within, a gigantic bald man, blindfolded, was strapped to a chair. Another man stood beside him holding what, at first look, was an electric shaver in his hand.

Now Amanda saw the jagged disk attached to the top of it - a bone saw.

"What do they collect?"

"They collect our screams," the bald man said.

The saw began to spin.

Chapter 10

Rescue!

The man smiled broadly, waving his arms as he approached from the forest.

And now it all seemed so silly, getting stuck out here like this. She was an adult, a grown woman.

But there was a cliff beyond that flimsy rail, a huge drop, and she'd lost control of the big truck through that last turn. She'd been petrified.

But now they'd come for her.

Blackness again. Night. Time to sleep. But it was so hot in here; she was burning up. She couldn't see the flame touching her skin, burning into her. Couldn't see anything. She was so tired. It was nighttime. She only wanted to sleep.

Nothing but snow. An unending, unyielding whiteness outside. Then gray shadows, indistinct, ghostlike.

Fangs slashed the windshield. The jarring clash of bone on glass.

What the hell was that!

The cab shuddered. A foamy red gout of matter splashed across the windshield.

Blackness. A bee sting, a new heat spread over her skin. The smell of singed hair, acrid then cloying.

Wolves hidden in the forest, swift shadows between the trees. The waving man hadn't seen them either. Now he ran to the car...

Another sting, and she was suddenly cold again; fire and ice.

She was safe in the car. Keep the doors locked! Just stay where you are. But the man would die if she didn't let him in. In the end, humanity got the better of her.

She unlocked the doors.

Blackness. Thank God for the blackness.

The man had a gun.

She was exhausted. It was dark again and Amanda
wanted nothing more than to drift away, to sleep.

-=-=-=-=-=-=-=-=-

Kristi tore the sheets away and dashed to her bathroom. She
barely made it.

The ball of hot pain in her stomach had yanked her
from her dreams as surely as Mom yelling, *"Fire!"*

She splashed cold, bracing water onto her face,
daubed it away with a towel. Her skin looked sallow, her eyes
yellow. An odd tingling in her hands and feet. She held her
hands up, half-expecting to find an army of ants marching
over her knuckles.

Why do I feel...sad?

A torrent of tears rushed down her cheeks.

Her stomach knotted again, she sprang to the toilet
and nearly exploded there.

God. What is going on?

A shower would make it all better. Cold water to stop
the fire. She called up the presets from the panel beside the
faucet and tamped the temperature down ten degrees.

Fire? Why was she thinking fire?

Now the water was just uncomfortably cold.

Exhausted, shaking, Kristi stepped into her slippers, wrapped herself in her bathrobe and shuffled back to her bed, barely dragging the slippers along with her.

The word had torn through Kristi's dream. She had distinctly heard Mom scream, *"Fire!"*

No she hadn't. The house was dark, silent. No one had said anything at all, and Mom was gone.

-=-=-=-=-=-=-=-=-

Reed slid into a pair of snow boots that actually fit, no more oversized Lugs until spring if he ever wore them again. He tugged his ski jacket on, and made his way into the great cold whiteness.

"God," Reed coughed frosty breath into his gloves, clapped his hands together; greeting the cold air the same way he did every morning. Dog responded with a quick bark then bounded through last night's snow to find one of her normal relief spots.

Dog had a pretty regular schedule, and pretty regular places to do her business. And true to Reed's sanitation plan, the snow was saving him from a lot of pick-up duty.

He carried her less and less now; Dog was already more than an armload. Amazing how quickly they grew up. He wondered if Mom had felt the same way about him.

Don't be angry at your father. It's not fair.

Where had *that* come from?

He wasn't mad at Dad anyway. Well, maybe he was. Yeah, he guessed he was.

Reed would have gone looking for Mom right away. He wouldn't have waited for a couple hicks in a stupid Sno-Cat to take their sweet time lugging up the road to look for her.

Reed would have grabbed one of the Ski Dos and headed down the road himself. *That's what Dad should have done.* What Reed would have done if Dad hadn't ordered him to stay put.

He would have disobeyed his father and done it anyway if he hadn't already been half-frozen and hurt.

If he hadn't fallen into the water like a total idiot.

Reed had searched up and down the road to town dozens of times since then.

Your father has too. His Mom's voice, from somewhere deep in his head, a "coping mechanism" is what his shrink would probably say. A memory, like a phantom limb. Eventually even that would fade. It was hard to think she was actually gone. But she was.

"But he was too late. Don't you get that, Mom? He was too late!"

Dog barked at him. A wake-up call.

"Hey girl, wanna go for a ride? Huh? Do ya?" He roughed up the thick fur behind her neck, "sure you do."

In minutes, he had a Ski Doo gassed up and they were on their way. But it wasn't the main road they were headed for today. They were making a bee-line for the creek.

It wasn't blistering cold, at least not once you got used to it anyway. The wind actually felt good on his cheeks. The sky was clear and the snow gleamed like white plaster on a hot summer day.

He took some of the hills too fast, but Dog was used to his crazy driving now, she knew how to keep her feet, and he was strong enough now to keep them balanced and upright. He practiced fencing every day, traveling up and down the strip in a crouch, working his legs and perfecting his parries, "building a foundation" as Kristi said. It turned out she wasn't a bad teacher – even if she was a bossy *bee-yotch* sometimes.

Okay, maybe he was even a little proud of her.

Kristi's door had been shut tight this morning when Reed trudged by with Dog in tow. Not one chirp from inside. Maybe his sister was human after all. She'd actually slept in for once.

His other world, Mythykal, was a heartbreaker. The Blogosphere was up in arms - posts everywhere, articles on Technorati and Inquirer.net blasting PureArts for leaving the door open to hackers by taking the Open Source road. Tom's Hardware and CPU had even weighed in. The Mythykal hackers, the so-called "Guardians," had walloped a whole warehouse full of servers and taken down home PCs everywhere – not even the Mac guys could crow this time, proprietary OS or not, they went down too.

It had gotten the FBI's attention – it was actually a cybercrime after all, but the Blogosphere knew Mythykal was just a stupid "computer game" as far as the feds were concerned. Reed doubted hunting down it's attackers would rate being what they'd call a priority.

When you logged onto Mythykal now, all you got was a banner stating Mythykal would be back soon.

"Load of shite!" Porsche would have said.

WyldChyld was on Facebook. Her real name was Maxine Day. She was nearly two years older than Reed, and belonged to a group called "Suicide Girls." She had a lot of tattoos, and she didn't mind showing them off on her webpage. They Skyped and traded music – it turned out they both liked the same music, but outside the world of Mythykal talk was awkward; DeerSlayr and WyldChyld had a real bond, they fought side by side, they were almost…hell, *lovers,* really.

But as hard as they tried, outside of music, Reed and Maxine didn't really have that much in common.

Reed crested the top of a ridge and pulled to a stop.

From here he could see the point of their neighbor's roof - completely blanketed with snow now, even the chimney was hidden but for the ribbon of smoke curling up and away from it. With the snow cover, the perfectly cone-shaped pines surrounding it, the place looked homier than ever. Like a Christmas card.

This had become his favorite view.

He knew next to nothing about his neighbors – only the family name, Morgan. It was neatly carved into a great round of cedar at the head of their drive, a cross-section from a big tree they'd likely cleared building their property.

He wondered if they had kids.

One day he'd bike over and have a look.

Dog barked, restless now. Ready to play.

Just below the ridge lay the dark depression leading to the creek; the thick foliage held so much snow now it looked impassible. He knew it wasn't though. It had taken some time, some courage to come back to this place. The memory of that thing in the water, twisting over to stare up at him with another set of wide, silver eyes, sent shivers up his spine. He had stood in that very water, his legs numb, barely able to move…if that thing had chased him, bit him – *if it had even touched him…*

Yep, it had taken some time, but he'd been back here quite a few times since then.

Only one thing had the power to trump his bad feelings about the place.

"What do you say, Dog? Think you're little friend is down there today?"

She replied with an excited bark, squirming nearly out of his grasp.

"Well, then let's check."

He started up the Ski Doo again, pulled as close as he could to the ravine without sliding over, and the two of them hopped out, Dog barking nonstop.

Sure enough, the pit bull answered Dog's call. Reed let Dog go. She bolted down the ravine. He smiled, feeling that little jump in his heart; that odd lift again.

Getting to the creek was tougher today than ever; Reed had to slide most of the way down on his butt. That was okay. He'd walk through a brick wall to get down there if he had to.

The girl knew his schedule now. She didn't always show up. Sometimes only her dog appeared even though Reed knew she was out there just out of sight, watching them. She wouldn't let her dog stay on his own for long. He was a tough little guy, but there were even tougher things in this forest and she knew it.

But Reed was okay with that. Even if she didn't come out and smile for him, he just liked knowing she was there, and he was pretty sure she was smiling for him in any case.

He was also pretty sure she wasn't exactly in the country legally. She did speak a little English, but she was scared of her own shadow. Oregon made it pretty easy for *illegals* who made it this far up the coast – you couldn't even say "illegal" at school without being shouted down or called a racist. They were *undocumented immigrants*. There was a lot of farming, wineries and stuff in Oregon, so he guessed that's why the government turned a blind eye. Illegals could even get a driver's license here – so in a way they *were* documented. With all the terrorist things happening, Reed thought it was pretty whacked that everyone could walk in and get an ID, but if that's what got *her* here, it was cool with him. She was what Mom would have called "a gentle soul," and he knew that if such a thing were possible, she was even lonelier than Reed.

And hell, *Paco* and Dog were best buds now. Reed had gotten the dog's name out of her at least, although she still hadn't given him her own.

The dogs were on this side of the creek today, chasing each other, wrestling and nipping at each other – a game Reed called *Romp'n and Chomp'n*.

And suddenly there *she* was – his illegal Goddess, the prettiest girl in the world, returning his wave as he knocked fresh snow from his favorite boulder and sat. With her smile, that lightheaded feeling came, the sense that all was well in the world.

She pulled a rolled-up blanket from the pack she carried. Steam came up with it.

That was a signal to Paco – he tore away from Dog, plowed his way through the snow for the bridge, Dog at his heels.

The *bridge* wasn't really much of one – just a support of the most stable rocks Reed could find, spanned by two rot-flattened logs. He'd left holes for the water to pass, and packed everything else with snow and ice – winter was the glue holding the whole thing together. It would be solid enough until spring, he guessed. Once things warmed up he'd take more time with it, maybe even haul some concrete down here for mortar.

Paco and Dog didn't seem to mind the rickety nature of his bridge. They shot back and forth across it without hesitation.

Whatever it was his goddess had cooked, Reed could smell it now too. *Wow!* His stomach growled as she broke off pieces for both dogs.

Then she pulled another wrapped treat from the bag and held it toward Reed. Her smile was wider than ever. In any language that was an invitation.

Now his heart really jumped for the skies. It actually felt like that – like his heart had leapt high into the air, taking him with it.

He tested the bridge with one push of his boot; *still solid.* Still, he moved over it quickly, hazarding a quick glance at the pool. The slower water had skinned over with ice, but he could still see shadows beneath it…*moving shadows.*

His feet landed securely in the snow on the other side of the bridge.

"Buenos Dee-az?" He said, clumsily.

"Morning," she laughed as she unwrapped the blanket, and handed him something warm wrapped in brown paper.

He smiled sheepishly, nodding as he took it. It smelled peppery and good.

"Thank you." He wouldn't try Spanish again today.

"Well…come," She said.

A thick, grilled homemade flour tortilla wrapped around cheese, potatoes and eggs with peppers and the

tastiest ground meat that had ever met Reed's tongue. He
tried not to gobble.

"God – this is so frickin' good!"

She offered a wide grin; not fully understanding the
words.

The pups barked at their feet, complaining. They
would *never* be full.

She unwrapped another treat and fed them. She gave
Reed another. He could easily have eaten half a dozen of
them.

She showed her empty palms to the pups.

"Nada."

She let them inspect her empty knapsack. Satisfied
there was no more food hidden inside, satisfied with that
evidence, romp'n and chomp'n renewed in earnest. They
took off across the bridge.

Reed and the girl smiled sheepishly at each other.

The kids are gone. It's just us.

Okay, time for the whole Tarzan thing, Reed thought.
He pointed to his chest.

"Reed."

This time, she nodded and repeated it. Then her
fingers touched her own chest.

"Malana."

The skies open. Celestial choirs break forth in song!

Now Reed wished he had taken Spanish. He was such an idiot. But who knew? It wasn't like he expected to hang with the homeys in Hillsboro – a town west of Portland lovingly referred to as *Hillsburrito* for its heavily Hispanic population.

"Umh…" she said, suddenly. "I…go…ummh." She shook her head. "Go. I have go. Paco!"

His chest heaved. The visit was way too short. But, this was a huge step today. *Huge.* Like he'd leveled-up. *No, quit thinking that way.*

"Okay," he said. *"Malana."* Letting her name linger, so great to be able to have it.

"OK. Reed."

Paco bounded back across the bridge. The sturdy little fellow nearly knocked Reed over. Reed clapped his thick sides, rubbed his shoulders. Dog galloped up right behind him.

"See you later," he said.

Malana nodded and started into the woods. Then she turned, an obvious question in her eyes. She thought better than to ask, and hurried into the forest. She was gone.

Where does she go when she leaves? Where did she live?

Reed started across the bridge – feeling good, but frustrated too. He had a strong urge to drop a big boulder in that pool, crush the monster lurking beneath the surface. If he didn't kill that thing he'd think about it every time he came here to see Malana. Reed stopped in the middle of the bridge, forcing himself to look for it.

There it was, a thick brownish shadow just under the skin of ice, almost motionless. Then it slowly rolled, the silver-whiteness of its belly flashing. Was it flipping over to see him better? Were those big silver eyes on the bottom better suited for seeing through ice? A wave of nausea rolled through him with that thought.

He had to kill it. This was his place with Malana, *their* special spot. No place for monsters here.

Reed crossed over, kicking snow until he found a big, nasty looking rock with lots of sharp edges. He wrested it from the bank, lumbered over to the water's edge, and squatted, feeling new strength in his legs as he pushed himself up, swinging the big rock forward and up. He hefted the boulder over his head.

Dog watched him curiously. Whatever he was doing, it looked dangerous. She whined.

Yes. The hideous thing in the water had indeed turned over to watch him. Silvery traces of those wide flat eyes flickered through the ice.

He guided the rock forward, his arms shaking from the strain.

It's not its fault. It is what it is.

Reed brought the stone down, dropped it in the snow at the edge of the creek. The stone moved slowly onto the ice, sending a snapping, spider web of cracks across the pool. Finally the big rock pushed through. He watched as it slid harmlessly beneath the surface.

He took a deep breath.

"Come on, Dog."

Reed sprinted for the snowmobile, smacking away branches and leaping the smaller obstacles, again feeling that new strength in his legs, as he forced his way up the hillside with Dog barking at his heels, finally overtaking him and beating him back to the Ski Doo.

One itch scratched. *But the other itch was so much stronger. He had to know where Malana lived.*

With Dog firmly in place, he revved the Ski Doo. It wasn't exactly nearby – but the Morgan house was the closest one to his. Malana probably worked for the Morgans, or maybe her parents did.

Could those burritos have stayed warm just wrapped in a blanket and stuffed in a knapsack like that? Even with the Ski Doo it would take a while to get to the Morgan place. It was a heck of a long hike through snow.

He followed the creek slowly north for a bit. He needed to think about this. It wasn't like she'd invited him to follow her. They had made great progress today. He could totally blow that now.

But then he revved it up again.

Kristi had shown him where snow had built its own bridge to the great beyond over their fence with the help of a lightning-blown tree. He guided the snowmobile carefully over it. As packed and stable as the snow seemed to be – there were pockets of air everywhere. If you hit one and dropped too low, the fence wire below could snare you like a big rabbit trap.

That could seriously ruin your day.

The top of the next rise provided, in Reed's humble opinion, one of the best views you could get up here: a great canyon of rock cut through the mountain, terraced by snow and trees all the way down to the river. It really was an incredible sight. But what he loved most about it, was something he couldn't see in daylight: at dusk there would be a bright yellow glow at the very end of the gorge, distant but warming: *the lights of Portland.*

Just below him the creek turned sharply away and the slope of its bank was much more gradual and forgiving. Beyond that was a tangle of snow and evergreen so dense you couldn't see much of anything. *A hidden place.*

Maybe Malana didn't live with the Morgans at all.

Maybe her home was right down there.

-=-=-=-=-=-=-=-=-

"I'm here, I'm so close to you! I'm here!"

But it was the sunrise, not Amanda, who'd woken Ken. He had left the shades open again.

The press of a key on his mixing console and the morning sun broke into narrow slits that soon disappeared altogether. Ken was left in blessed darkness again. His neck ached. It had been weeks since he'd slept in their bed. He wasn't sure he'd ever sleep there again.

These days he rarely left his studio.

Another press of the key and the shutters opened again. His eyes painfully adjusted, and the louvers revealed a clean, blue sky.

Somewhere out there, Amanda's soul was looking down on her surviving family along with all the souls of the lost.

So many out there; their troubles over now.

"Her troubles are over," that phrase was supposed to be comforting.

But outside of struggling through the seven deadly headstands of *Ashtanga's second series,* Amanda's life hadn't been troubled at all. The idea she was in a better place didn't ring true and wasn't comforting at all.

Just so much useless *death-speak.*

But what were people who loved you supposed to say?

You sent your happy, trouble-free wife to her death. Piece of bad luck, dude.

The truth was - people who didn't love him, who didn't know Ken at all had actually said worse things - if you could even think of anything worse than that. In the papers, blogs and chats, the *Runaway Mom* theories were bandied about like episodes from the latest *reality* show. The *troubled marriage of Ken and Amanda Carroll* had become one more chapter in *the Amanda Carroll story.* Amplified by the last she'd heard him speak, *ordering her into the snowstorm and to her death.*

He had himself to blame for the appearance of those words in print, to be endlessly dissected and thrown back in his face on cable and radio talk shows.

In a fit of self-pity, and yes drunkenness, he'd blurted them out.

But much worse than his own words coming back at him was something he'd managed so far to keep private; the bitter memory of his childish frustration when she'd called, his anger at being *interrupted in his work* by his wife.

The little rock'n roll fantasy he'd built for himself had been so important that the last words he'd ever hear from his wife had been an unwelcome interruption.

At least he hadn't blurted those feelings out to the press. That golden nugget he'd kept to himself.

The worst places in Hell are the private ones.

The red LED signaling voicemail had pulsed steadily for weeks: reporters, updates from Search and Rescue, from the Sheriff. Somewhere along the line his number had been leaked. The tone of the messages quickly went from concerned to crank.

The number was changed, and leaked again. Changed again.

Finally the LED went dark and remained that way.

His company had tacked an extra month of bereavement time onto his sabbatical. That was nice. His wife was dead. As a consolation prize they'd give him an extra month before telling him his career was dead too.

He'd held it together for a while; he'd insisted that he and the kids ate their meals together. They spoke to the Sheriff, to reporters, together.

But always beneath the surface the resentment, the blame, festered. And then he'd admitted what had been his last, loving message to his wife, *"Get back here now."*

The family meals became more haphazard, the talk more strained. Eventually it all ended. Eventually he'd crawled into this cave and rolled the stone over the entrance.

He hadn't showered or shaved in days, he didn't
know how many. His watch scraped the console as his
forearm crossed it; the band so loose now, his wrist so thin,
that the watch simply slid over and under, hung there like a
sinker.

He blinked at the beautiful day out there.

He shut the blinds.

-=-=-=-=-=-=-=-=-=-

Mark had greatly underestimated the wolf. Mortally
wounded, she'd gone much deeper into the forest than he
could have imagined. He'd imposed likely perimeters and
come up short each time. Today he'd simply moved in a
straight line from the road and taken that line much, much
further.

The snow had long since covered her tracks. But here
where her long run at escape had ended, her trail couldn't
have been more obvious; a terrible and final hemorrhage. The
cold had preserved her blood, bright as graffiti sprayed high
up the trunks of the surrounding trees.

A small patch of fur protruded from the snow
beneath an overhang of snow-covered branches. The half-
dome of ice and snow there looked like the backdrop of a
lawn nativity scene.

Mark stopped the snowmobile a few yards away from the dome and unbuckled a small shovel from the toolbox.

He dug and brushed the red snow and ice away.

She was a big wolf alright, a Gray. *Or kind of...*

"Uggh, that is nasty."

One silvery eye stared at him, socketed way too close to her ear. He had to force himself to examine her. There was barely a socket for another eye.

Swallowing the bile rising in his throat, he brushed the snow from her sides. His bullet's entry point had made a deep hole just under the shoulder. He probed for an exit wound and found it... *and something else.*

He shoveled quickly, sweating heavily beneath his jacket now, fighting to keep the nausea, his disgust, in check.

It took time to free her from the packed snow and ice. He kicked a stone beside her, used it as a fulcrum for the shovel, an awful ripping sound as he pried her from the ice. He crouched beside her, inspecting the fur on her flank.

Beneath his bullet's exit wound three other wounds evenly spaced, forming a nearly straight line. She'd been shot before – and not by a hunter.

Mark backed away, eyes scanning the forest around him. Acutely aware of the sounds of the forest, keenly aware of his situation. He slid the .38 Special from beneath his jacket, clicked the safety off. His skin tingled.

He was seriously alone.

And seriously outgunned.

Chapter 11

Sweet blue sky crossed with strands of wispy stratus, far below, a layer of fog had settled deep in the canyons. For Billy Hicks the view brought memories of cotton candy and summer fairs, girls in summer dresses, the sweet warmth of a sneaked kiss at the giddy heights of a Ferris wheel.

Childhood memories came more frequently and more vividly than ever these days.

Dad said it would happen that way in the later years.

"You forget what breakfast was, then that smell of shoe black comes outta nowhere and it's time to shine your shoes for Sunday School; but Sunday School was sixty years ago."

That's when you knew it was time to call it quits.

Hicks was sixty-two. Maybe it really was getting close to quitting time. Maybe there were important things he was missing these days…or just plain forgetting.

He hoped to God he never forgot how to fly.

Mary Ann coughed, a shudder through the fuselage that quickly smoothed out.

"You heard me, baby? Sorry, I promise I won't forget you."

The Sheriff pulled Mary Ann, the Piper Cherokee he'd named after the *other* love of his life, to follow the main road north toward the summit once again.

The forest was tangled and thick, broken only occasionally by clear cuts and new homes, most of those vacation homes. It wasn't exactly the suburbs; not yet it wasn't. No Fred Meyers up this way. No Starbucks. Most of the homeowners up here only stayed a few days, maybe a few weeks each year and went back to their lives when nature showed up.

Amazing how some folks could gather enough nuts to build a big house they didn't even live in.

Billy knew everybody who lived year-round on his mountain. No matter how big their freezers, they still came down to Cedar for supplies, or frequented the Tavern. Billy didn't drink, but he liked the Tavern ribeye. Shirley, the fifty-some year old waitress, was sweet on him. He couldn't remember actually paying for a meal there.

Over the years he'd come to know a lot of the part-timers as well. Some were folks who'd built up here expecting to stay. Eventually they'd come to understand that Cedar wasn't some backstreet borough of Portland, or Eugene, or even Corvallis for that matter. It was the wilderness. The *real* Oregon.

It was harsh. It could be deadly.

He passed over the Carroll property with a heavy heart. Their property would be up for sale before spring. They'd be long gone before a couple summer hikers would take a jaunt off the main trails only to meet the horror of their life. Billy had seen this one too many times. All the searching, all the news stories with their crawling tip line numbers, and sadly, inevitably, it would come down to that.

A thin curl of smoke from one of the Carroll's chimneys; probably one of those wood-pellet jobs, super-efficient, the smoke no doubt subjected to a half-dozen afterburners, catalytic converters, or some such contraptions to keep the emissions down and the EPA happy.

Throw a good cedar log in that damn thing. Makes the whole forest smell good.

He swung east just under the summit, early morning sunrays bursting over the white cornice met him like the watchful eye of God.

Billy smiled at that. People often said this was Billy's mountain. But Billy wasn't confused as to who owned this particular stretch of property. Billy was a temporary caretaker at best. And he hadn't been doing a perfect job.

Snow level broke more records than Tom Brady this year, but enough to cover a big GMC truck?

"What did I miss, Mary Ann? What did this old coot forget?"

He'd make one more pass before calling it a day, a wide loop east that brought him over the Morgan property; the Morgan's roof was so thick with snow Billy might have missed it completely but for the puffy gray column of smoke. Good, old-fashioned fire with good, old-fashioned firewood.

The Carroll and Morgan homes were a study in opposites for sure – and not just the fireplaces.

The Carroll's roof had been whistle clean. Milt Morgan's was likely to collapse if he didn't shovel some of that snow off.

"Milty, you know better than that."

Milt was somewhat of a character. A gregarious mountain of a man, with a long goatee and the biggest, shiniest bald head Billy had ever seen. His wife, June, was a tiny, mousy woman. The couple were a sight and a half. Literally.

Billy eased Mary Ann around for another look, brought her down low. Maybe Milt had taken sick.

Truth was Billy hadn't seen them, or heard Milt's butt-ugly red Dodge pick-up rattling around Cedar in some time.

Now he could just make out the truck between the snow-laden branches, half-buried in snow a good fifty feet from the garage where it should have been. Milt always complained about that old truck, there was always something broken on or off of her – but he hadn't bought a new one in thirty years.

"We know how that is, huh, Mary Ann? Just like me and you." He grinned, "My parts break down, but you never give up on me."

Billy sure as hell wouldn't leave Mary Ann uncovered out in the cold like Milt's truck was now.

Foot trails around the property. Doorways had been cleared of snow. They had that fire going. They were most likely fine.

He swung south, combing the switchbacks to Cedar once again. He'd make a point of giving Milty a call once he got back to the office.

-=-=-=-=-=-=-=-=-=-

Billy was surprised to find Mayor Lyle squatting in his office. Seated in Billy's chair, actually.

"To what do I owe this very distinct pleasure," Billy said as he hung up his coat. "And get the Hell out of my favorite chair, Lyle."

"It's a piece 'a crap, Billy. When you gonna buy some real furniture for this place?"

"When the county buys the Sheriff a new place for said furniture, that's when. We can't all have fancy, mayor-style digs."

It was a standing joke, Lyle's dilapidated office was in worse shape than Billy's.

Lyle harrumphed, grumbling nearly as loud as the chair groaned as he extricated his bulky frame from it. He took the one chair in the office with wheels that worked.

"You hear about those *butt-slapper* boys in McMinnville?" As usual, Lyle didn't come right out with what he needed.

Billy nodded. Sadly, by now everybody in the US had heard about the case. It had already made Oregon law enforcement a laughing stock. The chain of idiocy began with two middle school boys running down the hall during a class break slapping girls' butts. This act was supposedly part of a grand institution called "Butt-Slap Day," a tradition the school Principal apparently didn't have the nuts to stop with a reprimand. When a teacher's assistant reported the dastardly deed to the Principal, the fool actually called the police. That howitzer of overkill should have ended it. But instead of having the balls to act like a cop, give the boys a scare and tell them where those shenanigans could get them one day (and then giving the Principal holy hell for calling the police on a school discipline matter), the nutless goon who showed up in a police uniform arrested the kids! Even cuffed them.

The boys spent five days in jail. Twelve and thirteen year old kids in jail for *slapping butts.*

It burned Billy's butt just hearing about it – middle school boys handcuffed and confined behind bars for being stupid with puberty. If that wasn't child abuse, what was?

"Well now the Yamhill DA wants to put those boys on trial as sex offenders." Lyle drawled.

"Gutless fruitcake. Any judge with nuts'll throw that out before the paperwork skips halfway across his desk."

Lyle pursed his lips, his big red bulldog face doubtful.

"Don't tell me the judge is taking this one."

"Right up the shoot."

It made you want to spit.

"Now that you ruined the first sunny day I can even remember, what can I do for you? You see how busy it is around here."

Lyle glanced casually around the room, characteristically empty but for the Sheriff's volunteer admin, Helen. Helen sat behind a gargantuan monochrome CRT, the shell of which had been a putty color when they'd hefted it in here twenty years ago; now brackish with cigarette smoke and layers of handprints. Big as that monstrosity was, like Lyle, Helen was a large woman; the CRT did not begin to hide her or her lack of activity.

Helen was doing exactly nothing. But, to be fair, you couldn't so much as properly surf the net on that thing. Lyle nodded to her and she smiled cordially. He leaned toward Billy as best he could without tipping the chair.

"PC gone nuts – Political Correctness bull. Everybody's a victim - especially girls so you jail schoolboy cut-ups for a bad case of puberty."

"A scourge, Lyle. But exactly how does this foolishness affect law enforcement in the greater metropolitan Cedar area – besides making all Oregon law enforcement a joke?"

"Well, something related to it. The same PC bull crap. It's not a law-enforcement issue yet. But I guess it could be somewhere down the line."

Billy waited, patiently.

"Jerry Fields from the Forest Service came by yesterday with two other boys. One of them was a member of

something called the Center for Islamic Studies, the other guy
was from the damn ACLU. They say we need to install
footbaths for the Muslim Community in every Cedar public
restroom– including the one in this office and up on all the
trails."

"Footbaths? It is fifteen degrees outside. We're lucky
if folks wash their hands after they take a leak."

"Like I say, it's for the Muslim *Community.*"

The Center for Islamic Studies had taken over the
space formerly occupied by a head-shop that had operated
off Main Street since the sixties. The head shop had gone
under after the proprietor was busted for selling meth. Mark
D'Arc had been responsible for the bust.

There were a few Muslim families in the area, hardly
what you'd call a community, but they were good people,
good neighbors. Certainly the Islamic Studies folks had been
a welcome improvement over the previous occupant as far as
Billy was concerned.

"Billy, I'm not going to go along with it – next thing
you know, Catholics'll want Holy Water Founts on every
corner. It's bullshit. Can I get your support? ACLU can get
pretty ugly with all their lawyers."

Billy scratched the stubble on his chin.

"Ah, hell, Lyle. Sure it's bull – but is it worth the
mess? How much would it cost?"

"You haven't had so much as a new stapler in this office for ten years – let alone a decent computer. The county's broke and you think Cedar's got money to burn?"

It was nearly 8:30 AM. Billy had intended calling the Morgan's half an hour ago.

"Is that all you dropped by for Lyle? Foot cleaners?"

"No there's more there've been some complaints about the water in Cedar Creek lately. Most likely someone cut corners on their septic tank leach lines. Could be squatters. Or it could be worse. Maybe a meth lab."

"I'll check it out. Water been tested yet?"

Lyle nodded, "Should hear this afternoon."

Pot farms used to pop up like weeds here. He'd gotten a pretty good handle on it over the years with a little help from the DEA, and a lot of help from Mark D'Arc. The pot farmers were smart, grew the plants down in the dense parts of the forest, tough to spot – even with Mary Ann. A few of them had even gone underground – used all the new home construction to cover their digging.

E-Coli bacteria gave them away though. Sometimes even the lowest of the low could be your friend. You bring in extra folks to tend your crops, well everybody's got to go sometime. Sewage in the creek, good old intestinal E-Coli, was a dead giveaway.

Crystal meth, though, that was the worst. Runoff from that blight could kill you. And the runoff wasn't the biggest problem. Pot farmers could be mean sons of bitches, but the creeps who dealt in meth were outright murderers.

"I'll check it out. Have Joanie send those test results over to me soon as they come in. She still have any of that marion berry jam of hers?"

Lyle's wife was also Lyle's secretary, and made the best preserves and jams this side of the Mississippi.

"I think she might have a few jars lying around doing nothing."

"Well, have her send one or two of those too."

"I'll do that." Lyle hefted himself from the chair, this one stuck to his sides as he rose. He disentangled himself and set it down roughly where he'd found it. "You could use at least one decent chair in here you know. You could use that a heck of a lot more than a damn footbath, don't you think?"

"You're probably right about that, Lyle."

"Damn tail's waggin' the dog," Lyle muttered as he pushed arms that were too big through jacket sleeves that had mysteriously grown too small over the years. "You let one little group push you around – next thing you know, you've got ten pushing you around – ten little tails waggin' the dog."

Billy shook his head as he watched his old friend negotiate the snow and ice in the street from his window. If there were crystal methamphetamine labs on Mount Cedar, footbaths were the least of Billy's worries.

His call to the Morgan's went straight to an automated voice asking him if he'd like to press another number to hang up, or just hang up on his own. He managed to do it on his own.

Billy mentally checked off what he'd seen on his flyover: cleared doorways, signs of foot-traffic around the house, and they had a fire going. The heavy snow on the roof was a bad sign, Milt's truck sitting out in the snow was worse. They were most likely fine. But if they didn't pick up the phone next time, it wouldn't hurt to take a drive up there and pay them a visit.

But there was someone else he needed to talk to first. He punched in Mark D'Arc's number.

-=-=-=-=-=-=-=-=-

"Kiss, you okay?"

Ken rapped lightly on his daughter's door once again.

"Kristi?"

The soft commotion of comforter and pillows rustling from within. Finally, Kristi's sleepy voice.

"I'm okay, Daddy."

"Like some breakfast?"

The door opened. Kristi stood looking disoriented
and tired, wrapped in her blue comforter, her eyes puffy and
red. For a moment she was their baby again, one of the twins
wrapped in a blanket, with only their round faces, those tiny
hands in view. *Amanda, beaming as she cradled their babies in her
arms.*

"I could drink some coffee."

Instinctively, he held the back of his hand to her
forehead, the way Amanda would have. But it didn't really tell
him anything.

"Are you coming down with something?"

"I'm okay," she said again. "It's so cold in here."

"It's seventy-two degrees."

She nodded.

"You shaved," she smiled.

"Yeah, it was time to leave the cave."

She shuffled past him down the stairs. He couldn't
remember the last time he'd seen her this sleepy while there
was daylight. And she rarely drank coffee. She was definitely
coming down with something. He'd make an appointment;
get her in to see a doctor while he still had insurance.

They haven't fired me yet.

But his promotion was dead. He'd been set-up and
steamrolled. The "early retirement" announcement wouldn't
be far off.

"I love you, Daddy."

Just when you were standing on that precipice looking straight down into the abyss – your kids turned you around, gave you a reason to step away from the edge.

"I love you too, Kiss."

Reed's door, shut tight when his room was occupied, was wide open..

Once the eggs were scrambling on the griddle Kristi seemed to perk up. Before breakfast was over she'd drained two mugs of black coffee – tossing it down the way she'd normally chug orange juice – she'd gobbled two extra helpings of his signature basil and tomato scrambled eggs, with three slices of cheddar off the big wheel they kept in the chilled walk-in. He'd never seen her so ravenous.

"Once Reed gets back we need to sit down and plan things out as a family."

She glowered across the table at him.

"We need to stay *here*. Mom's here."

Ken sat back stiffly. When his shoulders loosened, finally, he shook his head.

"Honey, there's just no way…at this point. No one could stay out there this long."

"No, she's here. *She's alive and she needs us.*"

Kristi's eyes didn't waiver. No sign of tears, no breakdown coming. *She actually believes Amanda is alive.*

Ken had mourned alone, locked himself away and broke down. He'd reached a truce with his grief. But he'd made that journey selfishly, without his family, and now what?

Kristi cleared the dishes and loaded them into the washer quickly, efficiently. In moments she was dressed, shouldering her skis out the mudroom door.

The dishwasher churned quietly but for one plate that had lost its balance, clinking lightly, in rhythm with each sweep of the jets.

-=-=-=-=-=-=-=-=-

Reed had ridden halfway home before he stopped and looped back.

It was dumb. He shouldn't be doing this; *she didn't want him following her.* It had taken time to build her trust, just to learn her name. He risked losing that.

But now as he followed her trail he couldn't help himself.

Malana walked a long way to get to their property, a path that had already crossed the winding course of the creek twice.

Dog whined, looking forward to her mid-morning nap back in the warm, dry sanctuary of his room.

"Shhh, girl, we'll be home soon."

This is all wrong, at the same time he felt exhilarated, more alive than he ever had. They climbed a small rise and the landscape opened around them.

Here the creek turned east, the bed sank and flattened. A crosshatch of rotting logs rose from the far bank up to a wide, snowy meadow. Beyond the meadow, another thick tangle of forest crowded steep canyon walls. That deep patch of forest was the *hidden place* he'd seen from up above the ridge.

Malana's tracks ended just before the deadfall.

Reed swallowed. Now what?

The snow, hastily raked with evergreen boughs, was dotted with mud and pine needles.

God, could she really live under all that wood? She lived in a cave?

No, that was stupid; no one could survive out here.

A low rumble, from Dog's chest; Reed tapped her snout, just hard enough to get her attention.

"No, Dog," he whispered.

She snuffled. Looked up at him, wounded, but indignant. The rumble began again.

He swept Dog into his arms and crouched next to snowy hillock beneath the branches of a broad pine. He touched his finger to her lips.

She licked it. Still friends.

Still, the rumbling began.

A broad form appeared at the far edge of the meadow. He was a short man, but not a small one; broad shouldered, powerfully built. He kept to the edge of the forest as he walked, head swiveling, looking to the sky, to the high ridges of the canyon – and then directly where Reed and Dog hid.

Reed quit breathing altogether.

The clear mountain air seemed to darken around the man. Even before the tattoos on his neck came into view, before the line rising above his backpack became the barrel of a rifle, Reed sensed a danger beyond death in him.

Dog squirmed. When she began to growl Reed clamped his hand over her snout, she protested, her eyes wide with indignation and fear.

The man stopped above the deadfall. He took one last look at the skies, at the forest he'd just left, and descended the steep bank with practiced steps. Reed saw the rifle clearly now, a sight familiar to anyone who'd ever played a First Person Shooter game; an AK-47.

A lightheadedness, a surreal sense of not being, of not seeing what had to be there, swept over Reed. He felt detached and distant from this place.

Dog squirmed. The growl that would kill them both rose in her gut; yanked Reed back to reality. He clamped down on her snout again, hard this time.

Reed closed his eyes. What if he had to kill Dog to save himself?

God no. Please, God no.

He opened them as the man reached the creek bed, jaw working angrily as the man noted the same things Reed had – bits of pine needles, of frozen mud; boot prints hastily covered. His narrow eyes traced the path she'd made; just beyond that path, only a few yards above it. Reed stared back.

He fought the urge to pull himself and Dog into an even tighter ball. *Don't move, you can't move now, not at all.*

A curse in Spanish lifted on a frigid breeze.

The man turned abruptly, pulled the rifle from his shoulder, and Reed's heart beat like timpani in his ears, his boots slid down into the snow.

The man whipped the rifle around, striking a nearby log with the butt of it. He waited then struck two more times.

In the deep shadows of the deadfall, branches began to move. A rim of light shone from inside, and then Malana's face, her eyes fearful.

The man swore, pointed toward the shoddily covered trail, and slapped her. From where Reed huddled it sounded like the snap of a young branch. The man slapped her again, a nauseatingly sharp snap in the cold air.

The heat of anger flushed through Reed. The man had set his rifle down, it leaned against a log two long steps from him.

No. What the hell are you thinking?

And Kristi's words, "This isn't a game…you don't spawn a new eyeball when you lose one…"

There were twenty yards of deep snow between Reed and the deadfall. He'd be dead before he took three steps. All he could do was pray for his own safety while Malana, the most beautiful girl in the world, was beaten right before his eyes.

Nausea knotted his gut.

Malana didn't cry out. She only nodded. The man raised his hand higher. She cowered. He put his hand down. Malana moved out of Reed's sight. The man hefted the pack from his shoulders. He poured a wealth of tins and small sacks from it.

Paco appeared, finally. The man reached down to pet him but Paco backed away growling. The man shook his head and swore again. Even with the fear and hatred gnawing in his gut, Reed had to smile at Paco's good sense of character.

But the breeze that had blown those percussive slaps up the hill now brought the sounds and scents of Paco.

Playtime!

Dog broke out of Reed's grasp.

Reed pounced, flattening over her in the snow before the bark could leave her throat.

God no! No. Please don't make me do this!

Reed pressed his face into the freezing snow, but he could barely feel that. He could only feel Dog's chest, her wild heartbeat, her ribs compressing under his weight.

Please! Please!

He lifted his eyes only to see the man put his lips to Malana's. Reed watched them kiss. Dog struggled, and Reed pressed deeper, buried his own face in the snow.

When he lifted it again the man was gone. Malana's cave was hidden once more.

-=-=-=-=-=-=-=-=-=-

Leave it for the crows.

Reed had said that about the dead wolf.

But the wolf had been a *thing*, at most, the provider of a cool skull for a boy's wall or desk, a trophy.

Ten years must have passed since then; maybe a lifetime. That boy had passed through some mysterious portal now and was gone; a passage from complete self-absorption and bravado into emptiness and uncertainty.

Reed knelt before the sad hump in the ground. He hadn't been able to claw through the frozen earth, only to clear the snow. He'd found stones along the creek bed, many stones, and when he was done, Reed packed snow over the grave.

Today he'd murdered his best friend to save his own life.

If he ever saw Paco again, Reed wondered, would Paco back away from him?

-.=.=.=.=.=.=.=.=.=-

When his knock didn't seem to pry anyone loose inside, Sheriff Billy Hicks rang the doorbell.

The television had been going. Some sort of monotonous talking head prattled on behind the door, most likely one of those political talk shows everybody seemed to watch these days.

His eyes hadn't failed him on his flyby. Snow had drifted over the tire ruts leading to the garage, but work had been done around the doorways. There were fresh boot prints around the house and leading to and from the forest; a big blue snow shovel rested against the side of the house, fresh snow and ice still clinging to it.

Milt's rust bucket of a truck was still sitting deep in the snow quite a ways from the garage.

The talking head stopped abruptly. The front door opened with the pungency of fruit gone bad; a stale sickness in the air he tried not to react to as June greeted him.

June Morgan seemed smaller than ever. Dressed for church though it was Friday, she wore prim white gloves, a blue scarf covered her mousy gray hair.

"Morning, June."

"Morning, Sheriff."

"Everything okay? I think your phone machine's broke, I tried to leave a message, but it went straight to -"

Her smile faded.

"Everything's okay, Billy. Milton was sick, but he's coming along fine now."

"Sorry to hear that. Mind if I come in and give him my regards?"

Billy removed his hat, started to step inside, but mousy June stayed right there in the doorway.

"This isn't a good time. He's sleeping now – it's been very hard to get him to rest. *You know how he is.*"

"Stubborn as a mule, but at least twice as bright," he grinned. "Well, that's fine. You let him sleep. Tell him to get better for me, okay?"

"I'll tell him that."

Billy pulled his hat back on, and tipped it to her.

"By the way, that snow's getting a little thick on your roof – if you need help shoveling it off…"

"Our nephews will come by. They'll take care of it."

"They been by lately?"

"Yes, they have."

"Okay then. You have a nice day, June."

"You too, Billy."

She began to close the door.

"Milt finally bought himself a new truck?"

She looked surprised.

"Can't believe he left his old friend out there in the snow like that," Billy said.

"Yes, Peggy finally broke down for good. The boys have a truck. We still get around just fine."

Peggy. Billy had to smile at that, made him wonder how many men kept an old flame kindling in their favorite mode of transport. At least Billy wasn't the only one.

"Well, I guess we all break down sometime. Have Milt call me when he's up to it, could you?"

"I sure will. You have a nice day, Billy."

-=-=-=-=-=-=-=-=-

Well, that didn't exactly add up even.

Sheriff Hicks drove carefully back toward town. Even with snow tires and four-wheel drive, the switchbacks made for a tricky and treacherous journey.

Nothing criminal about leaving an old truck in the snow to rust, or being slow to clear your roof. June was an odd one. Showed a little more gumption keeping him out than he figured her to have, but there was no crime in letting your sick spouse sleep either.

His radio squawked on.

"Cedar One."

"You're killing me, Billy."

"Trying my best, Helen, but still you hang on. What you got for me?"

"You have an urgent message from Lyle."

"Lyle – not Joanie?"

"His Honor the Mayor, the big man himself."

"Nothing to do with damn foot washers, I hope."

"What's a foot washer?"

"Never mind. What's he got to say?"

"Water tests on the creek are in. Very nasty."

"E-Coli?"

"Positive, but that's not the worst of it."

"We have another meth lab somewhere up here?"

"Oh, it's a real batch of private reserve brewing this time. Benzene and other carcinogens, lysergic acid, and something they're not even sure of, probably another hallucinogen. They're cooking up something special in them thar' hills, Sheriff."

"Give Wes Davis at the Forest Service a shout. He'll need to post some of those 'unhealthful conditions' signs along the creek and wherever he can in town. That water's poisoned – so is anything anybody fishes out of it. Blame it on leaky septic tanks for now. Copy?"

"Already started."

"You are a marvel. Has Mark D'Arc called in?"

"Not yet."

"I'll give him a shout from here."

"Don't forget Lyle."

"Try as I might..."

"Roger that."

He tried Mark's cell first, but couldn't get enough signal. He craned his neck over the steering wheel, searched the treetops for a glimpse of the cell tower by habit - just the way everyone else on the mountain did. The only difference was Billy *knew* he couldn't see it from here. He flew right over that tower most mornings.

When he felt the wheels drift he eased up on the speed. He tried Mark on the two-way and couldn't raise him. Well, it wasn't like Mark carried that radio everywhere he went – and that was a good thing. It was already way too obvious he did more for the Sheriff than Search and Rescue. He'd played a big part in the turnaround of this whole area. Mark's parents dealt *crank* for the motorcycle gangs up here back in the day, before the name "crystal meth" made that garbage sound like rock candy.

One day his folks went missing; two weeks later they turned up in Hagg Lake wrapped in motorcycle chains. They'd likely still be missing if their killers had been bright enough to pick a lake that didn't drain half out every year.

The kid had been on a one-man anti-drug crusade ever since.

But it was dangerous work. A day didn't go by that Billy wished Mark had never gotten involved. But the truth was Billy couldn't fight the dealers without him.

So what did they have up here this time? The E-Coli was likely from a pot farm tended by folks with no proper plumbing. Most likely illegals who made next to nothing doing it - but still a hundred times more than the Mexican economy allowed them. Up here they'd work for some gang that cared way more about the plants than the hired help.

But cannabis plants needed warmth and light and room, and you weren't getting any of that above ground these days. Whoever ran this operation had smarts and some serious start-up money. Growing pot wasn't rocket science but digging a cave big enough for an underground pot farm took some doing – especially doing it undetected, and Billy hadn't seen a thing on his flyovers. But the other chemicals in the water suggested that and more.

Billy pulled to the side, shut off the engine and cracked open the door with a rush of cold that seemed to bite his bones deeper every winter. His boots crunched through the thin skin of ice over the snow as he walked toward the shear drop at the side of the road.

It had gone a few degrees warmer this morning, just long enough to melt the top snow layer. Then the temperature had dropped sharply. Those temperature fluctuations happened a lot up here, the skin of ice they formed made driving up here, hell, just walking up here, even more treacherous. This ice was a tiny taste of things to come though. The weather bureau was reporting a warm front rolling in from the coast. The *year-rounders* up here could handle the slush from that storm just fine, but a cold blast was heading down the Columbia Gorge. That forecast had serious ice storm written all over it - and that was something only God could handle satisfactorily. Everyone else had just better stay indoors.

Billy didn't have much time to figure things out.

From up here he had a clear view of the mountain for a good mile in either direction. Underground pot-farming took power and water. He followed the narrow cut over the west rim the power lines ran through. They had to tap those lines somewhere. They got the water they needed from Cedar Creek, polluting the hell out of it from that point down. There were maybe half a dozen places where the creek meandered close to those lines. All he had to do was to start at the top and test the water below those points till it went sour. Sophisticated operation or not, finding these A-holes would be easy.

Easier than finding the wreckage of a big SUV that slid off a mountain road. He looked down the pristine sides of the cliffs below his feet; half the pristine mountainside lay before him.

Billy Hicks, you are one senile old fool. They didn't find wreckage scattered over these cliffs because Amanda Carroll didn't wreck. She didn't drive out of town and run away either.

It was as if a bolt of lightning had struck him from on high, from a sky already growing dark with clouds, pregnant with the new storm.

She'd left the road all right, but not on her own.

Chapter 12

"Got away from you? *What do you mean she got away from you?*"

"She ran off! She's a *stupid fucking dog.*"

"*What happened?*"

"I told you. *She's fucking gone."*

Ken Carroll stood aghast. Who was this kid who swore in the doorway with glazed red eyes, his face wind burnt and lined. His son was quiet; painfully self-conscious. Reed was not cavalier; he was not cruel.

Dog wasn't a lost toy, she was his constant companion, *his best friend.*

How could this be his son?

He fought the urge to slam the boy's head into the doorframe. Finally, words came, not the right ones, because there weren't any right words for this – only ones he'd heard before, probably from an ancient family show on Nickelodeon.

"Dog's find their way. She'll come back," was what he came up with, but Reed's eyes told him something else. Just before the boy averted them, before he pushed his way past Ken into the house, they told Ken the dog wouldn't be coming back, *not ever.*

Ken felt his entire structure break loose from its moorings, as if his skeleton had simply unhinged itself, dropping bones one by one to the floor.

He found a chair and melted into it.

"*A stupid fucking dog,*" Reed had said.

And in an awful way Reed was right. He was talking about a pet not the boy's mother, not the wife Ken had lost.

Not lost. *Sent to her death.*

You killed her, just as surely as if you'd used your own hands.

And now for whatever reason, whatever circumstance, Reed had killed too.

Not just a stupid dog, *his best friend.*

Like father, like son.

Eventually, the tick of the kitchen clock, a fifties antique Amanda rescued from a Cannon Beach shop two summers ago, made its way through the fog in Ken's head. He rose with the stiffness of a man thirty years his senior.

The pantry was still well-stocked with all the staples, they could survive a cold winter here, but the niceties, the home baked cookies she'd kept in ceramic jars, the juice and fruit cartons, the sorts of things a mother would bake or bring home, those items were gone.

But home cooking wasn't what he needed now.

He found what he needed near the back of the long pantry on the highest shelf. Ken poured himself two shots of oblivion, and carried the bottle with him into his studio.

-=-=-=-=-=-=-=-=-

The first thing Reed did was move all of Dog's trappings; bedding, the cage that had become her sanctuary, the gnawed-blanket, chew toys, everything of hers he could find, down to the storage room.

In less than ten minutes it was all out of sight, gone.

Only the smell of puppy remained.

He sprayed the carpet with cleaner, shook baking powder over it all and vacuumed it away. He did what he could; but it didn't *go* away.

Then he sat on the edge of his bed and wept.

-=-=-=-=-=-=-=-=-

"Helen, I need you to call Lyle for me. You got a pen handy?"

"Sure do, Sheriff. Shoot."

Eschewing the GPS bolted beneath it, Billy Hicks unfurled the map across the dashboard, checking the coordinates while he drove.

"Tell him we need more of those water tests done at a few points I'm about to give you." He leaned over the map, steadying it with one hand, steering with the other.

"You wouldn't be looking at a map while driving, would you Sheriff?"

"Come on now, Helen, you know I'm a fool for safety."

"Roger all but the safety part."

"You *wound* me."

"You coming in soon? Storms about to break all over you."

"Roger that. Just checking out a *fool* notion of mine, won't take long."

He pulled to the side of the road, two clicks before the entrance to the Morgan property. If the Carroll woman had been carjacked in that big new SUV, all her attacker had to do was disable the GPS and keep driving to throw off the searchers. The blizzard covered their tracks.

Crashes, lost hikers, fallen climbers - all that was normal business up here. This wasn't Los Angeles, it wasn't even Portland. There had never been a carjacking in Cedar. There had never been a stolen car. The last violent crime had been the D'Arc murders, and that was fifteen years ago.

Maybe thinking of this as a carjacking *was* a fool notion, a way to justify how a woman had been lost on his mountain on his watch – and Billy hadn't been able to do a damn thing about it; hadn't even recovered her body.

Maybe. But it was worth another look at the Morgan place. Nephews who supposedly visited often and helped out around the place - nephews Milt had never mentioned before and Billy had never seen in town - a favorite truck left to rust away in the snow. June wasn't acting like herself - that was plain enough.

Late morning now and it was already growing dark; gray sky broken only by inky black clouds now. He didn't have much time before all hell broke loose – but fresh ice would make the main road pretty much impassible for days, he couldn't wait that long for a search warrant.

Hicks buckled on snowshoes, just hoping he was in good enough shape to get there and back in time. Hazarding one more glance at the gathering clouds, he took a deep breath, and started on his way.

.=.=.=.=.=.=.=.=.=-

Kristi Carroll watched those same storm clouds take out the sun. She'd already had a record run; there would be no rifle practice today, no need to push harder than she already had.

Her stomach had ached badly early on, the nausea coming over her so fast she lost much of that big breakfast against the trunk of a huge Sitka tree. But shortly after, her energy had blasted off the charts.

She was skiing faster than she ever had, a feeling more akin to flying than skiing. Bits of odd dreams had come to her, images so vivid she'd had to slow down several times, catch her breath and remind herself of what she was really doing - not sleeping but skiing, *and skiing dangerously fast.*

Thoughts of that Search and Rescue guy, Mark, had been so strong she felt him skiing right next to her at times. She had to admit it was a good feeling, a warming feeling.

But now she was thirsty. *So thirsty.*

She swung down to the creek again, snapping a good hole in the ice with her poles and refilled her water bottle as she done twice already this morning. Shadows darted beneath the hole, but she didn't take much notice of the fish. She gulped half the water down, filled the bottle to the brim again, twirled on the top and then she was on her way.

She'd taken a wide arc today, keeping an eye on the creek and the transmission lines for reference.

A sprawling valley of snow and pine opened below her, a dreamlike, postcard moment.

I actually live here.

She had passed a few cabins on her way, only two with smoke twirling up from their chimneys. The heavy snows had obliterated property lines and fences. It was all one big ski run. The mountain had indeed become her private playground. She was free, free as a bird.

Kristi took a hill and caught serious air. She landed soft as a glider, barely feeling the snow beneath her.

Yes, a bird. *She was flying like a bird now.* Sometimes her dreams let her do that, sometimes they didn't. But here she was, in real life, living out a dream…

Slow down!

A voice in her head – yes, but not her own.

Help me!

Kristi dug and rooster-tailed to a stop.

Mom?

You're not dreaming, you're here, you're skiing. What are you thinking? You're not asleep.

She'd heard that. She wasn't dreaming.

A gust of wind cut sharply through her jacket, beneath the sweats, cut right through her. She shivered for the first time since she'd left the house, and she realized that for the first time this morning she was actually *in* the moment.

The trees faded to white around her, bled into the watercolor sky like a mirage in the desert.

That was something she had dreamt.

Was she asleep now, dreaming on her feet? What was going on here?

Her stomach roiled. With no time to react a stream of vomit shot from her like a blast from a fire hose packed with orange paint. It spattered the snow, steamed, boiled there, and dropped out of site.

But not all of it disappeared, bright red spatters fanned out from the hole.

Kristi wiped her mouth. Her glove came away streaked bright red.

"Oh, God." She swallowed against the awful burning in her throat.

Her glove steamed where her blood had stained it. It bubbled there, boiled, gurgled up between her fingers. Kristi watched in helpless, numb horror as her own blood trickled over her palm, down the back of her hand. Her fingers broke through the liquefying glove, the flesh shrank, tendons shrinking, snapping, curling like burnt paper. The tiny bones of her fingers melted away...

She was on her knees in the snow. She had indeed thrown up. But…as gross as it was, it was normal as far as vomit went. She looked at her gloved hands. Intact. No red, no blood.

Okay, I'm okay. I'm okay. And she felt better now, so much better.

Fat flakes of snow collecting on her gloves and jacket. They fell slowly now, soon they would be coming down like nobody's business.

Where was she?

She scanned the mountain for the transmission lines, saw the thicker, darker line of trees where the creek dropped into a little canyon not far from their house. Above that was the hill with the view she and Reed liked so much – a vantage point they'd sometimes ride to on the Ski Doos at night, where they could see the glow of Portland.

She had to get to the tow line. Get back up to the house before the storm hit.

A straight line was definitely a shorter distance to the house – but she'd have to take off her skis to cross the creek at that point. If she swung south there was a decent bridge.

Hell, she could fly there in no time.

Quit thinking that way.

She ignored the other voice, her confidence growing again, rising like mercury. Endorphins for sure. *Just crazy ass endorphins. This is why you work out, girl!*

She planted her poles, pushed off and then she was flying again.

Help me!

Mom, where are you?

I'm here! Please help me!

Was she just crazy? Was she grieving? She didn't feel sad, not at this moment anyway. Right now she was feeling good, *unbelievably* good.

The truth was, she'd never stopped believing her mom was alive.

But no one was here, no one was speaking. There wasn't anything but cedar and snow here. The voice was in her head, in her mind.

She skidded to a stop, sucked more sweet water through the tube on her bottle.

Yeah, she needed that.

The tube gurgled and the water stopped flowing, then started again. Something rubbery and bitter hit her tongue. She spat into the snow.

A black dot with a tail wriggled in the foam for an instant, then disappeared beneath the snow.

"Oh, god *that is gross!*"

She held the bottle up to the fading sun. It was blue, nearly opaque, there wasn't enough sunlight to candle whatever was inside. She pulled the tube out, dumped the entire contents onto the snow.

Sure enough, there were more of those little things – black pollywogs. She felt lightheaded now, faint.

God, how many of those things have I swallowed?

What the hell? Pollywogs are baby frogs. They come in the spring, not winter.

She knelt down and took a good look. They weren't baby frogs they were some kind of fish. A couple of the little head parts had two tails. No, not tails. They were fused, she'd been drinking little Siamese twin fish. She might never eat or drink again.

Dizzy with nausea now. Her head throbbing.

God she had to get home. Get home fast and wash her mouth with a gallon of Listerine, flush her entire system out and fast for a week.

On another day seeing something that nasty in her drinking water would have been enough to make her collapse in a quivering ball. But she had too much energy now, was too high to let something gross stop her. She pushed off.

It was really starting to come down as Kristi poled her way up a low rise to see men hard at work clearing snow from a roof. Well, *two of them* were hard at work; they wore cheap jackets, wool caps pulled down over their ears, and they practically bulled the snow off the roof. The other four, dressed nearly alike in expensive black ski-jackets and pants, look like they'd never done a day's work, nor so much as lifted a shovel before; they poked the snow, kicked at it with the toes of their boots. If they'd been hired for the job they weren't worth the cash.

Still, snow collapsing the Carroll roof was something she didn't have to worry about let alone work to prevent; their roof was so high-tech it cleaned itself.

One of the black-clad men saw her, startled, he spoke sharply to the others; they all stopped working and turned her way.

She smiled and waved as she skied into the meadow. Only one of the men, slight and fragile, and probably the youngest - returned her smile and waved.

"Big storm coming!" She gestured to the blackening skies with one pole.

A few of them spoke softly to each other then one of them, the slight man who'd waved so quickly before, said,

"You are welcome."

She had to smile at that as she nodded and pushed on. Was he welcoming her to cross the property or just giving the best response he knew in the English language?

It was pretty funny.

-=.-=.-=.-=.-=.-=.-=.-=.-

By the time Sheriff Hicks reached his vantage point, the bulk of the packed snow had been cleared, and only two of Milt's *"nephews"* remained shoveling off the Morgan's roof. A brand new frosting of it had begun to stick right behind them. It was coming down steady.

His binoculars had fogged, but not so badly that he'd ever imagine a family resemblance between Milt and June Morgan and these boys. But maybe his nephews couldn't cut it and Milt had just hired some real help.

The garage door was still packed with ice and snow at the corners, tracks leading to it were similarly covered; it hadn't been opened in a while. Other than Milt's sad and disabled truck, Peggy, there was no other vehicle anywhere Billy could see. So how did the hired help get here?

Even from his perch, he could see snow had drifted over the seats. Milt might have left the truck where she died, but no way he would have left her windows open, let the snow build up in her like that. You didn't treat an *old flame* that way.

Whatever sickness had taken Milt had hit him hard; he obviously wasn't getting over it. He'd been incapacitated, or worse.

Billy Hicks, maybe you aren't a fool – but you are definitely getting slow in the head.

He didn't need a tape measure to see Peggy's wheelbase was narrower, with tires nowhere near as thick as the iced-over tracks leading up to the garage. The garage itself was a decent size, could hold one of those big GMC SUVs like the Carroll's just fine – but not with Milt's Peggy alongside; so outside the old girl sat to freeze and rust.

He fought back the lump rising in his throat. Sometimes being right was bad. Especially when the right answer came way too late.

But it also meant the Carroll woman might still be alive. The house was shuttered, he couldn't see a thing in there.

He got a better view of the men as they clambered down from the roof. The stockier of the two looked to be a real badass, the blue-black stain of crude tattoos, the kind that came with gang initiation and serious jail time, extended up his throat all the way to his jaw line. What were the chances June would have welcomed either of these two into her house? He dialed in on the neck of the stocky man's throat. *The Roman Numeral XIII was unmistakable.*

Billy reached for his holster, the strap holding his .45 Colt and released it with a "quip" that was barely audible.

He didn't hear the next sound at all, the ring of steel on bone, and all he felt was ice.

.-.=.-.=.-.=.-.=.-.=.-.=.-.

The baby's crying.

Very young baby — the famished, *"la, la, la"* of a newborn.

"Huh…" *Hungry.* Billy wanted to say the baby was hungry, but his lips couldn't quite form the word. He'd have to feed the baby somehow, but he couldn't get to it, couldn't even see it. The child was just out there somewhere in the endless blackness that surrounded him.

The *"lalala"* sound again, but it wasn't a baby's voice now, *a man's.*

"You are taking a great journey, my friend. A Holy journey."

Pressure. A needle prick.

"Owww…"

Lights now. A bearded face appeared before him, dark eyes sparkling, throwing stars. The face bled out into whiteness, *watercolor in the rain…* Wasn't that from a song? Yes, from another time, it was a happy time. Way back…in the Year of the Cat. Whenever that had been.

A cat's face close to his own. A kitten, no – a big cat, a cougar, *fangs wide, flashing.*

No fear. Only wonder at seeing such a thing.

The Wonder Years. That's when it was, that was the happy time Billy remembered. The wonder years of childhood when there *was still magic to believe in.*

The State Fair. Late summer in Oregon, clear blue sky, the gentle warming of the late day's sun with a cool rush of air. Flying. Flying on the Ferris wheel.

He'd cheated to do it. He'd cut in line to be next to her, and she knew it. She knew he would before he *did. She'd even hung back and waited for him, other kids had gone past, other boys. Sure, he'd cheated a little on this one, sneaking in line like that.*

But in the end, she'd really chosen him.

And now they were flying… the cornfields, the rolling hills and the snow-capped mountains in the distance.

And she was so pretty.

Yes, in the end, she'd chosen him.

That's the way it always was with girls. They did the choosing. Flying.

No…jostling, rolling…

He wasn't flying; he was back in the Ranger now.

A moment of wonder at that, *before the horror of his situation struck him.*

He wasn't steering. His hands weren't even on the wheel. He couldn't feel his hands.

Rolling. A blizzard. White on white through the windshield.

His hands were stuck in the shoulder strap. No not stuck, *wrapped and tied.*

Ghosts of trees blurring by. He knew where he was; knew *exactly where he was.*

The road turned just ahead, but the Ranger wouldn't be turning. Not without him. Not without his hands. There was only a flimsy rail ahead, and only empty space beyond that.

A bit of feeling in his shoulder: a dull sensation where the needle had gone in before. He fought the strap with muscles that no longer seemed to belong to him, pins and needles racing up and down his body, feelings awakening just beneath the surface.

He twisted, wound up, and drove his elbow into the console. Wound up and drove it again, his elbow sang with pain, the cover sprang open. He wrestled for the Bowie knife inside.

But the edge of the road, the canyon came fast. The rail didn't hold.

Flying…really flying at last.

The slight, bearded man watched the jeep crash through the railing and disappear into the beyond. Moments later the explosive shattering of trees reached his ears, trees that had no doubt clung to the bare rock for decades, one more affirmation to Amal of life's futility, just one more reason to let go of this life and embrace the next.

He touched his lips as the explosions echoed up the canyon walls. Soon he too would leave this life and this world for the next.

"Alhamdulillah," he whispered.

Chapter 13

The snow never stops up here.

Kristi changed to comfy sweats, her equipment and snow-covered outer-wear already hung and warming over grates in the mudroom to dry.

It had to stop snowing sometime. But it wasn't like some big dump truck in the sky emptied its load and moved on. As long as conditions were right - the temperature low enough, the moisture high enough - snow would keep forming and falling. Kristi figured the only real limiting factor was the Pacific Ocean, and that big dump truck wasn't going to be empty any time soon.

Firewood crib, planter, boulder...object by object, their backyard was disappearing into a barren white landscape of unrecognizable shapes. The snowfall had begun beautiful, become awesome, and now it was frightening.

It could go on forever.

The automatic blowers whooshed on again. They kept the doorways clear, one link of an electronic chain that kept the occupants of the Carroll home feeling cozy and safe; *normal.* The walkways were heated, as were the drains beneath them to carry the melted snow away.

They wouldn't be snowed in; if she *had* to get out of the house she could.

But then what? Where would she go from there?

Snow had risen halfway up the first floor windows, and a few feet past those blower-cleared doorways those same coziness-creating blowers had built a snow bunker that was shoulder high now. She would literally have to climb out.

She could ski or use a Ski Doo, but that soft-whipped topping she stared at now covered boulders, deep holes, throat-high wire fences; it created false ledges at the edge of the road. You could be sailing along a killer snow pack one second, free falling to your death the next.

Even with her skills, a trip to town would be deadly now.

As long as the power was on they were protected and warm inside. They had tons of food, gallons of bottled water if they needed it; extra fuel for the generators if the transmission lines went down. No need to feel trapped; they were sitting smack in the middle of an oasis here.

But one thing they lacked if things did go south was medical help. No emergency room. No big hospital nearby. She did know there was a Fire Station in Cedar, and there were Search and Rescue people like Mark.

But how would they make it up here in a blizzard?

The difficulty of getting out of here, getting out fast if she needed to, hadn't concerned her before. Now that thought wouldn't leave her alone, like a warning light pulsing on that bare edge of things Kristi Carroll, who'd always believed exercise and a balanced diet was all anyone needed to live, didn't know.

She just might have to leave, *to escape*. Because things weren't normal, *she* wasn't normal. She wasn't right.

It wasn't a matter of endorphins, it wasn't daydreams — *she was having feelings she wasn't even sure were hers; seeing things that couldn't possibly be real.*

And her stomach - out of nowhere, her stomach would churn and burn as though it's lining was peeling away, sloughing off like flakes of sun burnt skin, a little more each time it happened. The pain would come and go, and then she'd feel fine.

No, not fine, *numb*.

And their home wasn't right either. The blowers chugged on just the way they were supposed to, the furnace blew warm air through the vents, the lights worked. But it just

wasn't right. Except for all the expensive gadgets running on
their own, the house was eerily quiet.

The lights are on, but nobody's home. Literally

But Reed and Dad *were* home, Kristi could feel them
there, they were just…very quiet.

"Dog?"

Where was she?

From the kitchen she could see the makeup of the
snow was changing again. Big, fat flakes replaced by tons of
little ones, and they weren't floating softly anymore, they
streaked like stars through hyperspace. Eventually it would
pack and rise above the windows, little by little blotting away
the outside light. The view she had from here was the same
one toys get when they're being packed for shipping: all those
soft little Styrofoam beads piling up around them, slowly
snuffing out the glow of daylight over their heads. Total
darkness was eventual, inevitable. They were being packed
inside this house. Packed with snow.

"Reed? Daddy?"

Reed probably had his earbuds set on *destroy*. Dad
must be in the studio. But Dog heard all, barked at all, and
absolutely had to play with all. Kristi was home and Dog
hadn't bounded up to greet her, hadn't made any sound at all.

Sadness, exquisite and absolute, it flowed from downstairs,
filled the room… packed her in like a toy. Again, the tears flowed,

emotion so overwhelming her knees buckled. She dropped to the floor.

"*Help me!*" Mom's voice again.

Oh, God, no I am not right. I am not right in the head. Mom isn't here. *But she isn't far away.*

"Where are you?"

There was no answer. And as if a switch had been flipped, the sadness was gone.

Absolute dread took its place with a single revelation:

The water in the creek is toxic.

Every day I've filled my water bottle with mountain-pure poison. How many brain cells were gone now? How many esophageal cells? How much poison is in my blood? Do I even have red cells anymore? Do I still have a liver?

Stop.

She wasn't like this. She didn't worry, she worked out. She overcame. That's how Kristi was, had always been. She trained, she practiced and she won. She would win this too. She would fight the poison inside her and win.

But she needed help; she needed a doctor.

Then, as quickly as it had come, that feeling of dread vanished.

She didn't need anything. She felt great! She was strong, she was *invincible.* The spring was back in her step as she ran through the house. Kristi flew nearly to the ceiling, swam back down to the floor to plant her feet firmly on the hardwood again, her legs strong and resilient as saplings, her toes digging deep into the mountain drawing strength from its soil. She *was* the mountain. She *was the biggest, baddest thing on this f'ing planet!*

There was no ground below the last few feet of the den, only a drop-off; eighty feet of shear nothing until the rocks below. The ultra-wide, ultra-high den window there gave her a clear view of what was happening to the world north of their house. What had been green forest and blue sky for as far as human eyes could see was a stretch of pointed shapes now, not trees but tombstones leaning into a slate sky. *And so much snow...*

And just as quickly as her mood had changed, the snowfall broke, hesitated, as if the sky itself had taken a deep and healing breath.

Then the white rocks flew; rat-a-tat against the windows.

Even through those expensive double paned windows with their crazy inert gasses, through the walls themselves, she felt the hail strike like machine gun fire, in an all-out assault on their house.

Kristi listened, but now she watched it all from her lofty perch above the canyon...and smiled.

Eventually the white rocks gave way, fewer and fewer now, but the sky hadn't pressed *pause* this time, it had simply added warm water to the mix. Rain gushed, splattered against the windows, and sheeted down them.

Kristi knew exactly what this meant: *the danger ante had been upped.* In half an hour it would be ice, not snow, shrouding the outside world. Moving through the forest would no longer be death-defying; *it would be death itself.*

She nodded, acutely aware of these new odds.

"Bring it on."

-=-=-=-=-=-=-=-=-

There was nowhere to go. *No other world to escape to.*

DeerSlayr Wolfyn spawned in the Deadly Orchard ready for anything; ready for guards to encircle him, ready for banishment, amazed he had been allowed to spawn at all.

He and WyldChyld had broken every rule, they'd even used their combined powers to kill guards. Infractions didn't get worse than that in Mythykal.

Or did they?

Some of his loot was gone.

Raspberry. Syndee.

"Boss?" Raspberry, appeared, chest heaving, hands clenching, ever ready for the battle.

"Master?" Syndee spawned to sit in the crook of a tree above him as if on a swing, her long, shapely legs crossed, ever ready for...well, whatever a *succubus* was ever ready for.

"My emerald rune?"

His favorite minions glanced at each other then back at him, clearly puzzled.

"Master...you must seek out the Blue Hollow Wizard. He will help you find the Willow Wood Troll," Raspberry began.

"Defeating the Willow Wood Troll will bring you to level seventy five and give you the stones you desire," Syndee finished for him.

"We've already completed that quest. I *am* level seventy-five!"

Again, they glanced at each other.

"I'm..." Reed typed briskly, quickly checked his ranking.

"Level seventy-*four*..." DeerSlayr said, unable to hide a grin.

I'm level seventy-four. Because WyldChyld and I haven't done that quest yet...and the meeting of the Great Council hasn't happened.

The hackers, the so-called *Guardians*, had caused a crash catastrophic enough that Evanrud had only been able to fix Mythykal by restoring the entire game back to an earlier time.

DeerSlayr and WyldChyld were still in the game, the worst of their transgressions not only forgiven – as far as Mythykal was concerned *they'd never even happened.*

Perfect. He and WyldChyld could change things this time around, make their moves less obvious and go on the way they were.

"Let's take a walk…"

"Blue Hollow is a goodly distance, Master."

"We'll do that later. I feel a strong thirst coming on."

"Ah, the One-Eyed Eagle it is."

"To Bryn Shyre then."

Contact was simple now for DeerSlayr and WyldChyld. If either showed up at the Eagle and the other wasn't there, a coin tossed to the bilingual barkeep was all they needed, a message was instantly sent.

And there she was in a dark corner of the tavern, seducing a Malwor Archer. Obviously drunk, barely conscious, he held his stein with both hands, elbows balanced precariously on the short table before him, his eyes focused squarely on the deep cleavage WyldChyld so generously presented him.

The Archer would follow her to an upstairs room, or to some deep place in the forest...where she would seduce, then summarily kill and rob him.

DeerSlayr hated her methods – especially the seduction part.

She acknowledged DeerSlayr with a simple raise of an eyebrow, keeping her attention, her charms, focused on her prey.

DeerSlayr rolled his eyes; he ordered mead for himself. Surreptitiously watching WyldChyld as she lured the Archer upstairs. Not so much luring as carrying him up the narrow staircase. The man was draped over her shoulder, feet dragging, head lolling. Easy prey.

Despite the little tug inside he recognized as jealousy, DeerSlayr smiled. It wasn't like the bastard would get anything more than the chance to re-spawn later and recollect his body and whatever belongings WyldChyld hadn't valued.

Served him right.

The moment his drink assaulted his tongue DeerSlayr sprayed mead over the counter. He slammed down the stein.

"Barkeep – what in the name of Odin's gray beard is this?"

The troll raised himself up – short yes, but a substantial presence, wide as he was ugly.

"It is what I must serve these days."

"It's not *mead.*"

The troll nodded, somewhat deflated.

"It's NA mead."

"NA?"

"*Non-alcoholic.* Where have you been?"

"What?"

"One of the new rules."

"What new rules?"

The troll shook his gigantic head.

"It's changing. It's all changing."

"What do you mean *it's* changing?"

"The world, brother. The game. Tavern owners like myself were hit first – but you'll all feel it soon. Between you and me, brother, it stinks. There's a Great Council meeting tomorrow intending to explain it all."

DeerSlayr shook his head.

"I believe I'll avoid that meeting."

"Well, you'll see the changes one way or another, it's inevitable now." He leaned in close, dropped his voice to a whisper.

"You're little Malwor friend will need to change her ways too."

"Hah, she'll always be a thief."

The troll shook his head again.

"The thievery is fine, for now, she can always re-spawn a hand…it's her *wardrobe*. She'll be needing to keep those generous charms of hers under wraps."

"What?"

"No hint of sex and a flesh-price for thievery. Pains me brother, but that be the way of things since the Guardian's got their way."

"Got their way? *Those hackers?* They should have been arrested."

"Should have, would have, and could have. But once the *given-in* is done it makes no difference does it, brother? Now they be here, and we be here to accommodate them."

DeerSlayr had a sudden urge to break something, start a fight, to tear the tavern to shreds. If he'd been allowed to bring it inside he would have buried his axe in the barkeep's broad skull which, he knew, was exactly why weapons weren't allowed. But another thought quickly refocused his anger.

"There's *no alcohol* served here?"

"None served *anywhere* in Mythykal."

His bar stool crashed to the floor as DeerSlayr leapt up the staircase, two steps at a time.

"Barkeep - what room does WyldChyld use? Quickly!"

"You're not allowed up there without business!" The big troll protested.

The bouncer, a big brute of an Orc, thumped toward him. DeerSlayr buried his head in the Orc's gut, head-butted its ugly face on the rebound. The Orc rolled to a neck snapping landing below.

Eight doors in the hallway. He splintered three before he found WyldChyld.

She was naked, tied to the bed, her face bloodied, her lips torn. The Archer waved a broken bottle in DeerSlayr's face. Very sober, very narrow and cruel eyes, sparkled behind the jagged glass.

"Watch me kill this Glokkun faggot," the Archer said to his online friends.

"Join you're mother in hell, Malwor scum." DeerSlayr said.

Clearly the man hadn't expected a response in his own language – until this moment, all Malwor-speak had been scrambled to him. He hesitated.

DeerSlayr's powerful hand snared the Archer's wrist, wrenching it downwards with bone-crushing force. The wrist snapped like a dry twig.

The scream was piercing, the scream of a child.

DeerSlayr punched the man hard in the stomach and the screaming broke off. The Archer's eyes wide as the full moon now, his broken bottle was in DeerSlayr's hand now. DeerSlayr punched again; warmth sprayed over his hand.

The Archer's legs gave way and DeerSlayr released him to crash against the bed's wooden frame, the force tearing the gap in his stomach wide open. In horror he watched his intestines snake to the floor.

WyldChyld's expression mirrored the Archer's.

DeerSlayr tore off the man's helmet, wrapped the long golden locks in his fist. He held the bottle to the Archer's terrified face.

I'm not a warrior anymore. I'm a killer.

He punched the glass through.

DeerSlayr carried WyldChyld down the staircase in his blood-smeared arms. Guards waited for them in the tavern, swords drawn.

No chance of disguising their alliance now. There would be no reset this time.

"No murder in my tavern!" The troll roared.

"What about *rape?*"

"She came for skullduggery, her favor was returned in kind."

"And so I returned the favor."

"That you did."

The guards circled them.

"I obeyed the law, I carried no weapons here. I still carry none."

"Patrons, leave my tavern!" the troll's voice roared like an avalanche of boulders.

Still, in the tavern; Dwarves, Elves, Archers, all waiting, all looking forward to the show.

"LEAVE NOW!" The stairway shook beneath the thunder of his voice, steins crashed to the floor. The yeasty sourness of spilt NA mead, the stink of the Troll's breath carried through the tavern, a poisoned wind. Patrons tripped over each other now to flee. DeerSlayr steadied WyldChyld and together, they headed for the door.

"Not you two. Guards, sheath your swords." The Troll's voice was calm and strangely human now.

The guards obeyed, standing at attention, their chests drawing breath, heads moving from side-to-side, eyes watchful, hands clenching; the movements of programmed life.

"These guards and more are yours when you need them," the Troll said.

"What?" DeerSlayr was genuinely stunned.

"What the…!" WyldChyld stifled her last word. Shocked not by the offer, but by her new clothing – she was covered head to ankle now in thick robes. "What is *this crap?"*

The Troll shook his head.

"There's nothing I can do about that." He gave a very human sigh, "wish there was, believe me. Mead anyone?"

"Not that swill."

"No…the *real* stuff."

Two steins appeared on the counter.

DeerSlayr squinted at the Troll, he understood at last.

"You're Evanrud – the programmer."

The Troll nodded morphing into another avatar entirely; now it was the Malwor King who served them from behind the bar.

"Why can't you just…" WyldChyld shrugged, "you know, write a new program? Make the world anything you want?"

"The world's not mine to change anymore. We had to get bigger to make the game bigger. We thought we could keep the integrity too. Looked like PureArtz wanted that too, at first. I mean, that's what they bought. Big mistake. They don't care about Mythykal like we do. We had something great here and just gave it away."

He raised his stein. WyldChyld and DeerSlayr slowly did the same.

"We sold out. There's not much I can do now. I have a contract. But players like you guys…*that's* another matter."

"If you can't fix Mythykal and you wrote it - what are we supposed to do?"

"The same thing you've done all along – *resist*. Break the rules; you two already figured out how powerful Malwor and Glokkun can be when they team up. Start with that."

"I don't get it." The Reed part of DeerSlayr was genuinely confused. "The Guardians are part of PureArtz? They hacked themselves?"

"No; nothing to do with PureArtz. They're just really organized hackers – real pros. We're not the only game they're attacking. All the big publishers are running scared. PureArtz tried to appease them – they gave them their own Mythykal territory and thought they'd be happy. Idiots. But the Guardians hate the genre, they want everyone to follow their stupid rules. The publishers are too spineless to fight them. PureArtz was first, but they've all caved."

"So it's some right-wing Christian group?" WyldChyld was seething now.

"Hah! I wish it was. Do you know a lot of Christian women dressed like you are now?"

With that, King Evanrud went silent; except for his fingers which drummed with lightning speed, his avatar ran through the usual bank of programmed "at ease" motions. Finally the light returned to his eyes.

"You need to go now."

DeerSlayr nodded.

"So what are you going to do?"

"The only thing I *can* do at this point," he grinned, wryly, "introduce chaos into the system."

"Chaos like us?"

"You've got it. Good luck. I'll help you where I can."

With that, King Evanrud became the Troll bar-keep once more. He bellowed,

"Out! Out brigands! Out of my tavern!"

They blasted through the doorway, scattering clients who had waited near the entrance.

Once in the street, they parted ways without so much as a nod.

"Boss?" Raspberry said.

"We're headed for the Pyrian Spring. Where's Syndee?"

The big red Orc shook his head as DeerSlayr mounted his winged steed. Raspberry nodded to a slender young boy sitting cross-legged on a roof across the street. The boy smiled coyly at DeerSlayr.

"God no!"

"One minute she was there, and then…*this* was there."

DeerSlayr grimaced.

"This is *not* going to work."

-=-=-=-=-=-=-=-=-

DeerSlayr had assembled all his minions on a high ridge overlooking the spring – minus the transformed Syndee whom he'd already decommissioned and archived.

WyldChyld, her own band assembled on the other bank, shook her head.

The world they knew here was ending – in many ways had ended already. A series of skirmishes, but no decisive battle, no real war. In the end, the magical world of Mythykal had been, as Evanrud said, "given away." And there was precious little anyone could do about it now.

Another spring, another world entirely had pushed its way into this one; one choked with snow and ice and sadness. The stream emanating from what had been a gush of sparkling crystal water, was an ice-covered swamp that pulsed with a greenish glow.

"Ever drink from this spring?" He asked, at last.

"A little learning is a dangerous thing…" WyldChyld said.

He had to laugh at that.

WyldChyld had managed to extricate her face from the concealing veil; all damage removed now, no blood, not even a bruise stained her porcelain white face. Aw, the *miracle of spawning*. You recovered from mistakes quickly here. At least that part of this world hadn't changed. That part was still different from the *real* world.

But that outfit…except for the fine-features of WyldChyld's face, her long-lashed eyes, you wouldn't even know a girl was in there. No more fleshy curves, no more cleavage.

At least she still *was* a girl.

"Thank you," she said, "for what you did back there."

"I should have figured it out quicker."

"*Tell me about it* - I knew they were changing the rules. I should have known he was faking it."

"It doesn't bother you – what I did to him?"

"No. He deserved it. It bothers *you* though. I can tell."

"No. Not that much."

"*Hah*. You're sort of naive."

"Thanks."

"No, it's kind of sweet. But it's good to know you can be cruel."

"No it isn't."

"Yeah, it kind of is. You don't know me, I mean, we're not even friends on the outside."

"Yeah, well we're completely different out there."

"What was your first thought when you saw me at school."

He smiled sheepishly.

"I thought…I don't know, I thought you were cute, I thought you were sort of a rebel, I guess."

"You thought you could fuck me. *You thought I'd be easy.*"

DeerSlayr felt like he'd been slugged square in the stomach.

She nodded, "My mom's boyfriend thought that when I was eleven."

"Jesus."

"When you know *you* can be cruel – it makes it a whole lot easier to see that in other people."

He had no idea what to say. Wasn't even sure he should say anything.

The sun was falling fast; blue shadows from the pines stretched their long, gnarled fingers across the bed of the sickly stream.

"We can't change it, you know," she said. "It's over."

He nodded, "I've been thinking the same thing."

"So what do we do? Just walk away?"

"We could. Or we could fight – make things a little painful for those *ass wipes.*"

"We can't even *see* those ass wipes."

"Boss!" Raspberry thrust his sword toward the woods. Their minions galloped down the hill to protect them.

Now DeerSlayr saw the enemy too: little more than pixels shifting within the shadows. Instantly, those shadows boiled with life. DeerSlayr readied his axe.

"Fight, or log off, WyldChyld. *They're here.*"

-=-=-=-=-=-=-=-=-=-

It could hardly have been called a fair fight.

Raspberry's strength and skill with his massive Claymore sword – a weapon with which he'd often cleave enemies with one blow – was all but useless against an unseen army. DeerSlayr fought on, spells wasted on empty space, his axe finding mostly tree trunks and stone, even while his own life drained from the stabs and hacks of invisible daggers, he saw Raspberry torn like a Piñata before his eyes, saw the great Orc's insides scattered along the bank, red blood streaked the greenish water, flowing downstream.

WyldChyld strikes also came up mostly empty, she too began to falter and fail. Her raptors with their bird-like reflexes fared better, they would go on fighting even after DeerSlayr and WyldChyld were dead.

Their illegal alliance had given them power over the guards, had even helped them vanquish several of these invisible cowards – but now there were just too many.

We could use a little help here…

Life-force exhausted; DeerSlayr dropped to his knees, he managed to lift his axe one more time, only to see his arm pinwheel across the stream, hacked away at the elbow.

WyldChyld somersaulted high into the air, landing beside him only to reach a similar fate.

Her raptors protected her body as long as they could.

Come on, E…where's that help you promised?

.-=.-=.-=.-=.-=.-=.-=.-=.-

DeerSlayr re-spawned as quickly as he could.

Collecting his body and those of his minions was a sad and bloody task. His biggest fear wasn't that the cowardly Guardians might reappear and attack him, but that WyldChyld had decided enough was enough and gone on to other things.

It isn't fair. It shouldn't be like this.

But on another level things were much worse than that. No matter how deeply he had immersed himself in this world, no matter how real it had become, *it was a game after all.*

But Mythykal was the only world he had now.

He hated Evan and his brother for selling out, for giving it away. How could they possibly think a huge conglomerate like PureArtz would care about Mythykal the same way they had?

They'd been naïve – just like WyldChyld said *he* was.

It's good to know you can be cruel –

They'd trusted too much – the way she trusted her mom's boyfriend – before he'd raped her. WyldChyld had learned. Now she defended herself with the same weapon, had built a cruelty all her own.

WyldChyld liked him, he was pretty sure of that. But after what she'd been through - how could you really be close to anyone? Especially guys? Now she lived to break hearts.

So much to think about. He'd been dragged into adulthood, initiated into a secret society he wasn't ready to join, one he never *wanted* to join.

Yeah, he could be cruel all right. He'd never forgive himself for what he'd done. If that was adulthood, he didn't want any part of it.

WyldChyld blipped back into existence on the other side of the stream. And just like that – his heart leapt, and the entire world lifted into the sky with it.

She smiled when she saw him trudging through the cold current to her.

"I heard your *prayer* to Evanrud," she laughed.

"It wasn't a prayer."

"Hell it wasn't."

He shook his head.

"Well, whatever it was – I think he might have answered it, look."

A new object near the water's edge: a large, gold goblet.

"If you read Pope, I guess you'll want to toss quite a few of those down," she said.

"You know the Pierian Spring is mentioned all the way back in the *Satyricon*. Of course they spell it wrong in Mythykal.

'Like everything else. *You actually read!* I'm impressed!"

"My Dad said that when I quoted Edgar Allen Poe once."

"Poe's awesome. Maybe we do have something besides a couple songs and this stupid game."

That thought hung out there for a hopeful moment; but the self-conscious Reed cut it off before DeerSlayr could make it grow.

"So what do we do now?" he said. "My best stones are gone, my favorite axe. Our minions are weak, and we've both dropped three levels."

"Yeah, they've changed the rules again. We lose more powers when we die now."

"They'll just wear us out, keep killing us until we can't come back at all."

"Cowardly bastards are what they are."

"So…the question still is – what do we do? We can barely even see them."

"I'm seriously thinking of canning it. Mythykal isn't the only MMPG out there. We can find a game that hasn't been hacked yet. Another world."

DeerSlayr gave that some thought. Finally, he shook his head, no.

"PureArtz gave in because they're afraid of these nut bags. The other publishers won't be far behind. We're better off fighting them in a game we know."

"But they keep changing it."

"*E* said it's *our* game now. Let's change it back."

WyldChyld took a deep breath. She raised her robed arms and shook her head.

"All right. This goes first."

She tore the robes from her body and threw them into the stream. No armor remained; barely a ribbon of cloth covered her. Her flesh glistened. DeerSlayr felt the thud of his chin against his breastplate.

"*Hold that thought*, caveman," she grinned. "Better summon what's left of our minions."

The deep shadows of the forest were already alive with shifting pixels. Tiny squares of gray, shuffling, reshuffling.

"Crap, here we go again."

With a mouse click their minions joined them, ready for the fight.

"Okay," DeerSlayr said, "let's plan this time. Put the Raptors out front – they're faster and their eyes are better. Maybe they'll slow the Guardian's down for the Orcs. The Guardians stand out better in the shadows, so let's put our backs to the stream and watch the forest. If they get around us they'll splash through the water and we'll see that too."

Their Raptors took the front, the Orcs and other minions closed ranks behind them.

"All right." WyldChyld said. "It's a good day to die. Looks like they brought a whole army this time."

Pixels raced through the shadows like angry ants.

"Come on E – *we could use a break here.*"

By the time DeerSlayr had pulled a new axe from his armory, a row of guards had appeared just behind the minions with swords drawn.

"*Dude!* It won't be so easy this time!"

The movement in the shadows slowed to a crawl. DeerSlayr was pretty sure what that meant. The Guardian hackers didn't like the odds now.

WyldChyld turned to him, her sword pulsing with the glow of a powerful spell. She smiled and DeerSlayr nodded.

In a heartbeat, the pixilation ran everywhere outside their small circle of protection. The Guardian programmers had *indeed* summoned help – an army. So many of them that WyldChyld didn't even aim her freezing spell. Green lighting arced from her blade, blasting in all directions around them.

WyldChyld couldn't hide her revulsion at its effect.

A dozen Guardian warriors had frozen in place. Cast in pale green ice, they weren't human figures at all but snakes with dozens of short limbs and fanged with long, curved daggers. Some coiled around branches, others lay frozen in mid-slither on their bellies. Cracks raced over them like spider webs. Their collapse sent a fetid green cloud into the heavens.

The Guardians didn't wait for another spell.

"Here they come!"

Slithering through the stinking cloud, their forms painted by the settling green dust, they were easy prey for the Raptors, who snapped up dozens before the guards charged, hacking the first wave to pieces. DeerSlayr walloped the few who made it past; wriggling tubes of meat splattered the rocks at his feet.

Pixels spun from the snow, from rocks and trees. The Guardians swarmed from the forest. Another freezing curse. Another cloud of green dust.

More Guardians splashed into the stream.

"Keep the spells coming!"

He chose another axe, held one in each hand and swung them slowly, testing their balance as the first snake slinked toward him, its form clearly visible in the rippling water.

He lay into it with both axes, snake head and limbs spinning away downstream as DeerSlayr waded in, slicing cleanly through the gut of another, burying his axe in the head of the next, so much Guardian blood flying now that a pink mist hung in the air, making it even easier to see them.

"Come and get me assholes. I can do this for days!"

But it wasn't so easy behind him.

"I'm running out of spells!" WyldChyld hollered, "Raptors are dead!"

"Hold as long as you can!"

"They fixed the textures – I can't see them anymore!"

"Everyone! Into the water – make them slither through it to get us!"

A bright flash in the corner of his eye. On the other side of the stream – the golden goblet suddenly pulsed with new energy. *He'd forgotten all about it.*

The water between DeerSlayr and the goblet was filled with snakes; they'd have him before he waded halfway across.

Am I a complete idiot?

The goblet wasn't the point E was making; *DeerSlayr was waist deep in the goddamn Pyrian Spring.*

He chopped wildly at the surface, splashing, holding the Guardians at bay as he dipped his mouth into the stream, gulped in as much as he could.

He could see them!

A few snakes on the far bank, in the water and forest beyond. They looked flat now, 2D, but they were *plainly* visible. And there weren't nearly so many as he'd imagined.

Ray-tracing. It was Evanrud that he heard. *I turned theirs off.*

"What?"

Never mind.

"Drink the water!" DeerSlayr shouted. *"Everyone drink the spring water!"*

The surviving guards and minions were all in the stream now. He was glad to see Raspberry still with them. Those in front swung their weapons wildly, ineffectively at nothing - letting the others drink. Those who drank quickly replaced the front line – and seeing the enemy now, quickly dispatched them. The Guardians fled. For the first time, he heard them scream in rage and terror. Raspberry and two of the guards ran down the remaining snakes, chopping them tail to head.

"We did it!"

Snake parts littered the landscape, the stream ran with Guardian blood.

All of the living had suffered wounds, some, their last bits of life-force waning, slowly began to dissolve. But they had won this round.

"What now?" WyldChyld a wide grin; her nearly bare chest heaving from the exertion, glistening with sweat and blood.

"So you're still in the game?"

"Hell yeah! *It's fun again.* What's the plan?"

"Kill the badly wounded so they'll re-spawn quickly, Raspberry and the others need time to grow their health. Then we spread the word - ride to Bryn Shyre – get the Malwor and Glokkun to pull together the way we have. We'll pick up as many fighters as we can along the way. Text your friends – give them the code so we can all talk."

"So what's in the water?"

"A program patch. I got a message from Evanrud – something about ray-tracing."

WyldChyld nodded.

"Got it. It's a way of rendering transparency and reflections – the water must be a patch that turns ray-tracing off for whoever drinks it – so anything transparent like glass or those snakes, turns opaque."

"So that's why they look like cartoons now?"

"Yup."

DeerSlayr called up a territory map and quickly traced the stream.

"The Pyrian Spring doesn't run all the way to Bryn Shyre; so let's carry it with us."

"Everybody, empty your flasks," WyldChyld ordered, "fill them with water from the stream."

"I'm pretty sure our packs and saddle bags are watertight too. We can dump out most of our rune stones, we don't need magic to fight the Guardians if we can see them."

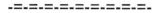

They were set upon by Guardian patrols twice along the way. The attacks were repelled without a single loss to their band, the ranks of which had swelled with the addition of their friends and minions, with every traveler, Glokkun or Malwor they passed along the way. By the time they reached Bryn Shyre *they had an army of their own.*

"This won't be as easy as it seems," DeerSlayr said as they rode through the gates, joined by the city guards, holding their weapons high.

WyldChyld nodded, "They're bound to switch tactics."

Above them, shutters flew wide, windows filled with the wide-eyed faces of the citizens of Bryn Shyre shocked to hear the clatter of hooves on cobblestone, the marching footsteps of a thousand warriors.

An army of Glokkun and Malwor, Trolls and Warlocks, and every other sort of creature imaginable. Storekeepers left their shops to watch and their patrons followed them into the streets.

"People of Bryn Shyre!" DeerSlayr shouted. "Take back your world! The Guardians can be seen and they can be killed! Drink the waters of the Pyrian Spring and you'll see them."

WyldChyld threw a flask to a stunned Archer at the side of the road. The man caught it and pressed the flask quickly to his lips.

Others took her lead, flasks began flying into the growing crowds.

"Drink! Drink and defeat them!"

"Boss!" Raspberry called, he pointed at a robed woman slipping into a throng gathered on the corner just ahead of them. *"Guardians!"*

The young woman's image blurred, stabilized. A hastily executed avatar switch, a motion so quick DeerSlayr would never have seen the form of a snake inside her if not for Raspberry's warning.

"Get back! Get away from her!"

But it was already too late.

An explosion of blood and limbs so bright and loud it seemed to swallow everything around it.

Broken bodies, limbs, dropped, smoking, into the street. Flames raced up the storefronts. Screams and panic, those still capable of running trampling the wounded who sat stunned, blind, and bloodied.

All around them, more villagers blurred, quickly changing with a flash of the telltale snakes.

One more terrible explosion and Mythykal was gone.

-=.=.=.=.=.=.=.=.=.

Reed's display flashed blue and went dark.

"Goddamn it!"

He knew the drill: bring it up in Safe Mode, find a restore point and start again. He wondered how far back Evan would have to bring them this time to get things to work.

What do you really care? It's just a stupid game.

He watched Microsoft's Window's program slowly figure itself out, gingerly righting itself like a fallen racehorse testing its injured legs.

Just a stupid game.

Dog's corner of the room was painfully empty. When her picture appeared in a slideshow onscreen, the tears came. He wiped his face with his sleeve and shook his head.

Sometimes it's good to know you can be cruel...

So what did he do now?

He had yet to report Malana's boyfriend to the police. The guy wasn't hunting deer with an AK-47. He was a drug dealer at the very least, and that tattoo was some sort of gang thing; he might as well have painted "killer" on his forehead.

But if Reed said anything to the police they'd deport Malana for sure.

Hell, he'd be doing her a favor. She was living in a damn cave in the middle of winter. She couldn't possibly want to be in America *that* much.

The image of her kissing that guy after he'd slapped her, a hot dagger in Reed's chest. But not nearly as sharp nor deep as the pain of what he'd done himself. The two acts would be with him forever, forever connected.

WyldChyld was right. Reed had seen cruelty in himself; now he saw it plain and simple in Malana; you couldn't let someone treat you that way if you didn't think you deserved it. As pretty as she was, as sweet as she seemed, it was in her too.

Once WyldChyld had been too innocent to recognize it. Now in Mythykal she was a seductress, a murderer and a thief – she practiced cruelty to keep her sense of it sharp.

I'm learning too much and learning it way too fast.

But that's just how it is. You have to grow up sometime.

He logged in, fingers drumming as he waited for the Mythykal servers to answer his ping. Normally, there would have been thirty or more servers waiting to suck him into the Mythykal melee. Only five showed in the window now. Then four. Three. Reed watched, helpless, as one by one each server blipped out and went dark.

The Guardians couldn't play and win; now they were taking the ball and going home. Just like that it was over.

He had nothing now. Absolutely nothing.

Chapter 14

Kristi flew through a world of spun glass trees and waterfalls. It wasn't Cross-Country, it wasn't even slalom, it was uncontrolled sliding at best, but she had no fear and no intention of slowing down.

A hill of ice rose up before her. Yesterday this hill had been a boulder, now it was a highway to the heavens if she took it right.

And take it she did.

Kristi tucked and flew, snapping row upon row of icicles off an overhang of cedar branches. Below her, the entire valley opened wide.

She took flight, opened her arms to embrace it.

No, not arms...wings.

She soared over the world of ice. It was all there beneath her: her house, the houses and cabins of their mountain neighbors dotting the mountainside, framed in tiny squares of snow, the little toy-like town of Cedar with its log buildings, streetlights encased in ice like everything else, all glistening, all frozen solid. No motion anywhere but hers.

She began a slow, easy descent.

Halfway between her home and Cedar, a small half dome of ice leaned into the mountain. It was deep in the forest, a grotto formed by young trees bent and broken by their burden of snow. A man knelt near its entrance. She recognized Mark's jacket and her heart flew as high as the mountain.

She touched down lightly, perfectly, on the slope behind him.

Whatever held Mark's attention so firmly was completely hidden by his broad shoulders and back. She'd ski up behind him, tap his shoulder as he worked.

But he wasn't working.

He wasn't moving.

And then she was flying again. Up, up, and away from this place.

Mark shrank to the size of an ant, the half dome of ice, the town of Cedar, the forest - all things drew far away from her now, their shapes and color bleeding out to a dull formless gray.

Only sadness remained.

-=.=.=.=.=.=.=.=.=.=-

The lights are on.

Wide awake now; the sadness from her dream not fading so much as settling into her like the trace of foam from a receding wave.

Outside, an absolutely clear, blue night. The cratered face of a frighteningly large moon hovered beyond the iced-over pines.

She'd never seen *anything* like the scene before her now.

Their back yard was gone. Snow had brought the forest floor halfway up the side of the house, and inches more of ice had turned that floor into a slick skating rink glowing blue with moonlight trapped within. Ice completely sealed the outside walls of their house, and every exposed branch, twig, or cable looked to have been preserved in a cast of thick glass.

Her breath caught in her throat.

A woman stood just at the edge of the forest, the moon casting a rim of blue light around her robed form. And not just ANY woman.

'Mom!"

Yes. But was her mother actually standing there, watching her? No.

I am seeing these things. But they don't exist.

But there is a reason I see them.

She held up her hand, closed and opened her fingers; the wave of a child. Nothing but a stare in return.

It's me, it's Kristi, your daughter.

No change, no change at all. Just a stare.

Kristi closed her eyes. *She doesn't know me anymore.* When she opened her eyes again, her mother was gone.

-=-=-=-=-=-=-=-=-

Kristi prepared the breakfast to end all breakfasts. A meat-lover's paradise of ham, bacon, and sausage with hash browns and mound of cheddar nesting two duck eggs. A deep skillet of protein and fat.

She was eating a lot these days; burning it off faster than she could possibly take it in. Hollows had formed beneath her cheekbones. No longer able to stay put on her wrist, her watch was zipped into her jacket. Her rings, oversized now, were tucked away in her jewelry box. She didn't need the scale to tell her that not only her weight, but her body mass index was in free fall.

The nausea, the pain in her belly were becoming constant companions. But she could deal with all that.

She was stronger than ever; her slalom times better than ever.

She was sure she'd downed several gallons of good clean distilled water since her return yesterday. If her bottle ran dry on today's run, she'd go thirsty. She wasn't going anywhere near that gross creek water again.

The back windows offered a bleak view indeed. If there had indeed been a break in the storm last night, if she really *had* seen a full moon and a clear sky, she'd surely woken smack center in the quiet eye of the storm.

Outside the rain had picked up again, freezing where it hit, the frozen landscape growing thicker with each drop.

What made her think she could survive a run in that, let alone ski through it? *What insanity made her want to?*

Right after you got home yesterday, you went right back out in it. You went right out there and skied over the ice and freezing rain and you weren't killed.

She'd done it because she knew she *could.* Lately, there were times it seemed *anything* was possible.

And then again, just maybe it was possible she was going insane.

Yes, that was very possible.

She was nearly convinced when she found her holster empty. She was careful, *meticulous* with her competition weapons. You had to be.

She mentally retraced her every movement from the moment she returned home yesterday. *She* hadn't misplaced anything.

Kristi raced upstairs to Reed's room. *Her pellet gun wasn't a toy – it was dangerous.* If Reed was playing with her pistol and didn't kill himself with it – she'd kill him herself.

Reed was gone.

Dog's crate – her entire bedding area, her basket of toys, all of it gone.

A feeling so sad inside the house yesterday.

And the same way she'd mentally retraced her own steps, Kristi ran through the emotions, the sensations that had passed through this house. She accepted this ability of hers now without hesitation, no longer questioned its very possibility. She simply flipped through the Rolodex of anger, of sadness, of horror, of every feeling that had burst through here: Reed's heartbreak and anger, their father's sense of horror and despair. It all added up to one terrible answer.

"Oh, my God…"

-=-=-=-=-=-=-=-=-

He had to talk to Malana.

Reed huddled, shivering in the very same place where yesterday he'd killed his own dog to save himself. Only now the place was dark and choked with ice. Raindrops freezing onto his visor and gloves.

He was half-crazy with anger and exhaustion. He'd rolled the Ski Doo on the way and nearly crushed his leg beneath it.

Once the Mythykal servers had blipped out, taking his other world with them, the real world come crashing back on him. All night long he replayed what had happened in this place, tried to change it. But he *couldn't* change it, not even in his head.

Maybe Malana really *was* cruel, even evil. He was, and maybe the entire world was.

That gang-banger piece of shit had turned him into a frightened baby yesterday. He would eventually call the police or ICE, or *someone*. Have that gang banging piece of shit's ass put away or deported. He would make that call soon.

But he had to see Malana first. Talk to her.

He cradled one of Kristi's pellet guns beneath his parka. It was no AK-47, it wasn't even her .22 rifle, it was basically a fancy air-pistol, and you'd probably have to stick it in someone's eye to kill them. But it *looked* deadly. It was better than nothing. And he wouldn't have to use it anyway.

That asshole had come and gone by this time yesterday, and he most likely didn't bring supplies every day.

Reed waited five more minutes, his eyes on the far edge of the white plain where the man had first appeared. No one emerged from the forest.

Reed let another minute pass, eyes on the horizon. He unwrapped himself from his cold perch as painfully and slowly as a stomped ant. The rollover had been harder on him than he'd thought. Adrenalin had brought him the rest of the way. He limped slowly down to the deadfall, slipped, cracking his already sore knee and skidding halfway down the hill on his butt.

He came to a sliding stop just before her hidden doorway, managed to get on his feet and stood there pelted by the frozen rain, suddenly petrified as his first clear thought of the day came to him.

What if the guy slept with her last night?

He closed his eyes, reached into his parka and touched the pistol's grip. Then he pulled off his glove and rapped loudly on the overhanging log. The gun crashed to the ice at his feet. He dove on it – scooping it up just as he heard something very familiar coming from deep within the cave.

Paco. Not a warning sound, a welcoming one. Paco knew who'd come calling.

Ice cracked and snow fell, the hinged door moved away. Sour smells, sweat, dog crap and urine, so strong it made him step back.

Malana's face appeared from the darkness behind the door. Eyes huge. He covered her mouth with his hand before she could scream. He pushed her back inside.

"*No...no...it's okay. Malana, it's okay. Don't scream – please don't!*"

When she saw the gun, she tried to scream.

He shoved her away and pulled the door closed behind him. The smell of too much life in too little space was overwhelming now. It was so cramped in here. A small propane stove. Battery powered lights, and rough blankets. A few books. In the dark recesses he saw Paco lunging against a chain, his barks were concussive, pounding Reed's ears like a pistol fired at close range.

He set the gun on her bedding and held up his hands. For a second he thought she might grab it and use it on him. But she stayed put, breathing hard, hyperventilating, near fainting. Tears in her eyes.

"I'm sorry. I'm sorry. I just...I just wanted to see you."

She shook her head.

"No!"

"I'm sorry. I'll go. I'll go."

She said something in Spanish. Maybe a prayer. And then she cried.

"They will kill you." She touched her breast. "Kill me too…"

"Come home with me. Mi casa. Live with us."

She shook her head.

"Go!"

"You can't live here like this!"

"Go. They will kill my brothers!"

"Your *brothers?*"

God, it made sense. *He was a complete fool.* The anger, the kiss. Her brother was only trying to keep her hidden and safe.

"Who? *Who will kill them?*"

She didn't answer. It didn't matter.

He squeezed past her to the back, and unchained Paco, the pup leapt into his arms licking and sniffing. Reed knew exactly what the dog wanted.

Where's Dog? Where's my other friend?

"Hi boy, just me."

"No! Paco!"

"Get your stuff, Malana. *We're going."*

He dragged her crying up the frozen hill. Finally, used to having little choice, she gave in. Reed was too cold, exhausted and naïve to understand any of that. He only knew he was doing the *right* thing for once. No one should live like she was.

Paco was having a hard time with the ice. As tough as the little guy was, he wasn't built for this weather. His paws were freezing, slipping over the ice. Reed scooped him up and shifted the stocky pup to his shoulder, barely able to climb the icy bank himself, he clawed his way forward, the rain coming down harder now, trying its best to turn them all to ice sculpture.

This was no way to run away. We're way too slow.

Paco growled before Reed had even processed those thoughts. Reed's heart pounded, a hot ball of steam rising in his throat. That hadn't even reached the top of the hill, that awful place and he knew exactly what that growl meant.

Malana's brothers were coming.

Reed took wider strides, pushed harder; he slipped to his knees and slid back. He struggled to regain his footing, feeling the warmth of his blood streaming down his shin this time.

"God!"

He stomped his boots through the ice. Wind whipped across the meadow, screamed through the pines, burning his cheeks and nose. It was even slower going, and painful where his heel struck the ice, but two more strides and they'd top this hill. Beyond that, some five feet of level footing before they came to an even steeper one.

Then they'd be at the Ski Doo. Then they'd be home.

"White boy!"

Malana dropped to her knees, *"No, Esteban, no..."*

To Reed, it was as if all the ice outside had found its way into his veins. There was nowhere to go. Perfect target.

Reed turned slowly back to the deadfall.

Paco growled, she wrapped her arms tightly around him.

It wasn't the brother he'd seen yesterday. This man was skinny, younger – and pointing an AK-47 directly at Reed's chest. Heat spread from his crotch, running down the inside of both legs. The pee came freely, he couldn't stop it.

The man shouted something in Spanish to Malana. She spoke back to him over the rain.

He motioned her away from Reed with the barrel of his rifle.

She's in the line of fire now, Reed thought, dully. *The last thing I'll ever see is Malana moving out of the way.*

She didn't move.

"Malana!"

She shook her head defying him again. Her brother swore.

The barrel moved back in line with Reed's chest.

Karma had come to Reed. Malana had told Reed *they* would kill her brothers; whoever *they* were Malana's brother was afraid for his *own* life. Today Reed and Malana were Dog. Her brother would kill them both to survive.

DeerSlayr would have fought to the bitter end.

But now he was only Reed. Scared to death yesterday and peeing his pants today. Reed wouldn't die heroically like his alter ego always did. Reed would just die ugly and with pain. There would be no reset. He would not spawn somewhere safe.

His knees began to shake. A gust of wind so strong and cold it lifted him.

Malana's in the way. He can't see my hands. The air pistol was just under his parka; he could reach it.

"Malana…" Pleading this time. He bit his lip. This was his sister. *His own sister.*

Reed slipped his hand beneath the parka, over the grip. He found the safety and clicked it off. There would be no turning back once he drew the gun. Her brother would fire that AK-47 and they would both be killed. He and Malana had no chance at all. *The wind howled up from the field, slapped their faces with icy rain.*

The man took one hand off the rifle. He swatted the rain from his forehead.

Reed would die fighting; *he drew the pistol.*

It slipped through his fingers. Petrified, he watched it slide all the way to Malana's feet.

Reed dove for the pistol, fought it back into his hands.

Malana screamed.

Her brother didn't seem to hear, he swatted his forehead again. It wasn't the rain striking him – Reed saw something like black bugs land on his forehead, sticking there. Her brother didn't seem able to swat them off.

"Mal..." His tongue fumbled. The man took one faltering step forward and dropped, his rifle coughed bullets in explosions of ice and rock at his knees.

"ESTEBAN!" Malana bolted down the hillside, tumbled and fell flat, skidding only a few feet from her brother, screaming. She crawled to him on her knees.

"Reed! Run!"

Kristi leaned against a tree on the hill above him, the butt of her .22 pressed to her shoulder, the strap wrapped around her arm.

"Damn it! Run!"

And then Reed did run, but not in the direction Kristi intended.

He crashed down the frozen hill, wrenched Malana back. Paco was already tearing into the stricken man, whipping him side to side. Fresh blood spattered the snow and ice.

Malana wailed, she ripped away from him and Reed nearly tore her arm from the socket.

Kristi screamed, "What the fuck! Leave her!"

"They'll kill her!"

"Fuck!"

Kristi ran sideways down the hillside; grappled for the girl's free arm. They fought the girl back up the hill to the waiting snowmobiles.

"What did you make me do? God damn it, Reed! *What did you make me do?"*

Kristi's skin was nearly transparent and alabaster white beneath. Reed had the frightening feeling he was staring directly at his sister's skull.

"I *killed* someone, *murdered* him," she rasped. She'd barely turned her head to one side before she vomited onto the ice.

"His gun, I'll get his gun!"

"God damn it, Reed!"

"Hold her!"

"We've got to get out of here!"

Reed disappeared over the side of the hill.

Kristi revved the motor, glowering at the girl. The girl blubbered, took a good look at the fire in Kristi's eyes, at the raisin of blood clinging to the corner of Kristi's mouth, and went silent.

"You got that right, bitch" Kristi rasped.

Chapter 15

So high in the blue sky.

Rolling hills, a green and yellow patchwork of fields ripe for harvest running all the way to the white peak of Mount Hood. Air sweet with freshly cut hay, the aroma of prizewinning BBQ and Marion berry pie. The midway, the games of chance and skill, a world spun only for the young, was spread out below.

And they were at the very top of it all, with no one to answer to but each other. She moved toward him, their lips touched.

A warmth, a sweetness beyond imagining.

Her name was…

"Mum…mumm…"

Tongue and lips thick, dry; too clumsy to mouth the words.

"Mary Ann," she whispered for him.

But the day had already turned to night, late summer to late fall, and the cold had swept her warmth away.

-=-=-=-=-=-=-=-=-=-

Alive.

Oh, why did he have to wake from that dream? *Why did he have to wake at all? So he could watch himself freeze to death piece by piece? Did he really need to be awake for that?*

Billy Hicks surveyed his situation again; more clearheaded now, but no better off than yesterday.

He'd been conscious enough, able enough, to claw himself an upward angling hollow into the snow with his good hand, a rough channel to carry the water away. He'd been through enough mountainside rescues, successful and not, to know the drill. Once you protected yourself from the wind, it was the snow and ice that made you feel cold, but it was the water that robbed your body heat and killed you.

You had to stay dry.

High and dry.

Well *high* he was, *dry*...he mostly was. His right elbow was swollen, painful to the touch where he'd struck the storage compartment, but not broken; his left hand was another matter... The pain was gone from his left foot and that was actually a bad sign. The county's Jeep Ranger had taken his boot with it, and he hadn't been able to keep the foot dry. He'd be lucky to come away from this with a toe down there.

Who the hell was he kidding?

He used his forehead to crack open the new crust of ice that had formed over the door of his little nest. Billy stared straight down two hundred feet of rain-swept, iced-over rock, littered now with the twisted metal remains of that Jeep.

He wasn't getting out of this with any toes. He just plain wasn't getting out of this.

Billy Hicks was already dead, with a slow stubborn heart that just hadn't gotten the message yet. That's what aging reflexes and just plain stubbornness did for you.

At least the pounding headache was gone, and the drug hangover with it. He twisted slowly over, careful not to overstrain the broken trees that held his life precariously in their clinging roots.

Only a tantalizingly few feet of ice-covered rock and snow rose over him; just above that the icy ledge of the road sang like a damn Siren to a doomed sailor.

Just try…you can make it.

Sure, just use your one good arm and one good leg and whip yourself right up there to that nice solid-looking shelf of ice that'll likely

snap off the second you put your weight on it. You can collect all the
parts and rebuild your Jeep on the way down.

Better to sleep, maybe call up that dream again.

If only.

He closed his eyes, but sleep wouldn't come. Comfort
wouldn't come. Mary Ann wasn't going to sweep him happily
up to the angels. Life wasn't easy; why the hell would death
be?

"God damn it."

Mount Cedar, *his* mountain, had saved his life. Or at
least spared it for the moment. Maybe there was a reason.

Something terrible was happening on his mountain, a
malignancy had taken root and festered on his watch. Drugs
were part of it, but drugs only fed the *real* poison. He'd seen
the men; he'd heard them speak. With the collapse of the
Middle East, the rise of ISIS, the attacks already happening in
our country, what made him think his mountain was immune
to terrorism? As usual, he'd figured it out too late.

Old fool.

He'd like to live long enough for Lyle's ACLU friends
to come calling. He'd give them a footbath all right; give
them one they'd damn well never forget.

Now, he just had to figure out that "live long
enough" part.

Helen knew roughly where he was. Anyone on the
road would see the trail the Jeep had gouged down the
mountainside from any number of switchbacks along the
road. But the ice storm had been vicious; no civilian would be
on that road now and Search and Rescue weren't likely to pay
him a visit any time soon either.

The rain and hail had stopped and snow fell quietly
once again, but that was just nature ratcheting up the ante in
that sweet, gentle way she has of doing things, of sweeping
problems like pesky humans out of her life. With a layer of
powder over ice nothing but a helicopter or mountain goat
could reach his perch - and the mountain goat would have
better sense than to try. The nearly black canopy of clouds
overhead had "more ice on the way," written all over it.

No helicopter was coming. He *was* Search and Rescue
now.

What he wouldn't give for Mary Ann. Not the one
who'd ultimately let him down, the one who *never* had. Bad
conditions or not, he'd give anything to be sitting inside that
old plane.

"You're doin' a lot of thinking for a man with no time, Billy."

He gathered himself to a sitting position, worked the
stiff fingers of his left hand. As sore as the swollen knuckles
were, as dark as that blue line was across the back, the hand
worked as if the bones weren't broken – at least not broken

clean through. Green stick fractures. Damn, it hurt like the Dickens though. How much weight could it take? He worked his right arm, the elbow

"Quit your whining, Granma. You think you got it tough?"

Once more, he viewed the theater of rocky death below him.

"Yeah, well maybe you do."

He wouldn't look down again.

"F'n baby."

Not many choices around him either. Beyond the few feet of snow that sheltered him, the nearby rock was encased in ice. *No ice axe and a bum hand.* A yard from the end of his perch, three saplings clung to cliff. They too, were sheathed in ice. Chances were good he'd have only one chance to leap from this little Robin's nest. With no feeling in one foot, the push-off wouldn't be clean. The very act would likely send the unstable platform on its way to his Jeep, and him with it.

If you were on a sidewalk, hell, you'd take that like it was nothing. Not even a jump - just a good stretch, that's all.

But there was no sidewalk beneath him. There was nothing but frigid gusts of wind, a few clumps of packed snow under his feet, and a few iced-over saplings to grab with no guarantee their wispy roots could manage more burden than they already had.

If he managed to throw his arms around one of those fragile trunks, the grab wouldn't be clean either. The frozen branches thrust toward him like the spears of a Spartan phalanx.

"There you go thinkin' and bitchin' again."

He crawled as close to those saplings as he safely could, slowly, like a soldier testing for landmines. At the very edge of the shelf, he rose to his feet.

The mountain didn't give him a chance to think this time; he felt her give way beneath him.

Billy sprang, his arms flung wide.

Icy spears punched his chest with booming *"snaps!"* could have come from his ribs as easily as the branches themselves. He wrestled his arms around two of the trees, pulled his chest into the branches against the pain. A ribbon of heat ran across his temple. Blood flushed his right eye.

Don't let go. Pain means I'm alive. I'm alive.

But the saplings bent with his weight, began to give.

He groaned, forced his arms around another sapling. Rocks slid and crashed below, echoing for what seemed an eternity through the canyon.

Billy gulped labored breaths, his lungs and throat raw. Was his numb left foot touching anything? *His right one found nothing.*

He hung there, a feeling that something stronger than the trees held him. Maybe, it was the hand of God, maybe Cedar Mountain, or maybe they were one and the same.

His boot hit solid rock. Half blind, he clawed the ice, fought his way higher up the cliff to safety before the pain in his chest would force him to let to go, send him freefalling to his death.

Slipping. He was slipping back.

No. No don't think. Fight. Fight your way.

A vague sense of weightlessness caught him. Billy closed his good eye; certainly flying to his death.

It opened to nothing but snow and ice.

He forced his other eye open against the burning, and thick blood. Forced himself to really look.

"Dear God." He'd made it to the road.

Billy Hicks rolled onto his back. From this odd vantage point, he could actually see the cell tower he always searched for when he used that damn phone. The tower seemed to be kneeling in prayer. The storm had twisted it down to its knees.

And Billy laughed, even though each laugh lit a brand new fire in his chest and throat, he laughed like he hadn't since he was a kid.

-=-=-=-=-=-=-=-=-

Manuel Garcia-Garcia stood motionless above the frozen deadfall. The shock of what this nightmare truly meant, settling in.

They found Malana. They know.

They would tear her to pieces and then they would come for him. If those *Towelheads* didn't do the job, his brothers, his *clique*, would finish him, the second the money quit flowing they'd come for him too.

This fucked up everything.

Esteban lay in a pool of blood near the deadfall. From the entrance to Malana's hideaway, a messy trail led west up the hill.

Manny spat.

"Pendejo."

He picked his way up the hillside; eyes shifting, searching the dark sky, the shadows in the forest.

He had always taken care of his little brother, protected him; he'd killed more than once to save his honor. His brother was a fool. It had been Esteban's idea to bring their sister with them to America, one more mistake in a life of foolish acts.

There was no room for fools with the Arabs; more dangerous than wolves – wolves killed to live, these pendejos killed to die - with a murderous respect for timetables and ritual. *They did not like surprises.*

He tore his brother's face from the ice. His brother had been shot repeatedly, the back of his head was shattered but mostly intact, the holes in his face were small. If this had been the Arabs or DEA the few brains Esteban had would have covered the hillside.

He pried a .22 slug from the bloody ice, held it in his glove and spat his brother's name again. His brother had been killed with a toy.

Manny studied the trail. Malana had not gone easily, her tracks were broken, long in places as if she'd been dragged. She had fought her attacker. She'd been kidnapped.

Maybe Manny would go easier on her for that when he found her. *Maybe not.* She had left the hideaway before against his orders. She was careless in covering her tracks.

A package delivered to the Arabs before the big snow had triggered a chain of activity with them that ended last night with packing their small kits and incessant bathing. That meant their work here was nearly over. The one they called *The Chemist,* had taken out the cell tower. *Radio silence,* they said, until they left. Manny had been pissed as hell when they did that. The cell was the way he talked to his clique and to Malana. But that break in communications would work in his favor now.

He would keep Esteban's mistake silent until they left. *Whatever that took.*

He freed his brother's body from the ice, dragged it inside Malana's hideaway, and hid the entrance for the last time.

Manuel learned the rest of the story by following the tracks up the hill. He saw yellow in those that had faced his brother, Esteban had surprised whoever it was, scared the piss right out of the fag. So how had his brother been killed with a toy?

At the top of the hill he found the tree where the real murderer had lain in wait. The boot tracks were too small and thin for a man.

Puta. Pendejo!

His brother was killed by a girl!

The black clouds let loose, pelting him with slivers of ice and freezing rain. He pulled his wool had down over his ears, the hood of his parka over that. Manny reached for the cruel blade he kept just for little girls who gave him trouble. It was razor sharp on one side, bristling with crudely cut jags on the other. He fixed his homemade bayonet to the barrel of his AK-47.

He began a sure, steady march within the snowmobile trails, his boots cracking through the ice with the sound of snapping ribs.

-=-=-=-=-=-=-=-=-=-

"What have you done? Who is the girl?"

Ken's questions sounded more like croaks. He swallowed coffee and water in alternating gulps, trying to loosen vocal cords that seemed to have been packed away for years in dryer lint. Going from stone drunk to sober fast.

His daughter looked drained and limp, as vital and feisty as a de-boned trout.

Reed returned from the guest bedroom, found a chair at the table and melted into it. He stared at their centerpiece of small ceramic pumpkins and gourds; the one his mom purchased at Fred Meyer just before they'd left for Cedar Mountain.

Ken had woken to flashing lights on his console, to a dull thudding that became his daughter's fists slamming the studio door. *Now there was a strange girl showering in their guest bathroom, a different dog in the house;* fear and guilt hung in the air like a poisoned fog.

The fog was nowhere near as bad as the truth. Not even close.

The horrific torrent of events that burst suddenly from the two of them was nothing he could have prepared for.

Ken felt a terrifying tug - magnets of nearly equal pole and force - his absolute need to protect his boy's life and a powerful urge to strangle that life out of him.

"Voice control – dial 911."

The thin bar near the doorway pulsed green.

"What are you doing?"

"Reporting it – the way you should have the first time you saw him."

"We can't do that – *he's dead!*"

"Once he pointed that gun at you, Kristi didn't have a choice."

The pulsing stopped.

The bar glowed red. A woman's voice spoke, "fault."

"Voice control – *dial 9-1-1.*"

"The cell phones haven't worked all day," Kristi said.

"It's supposed to rollover when that happens. *Voice control* – roll to landline – *dial 9-1-1.*"

The windows rattled with the rising winds. The green pulsing stopped again, returned to red.

"Fault."

The bar returned to its normal blue.

"The satellite's connection's gone too." Reed shook his head, "we can't even talk through the computers."

"It's the ice storm. The cell tower and the dish are either frozen solid, or they've blown over. Nothing we can do but sit tight until it's over," Ken said, but the voice was someone else's, his father's maybe. Or the voice of someone *acting* like a father. The fragile tethers connecting them to the outside world were breaking, the full meaning of that setting like concrete around him.

Wind buffeted the house, the hardwood shook beneath them, dishes rattled in the cupboards.

The house went dark, sending them scrambling through drawers for flashlights.

Beeps and whistles. Every battery backup, every smoke and gas detector shrieked warnings.

A loud, snarling bark; a scream from the guest room.

"Malana!"

Reed slammed into a chair, toppling it as he dashed into the darkness beyond the kitchen.

"They're scared that's all" Ken called after him, "Just the wind; the lights going off." xxx

Ken found a Mag light and followed the beam of light into the den behind his son.

The den window showed a world as dark as the house. Silent white missiles exploded to powder against the glass.

Snowing again, *snowing hard.*

"The generator will kick in."

But it didn't, not right away, and now even the imposter's fatherly voice was failing him, shaking.

The generator found its heartbeat, the house filled with light once more. A soft chug as the snow blowers fired up.

"Voice control!" Ken ordered, *"Shutters – all. Close."*

The shutters whispered into place. At least, *most* of them did. A metallic squeal from the back windows and walkways.

"Fault."

"It's the ice. *Voice control. Blowers reset. Heat on.* The blowers are out of sync. Everything will work once they warm up."

But the squealing didn't stop. He'd have to override them from the main console before they burnt out completely. Ken took the stairs too fast, tripped and nearly pitched over the bannister. He caught himself and raced to the studio.

The stillness inside enveloped him. The walls and floor were free-floating, separated from the house, from the buffeting wind. It would take a bomb to shake him here, nothing less.

Two empty bottles of Belvedere vodka on the console, another half-empty bottle waited.

A shot would calm him.

He lunged past the bottles to the console and switched the blowers off manually. He switched off the uninterrupted power supplies and the warning lights stopped blinking.

He switched the console's display input to the security cameras. Eight windows quickly assembled themselves across the three monitors, roof, garage door, back door, front door, and four showing the first floor windows. The first floor window views were black.

Crap.

Jesus, can the snow really be that deep? He swung the other cameras in wide arcs. The small trees at the back of the house were gone, completely buried.

Yes, it really is that deep.

The shutters should have been closed when the storm began – but he'd been asleep at the wheel, they were likely frozen open and ruined. But no "fault" lights showing broken windows. No intrusions. They were safe. They had enough fuel to keep the generator going for two weeks if they conserved.

He pulled the electrical schematics, triaged the systems in the house, and began cutting power to the unnecessary spaces. Water and heat were priorities; he lowered the temperature across the board and shut the heat off completely in the master bedroom and the studio. They had enough sweaters and blankets for a small army. He could see from the roof monitors that the shakers and heaters had done their job. Of all the systems, the roof and attic drained the most power. He switched them to manual. As long as the cameras worked, he could manage the roof.

In a couple minutes he had the house down to barebones power. *Survival mode.*

This was a trial run, a good check of the system, the lines wouldn't be down for two weeks.

He kept telling himself that.

Reed picked up the weapon he'd *only* ever used in video games before.

The game developers had gotten every last detail of the AK-47 right. *He could operate this thing.* He was sure of it. Reed released the clip and pulled it out, pushed it carefully back in. He repeated the motions quickly, slamming the clip home this time.

The thing was a hell of a lot heavier than he'd imagined.

There was a wallop of a kick programmed into the games when you fired one of these, but as good as *physics engines* and *biofeedback mechanisms* were for some First Person Shooter games…actually hitting something real with a real AK-47 without killing himself would take practice. One thing Reed had inferred from the FPS games was a problem with the AK-47: built to work under the worst possible combat situations without jamming, *accuracy* wasn't its strong point.

But he'd only found one extra clip on Malana's brother; he couldn't waste bullets on trees and targets.

He hefted it to his shoulder, aimed into the mirror. *It wasn't Rambo looking back at him. It wasn't DeerSlayr Wolfyn. It was a skinny, pimple-faced geek with a big gun.*

What the hell am I doing?

His sister had *killed* the guy who owned this weapon - taken him out with a frickin' *target rifle*. Kristi was more Rambo, more DeerSlayr, than Reed would *ever* be.

All he'd ever done was play.

Screw that. I've got an assault rifle in my hands.

If Malana's other brother *did* show up, Reed would do more than play warrior. *He had his own gun now.*

-=-=-=-=-=-=-=-=-

The line across her forearm was thick and green.

Kristi's mom had taught her the trick. You took a
piece of gold jewelry and ran it over the softer areas of your
skin. If you saw a green line your iron's been depleted, you're
anemic.

Clearly, Kristi's iron well had run dry.

That line crossing her wrist spoke of other *unspeakable*
things. She'd never felt this weary and alone. The odd
connection she'd felt to her mother had gone dry too. She sat
propped against the bathroom wall, feeling the vibration of
water through the pipes to the guest room shower.

She'd barely had the strength to reach her bathroom
and throw up. And just when it seemed she couldn't possibly
have anything more inside her, it started all over again.

Finally it was her own blood she flushed away.

The green line on her forearm tingled.

"Follow me," it said, *"I know a way out of this. Don't use a
dull earring this time…"*

The water quit running through the pipes. Reed's *little
lost pet* had finally finished.

She'd been completely blind-sided. Nothing pulled
Reed away from his stupid computer games. He'd never had
a girlfriend, never played a sport. It wasn't like Reed to spend

those long mornings out in the forest with Dog. She *should have known* there was more to it, there was something up.

But who'd expect he'd find a girl *out there?*

If you'd paid half as much attention to Reed as your course times you'd have figured it out.

But for that, you actually had to be a sister.

Now Reed was messing around with some gang chick, and Kristi had killed to protect him. She'd eventually have to answer for that with more than her own revulsion and guilt. *They all would.*

She could go to prison. *So what that she had no choice?* She had to shoot the man – but that didn't mean she wouldn't be convicted. The legal system was just that crazy.

She pushed those thoughts back. *She'd welcome the police with open arms right now. Where you had two gang members, you likely had a whole nest of them.* A blind dog with no snout could follow the Ski-Doo tracks to their house..

Even through the closed shutters she felt the wind gusts out there, the icy missiles striking. Maybe the bad weather could help them. The same thing that made it impossible to call for help could be keeping them safe. *You had to be crazy to be out in weather like this.*

But *she* had been crazy enough to be out there only this morning. Creek water was all it had taken for *her.* For Reed, lust had done it.

How crazy could *revenge* make someone?

She slid up the wall for support; struggled to her feet. So strong and confident before, so weak and sick now - *how can everything change so fast?*

Sleep. You need to sleep.

Her bed with its 600-thread-count down comforter, beckoned.

No. You need to move, get your feet going, your legs. It's the middle of the day. It only looks like night now. But she was sick, *so sick.*

Movement was *always* the answer. She splashed water on her face and lurched downstairs like the Frankenstein monster learning to walk.

Maybe movement wasn't the answer.

You know what the answer is.

But she wasn't going to do that. *She wasn't going to drink that creek water again, not ever.* The depression, the vomiting – *the blood* – it was all because of that water.

But it put you on top of the world.

Kristi had sweat all the way through her workout clothes before she'd even reached the den.

Her head pounded. Noise intruding from everywhere at once, the buffeting wind outside, the slap of metal on metal, far-off but sharp, unsettling, as Reed toyed with that horrible gun. *He had no idea what he was playing with.* Chances were he'd end up shooting himself with it, *or all of them.*

"Power, I've got the power!"

God, it was happening again. *That message had come from Reed.* Something from some ancient kids show – *Grayskull? Jesus.* She didn't need anything else flying around in here head right now.

But the "else" kept coming, in disjointed phrases, feelings...

From her father now, a frightening brittleness, he was on the edge. Keeping up a front but his thoughts were scrambled, *all guilt, sadness and fear underneath.*

I don't want to know this. I shouldn't know this.

Each step down to their gym was a jarring, searing stab from her heel to brain.

Spanish. A whisper of a prayer from the guestroom - Reed's illegal alien girlfriend.

Fear. Nothing but fear in her.

Not a prayer.

Hate. Pure and evil.

But not from the girl.

Malana wasn't alone.

-=-.=-.=-.=-.=-.=-.=-.=-.=-.

"Dad! Reed!"

Kristi hurled herself up the steps toward the den.

Pounding and snarling from the guest room — the dog throwing itself at the door to get out.

The stench of new sweat on old; she smelled him before the butt of his rifle blasted the breath and light from her, sent her tumbling back down the stairs.

The basement floor pounded the last bit of air from her lungs. *Screams. Percussive blasts from a powerful gun being fired indoors, the impact of bullets thumping into plaster and stone, shattering glass, and splintering wood.*

She fought for the air her brain screamed for. *It was her own fear, her own pain she felt now, no room for anyone else's.* All she saw was a hovering grayness around her. And still gunshots hammered her ears. So many now, so loud the ringing in her ears wouldn't stop.

Reed had gotten his gun to work, returning fire, he had a fighting chance.

Swirling flashes of bright orange in the fading light. The fireworks in her head faded to blue and then she saw nothing.

-=.-=.-=.-=.-=.-=.-=.-=.-

Her stomach twisted. Hot, stinking breath, grunting. *Pain, sharp and deep.*

Kristi's eyes opened wide to yellow teeth, black eyes, and flying sweat.

She kicked, jammed her elbow into his throat. He was heavy, powerful as an ox. Her screams set the dog barking again.

He fought to control legs and arms, limbs that had been immobile and helpless before.

"KRISTI!" She heard Reed slamming himself into a door deep in the house.

She shoved against her attacker's with everything she had, breath sizzling through her teeth. His limbs like bulging pythons, flexing, prying her legs apart; she raked his face with her fingernails. Skin curled from his cheeks and blood filled the void. A sudden, hot wetness shot into her.

Oh God, no...

He groaned and for a second his grip went slack. Kristi kicked him away, slamming off-balance into the weapons rack behind her. Her hand grasped air, then gripped the handle of her epee.

The rifle was in his hands now, a cruel blade jutting toward her from its barrel. Blood ran from the wounds in his face. His wet penis bounced from the crotch of his dirty jeans. Laughing, he made a short, mocking thrust with the bayonet at the sickeningly inadequate weapon in her hand.

She yanked the waistband of her sweats up past her hips, unable to stop her lips from curling down, from shaking.

Grinning wide enough to show the blood in his teeth, he tipped the bayonet toward her crotch, mimicked her violation. A high chuckle, the sound a mean child would make gurgled from his throat.

"KRISTI!!!" Trapped upstairs, even if Reed crashed through the door, she'd be dead before he fired a shot.

She slipped her thumb in her waistband, slid her sweats back down below the point of her hips.

His eyes followed that waistband.

That was all it took.

The barrel dropped offline. She lunged, caught the evil blade with the thickest part of her own, slapped it off target and thrust forward in one smooth, powerful motion through his left eye, through the fragile eggshell of bone that held it to the back wall of his skull. She'd withdrawn and recovered before the rifle hit the concrete floor with a percussion so loud she was sure it had gone off.

She dove for it, swung the heavy rifle to his gut and pulled the trigger.

Nothing. *Empty.*

"Madr--!" Blood pumped through his shaking fingers, when his hands dropped, the cavity behind them a

sickeningly deep cave of blood. His one remaining eye blinked wildly.

A cloud of red mist expelled from his nose and mouth, as he shrieked.

Kristi reared back and slammed the bayonet deep into his gut till she hit thick bone.

"How does rape feel now?"

He croaked a windless curse in Spanish, something she could do to her mother. Kristi had heard it before, but never had it held the bitter meaning it now did.

"Wrong answer," she hissed.

She kicked the bayonet free and slammed it in him again. When she pulled it free this time his foul, steaming insides uncoiled at her feet.

The room spun. She would have feinted if not for Reed's voice; she pushed herself past the dead man, upstairs to the den, to the acrid smells of nitroglycerin and burnt sawdust, hanging in the air.

Still, it was a clean spring day compared to what she'd just experienced.

"Kristi!" Her head throbbed, trying to pinpoint the direction. The kitchen or garage.

"I'm coming!"

Wind whistled through dozens of holes in the walls and shutters. Swirling shafts of mote-filled light revealed a ruin of glass shards, splintered wood and drifting snow. The huge den window and theater screen were shattered; every piece of their furniture had been blown apart, the stuffing mixed sliding into drifts with the snow.

"*Where is he?*" Reed yelled.

"Dead. He's dead."

"*Was he the only one?*"

"I don't know."

But she could feel nothing from the house now.

"I think so, but I don't know. Keep your guard up. Dad?"

Where *was* he?

Glass crunched beneath her slippers, as Kristi picked her way through the suddenly unfamiliar and broken landscape of her home.

Shivering uncontrollably now, her breath a frosty cloud enveloping her, moving with her.

Silence.

Chunks of granite and black stovetop glass littered the broken tiles. In the mudroom, a chair, the bookcase of Mom's recipes blocked the bullet-riddled door to the garage. She shoved the bookcase and the chair went over with it, they thudded onto the snow-covered floor like tombstones falling in a cemetery.

Reed crouched in the corner of the garage, behind the steel tool cabinet.

"Are you okay?" His eyes were wide, but vacant. "Are you hit?"

I've been raped and I've killed people. I will never be okay again.

"Yes. Yes, I'm okay."

Blood had soaked one arm of his jacket through a blackened hole.

"You've been shot!"

He looked at his arm and nodded.

"I guess. It doesn't hurt so much."

He' in shock. We both are. But we'll be feeling this, all of it, soon enough.

And then she was floating, drifting away. An overwhelming urge to sleep, or was it to wake up? *This was a nightmare after all, wasn't it?* This wasn't their life now, it *couldn't* be. The cold, whistling wind shot through her, brought her back.

"Daddy?"

Something dropped in the pantry, they both swung their rifles toward the door. A whimper from inside as Kristi kicked the door wide.

"Malana!" Reed said running to comfort her.

Kristi ran too – with a far different intent. She shoved Reed aside, yanked the girl to her feet and slammed her, screaming, into the shelves. Cans, and bottles shattered against the floor.

"This bitch let him in! She let him in!"

Reed forced himself between them.

"Kristi! Stop! Stop it!"

Malana said nothing.

*"*You understand me, bitch! I *know* you do!*"*

It was all Reed could do to keep his body between the girl and his sister, a look of desperate horror on his face.

"Kristi! Let her be. Leave her alone!"

Kristi bit her lip. She looked her brother directly in the eye, and shook her head.

The bitch is dead. She just doesn't know it yet.

"Daddy!"

Kristi threw herself through the kitchen doorway to the stairs, kicking away the debris of chairs and cushions, remnants of a comfortable life that choked her path and clung to her now.

-=-=-=-=-=-=-=-=-

Malana held herself tight to Reed, wrapped herself around him.

Warmth against the withering cold, her tears washing over him. Her sobs shook them both. The protective fog began to lift.

"What did you do?"

Her grip tightened.

"No! Dad! Dad – we're here!"

He forced her away, ran down the path his sister had just taken.

"Dad!"

-=-=-=-=-=-=-=-=-=-

"Daddy? Can you hear me, Daddy?"

His breath hung like a low bank of fog, just inches above his chest as she knelt beside him. Blood soaked his midsection. His lungs labored, the sound of their efforts doubled somehow, a sucking sound just after each breath. A jagged line of bullet holes halfway up the wall crossed the studio door, how many of those slugs had passed through her father?

He couldn't have heard the shouts. Probably hadn't heard a thing in the studio before the shooting started, and then he'd only gotten as far as the hallway.

Reed dropped next to her.

"What do we do?"

She shook her head.

"I don't know. *I don't know."*

An icy blade of wind cut through everything; with it, the temperature seemed to drop another twenty degrees.

"Daddy, *what do we do?"*

"We need to see where he's been shot," Reed said.

Gingerly, she lifted the sweatshirt; an awful, wet sound as it tore away from his skin. She winced.

Two black holes, not bleeding so much now; the one just under his ribs bubbled, the look of it, the sucking sound it made as he fought for air was terrifying. Purple bruises growing beneath his skin. He was burning up.

He's bleeding on the inside. That's where most of his blood's going now.

A weak, wheezing cough.

Reed ran from the room and Kristi's brain seemed to float again; she fought the sensation, fought to stay conscious.

Barking now. The furious scrape of nails over wood. *The girl's dog — she's unchained it.* Kristi heard it pound the steps as it bound, snarling, downstairs. The sounds that came up from the gym next were grotesque. She almost *felt* the dog tearing into the bloody mess that lay there. Kristi tried to put it out of her head, but she couldn't.

A blood-curdling shriek. *Malana screamed her brother's name, fighting the dog, begging the dog to stop.*

"God…" Kristi was sure she'd faint now.

Then Reed dropped beside her again, ripping a length of duct tape he stretched over the sucking wound. They lifted their father together, and Reed pulled the tape around to their father's back. The sucking sound stopped.

"We gotta get the blood out of his lungs."

Without hesitation Reed took a deep breath, opened their father's mouth and exhaled into him.

Their father groaned, his eyelids fluttered. An awful gurgling deep inside him. He coughed out a bright red gout of blood; his eyes opened wide.

Kristi fought back the scream climbing in her throat. She squeezed his fingers tightly.

Dad moaned; his fingers squeezed back. His next breath was stronger. He swallowed hard.

His lips formed the word, "Kissy."

We're alive. Kristi thought. We're still alive.

Chapter 16

It's not Mark D'Arc.

Sheriff Hicks crouched closer to the tree trunk, stayed firmly under cover and hidden as the growl of an approaching Search and Rescue snowmobile lifted in the wind.

The engine cut, revved, cut again.

Whoever's driving that thing shouldn't be.

Sleet had turned once again to snow. That was a blessing if comfort was what he needed. But the snow was blowing down hard and fast. Powder over ice, visibility he could measure in scant inches at times; the conditions for any chance of rescue were worse than ever. No one should be out in this – let alone an inexperienced driver.

The wind gusted, dropped and the engine came through clear and strong. The snowmobile passed just below the hollow where the Sheriff hid, sliding and correcting just in time to avoid a tree. Sure enough, it was the big Search and Rescue snowmobile, the sound that engine made was all-too familiar, but Mark D'Arc wasn't in it.

The driver wore black, an Uzi strapped loosely across his back.

They either had Mark, or they'd murdered him. The pain of that was a fist, not to the solar plexus, but directly to Billy's heart.

The driver cut the engine, checked his bearings and drove off in a new direction. The terrorists were on the move, but apparently not the move they'd planned for. *This Bozo has no idea where he's going.*

Anger shoved sadness out of the way, forced Billy's tired, frostbitten feet to move. Just maybe he had a chance to stop them.

-=-=-=-=-=-=-=-=-

"We have to get help."

Their father lay on the carpeted floor beside his mixing console, they didn't dare move him.

Malana sat balled up in a far corner of the room with the dog in her lap; afraid to so much as glance Kristi's way.

Reed nodded, his teeth clenched tight against the pain. *He's feeling that gunshot now, alright.* Her own body was wracked with pulls and strains, and a sharp, stabbing sensation deep in her gut that reminded her, over and over, of exactly what had happened to her. She wanted so much to drift away to nowhere; in an awful way she envied Dad his unconsciousness. She'd been right before; the shock would fade, they would feel the full effect of this horrible day soon enough, and this was only the beginning.

She'd put Reed's arm in a sling. Maybe that was a mistake, he'd probably never be able to straighten it again. She didn't know what to do. Just didn't know. She'd had more than her share of bang-ups and bruises training, but she wasn't a doctor. How the hell had Reed, of all people, known how to deal with a chest wound? *The internet? Some stupid video game?*

"Do you know how the generator works?"

Reed shook his head, and she almost laughed. She felt a new pain from him now, before it even crossed his face.

"It's not your fault," she said, "I don't know either. It's just – we've let mom and dad do everything for us."

He nodded, "I can figure it out. It's just an engine. It's got a fuel tank and an oil tank like they all do."

"Okay." She bit her lip, "okay. What about ammunition?"

He shook his head, "gone."

"What if more of them come for us?"

"Jesus, Kristi, I don't know,"

I can't *make* bullets."

"I've got two full cases of pellets. Fill the pistol and keep it on you – and make sure the cycles are ready to go if you need them. But don't get on them unless you have to. They're dangerous with all the ice. The Ski Doos are more stable."

"You should stay with Dad, I'll go for help."

"You've got one arm. I'll go."

There's no way you can ski in this.

It seemed she could feel every bone settling painfully into place as she stood.

"I'll have a better chance getting to town on skis than a cycle."

"Are you crazy?"

"No," she said. *But I will be soon.*

-=-=-=-=-=-=-=-=-

Dad's lungs rattled, his breathing ragged and uneven again.

Malana soothed his father's forehead with a damp towel. She had waited until Kristi left the house before she'd so much as moved from the corner of the room.

Reed watched Malana comfort his stricken dad, the pain from his own wound growing now, fear with it. *At the heart of it all was this girl.*

Had Malana *really* let her brother in? Of course she had. He couldn't have gotten in without tripping an alarm.

When Hell broke loose Reed wasted all of his bullets hitting nothing but their house. In the end, he'd barricaded himself in the mudroom; Malana's brother had simply finished the job of trapping him and blocked him from the outside, content Reed was powerless to help. He'd been right.

Kristi had saved them all. Reed, true to form, had caused the problem and contributed nothing worthwhile once it blew.

Even now, all he could do was wait.

His father shone with sweat. God only knew what was going on inside him. How could Kristi possibly get help in time?

No way she even makes it down this mountain.

"Malana, stay here with my father. I'll be back. Do you understand?"

She nodded quickly, her eyes wide, terrified. Malana had lost two brothers today. She was in a completely strange world. It was *his* fault she was here in their house, not hers – it was Reed's fault her brother had come to kill them.

All of this was on him.

He pushed the thought away. *Kristi and I are the parents now. Concentrate on what you have to do.*

-=.=.=.=.=.=.=.=.=.

The gym stank with human excrement and of things that should never see day.

He tried not to look at the ruined thing on the floor as he found Kristi's pistol in the rack, loaded a fresh CO2 cartridge, and filled the gun with pellets. He strapped the holster with a bandolier of pellet tubes to his chest, his arm ached like a rotten tooth, throbbed with each movement.

When he turned back, the full gruesome picture of what had happened here overwhelmed him. Kristi's epee' had rolled all the way to the Nautilus machine, the jelly of her attacker's eye still hanging, frozen now, from the flattened steel tip.

Reality imitating DeerSlayr's gruesome fantasy rescue of WyldChyld. Below the spilled coils of the man's insides, the man's penis protruded from his pants.

Kristi was raped.

Reed shook. His entire body throbbed with anger and pain.

"Malana!" He leapt the staircase to the den, tore up the stairs to the studio.

Malana quickly stood, backed away from his father, from *him*. Paco circled, whined, seeing his friend, but seeing something terrible in his friend's eyes.

Reed's hand flew back.

Malana's brother at the cave, hand drawn back to strike.

It helps to know you can be cruel...

Malana looked up at him expressionless, she offered no defense, no resistance at all. Resigned to one more beating from one more man.

His hand dropped to his side, spent, an enormous and horrible weight on him now.

He trudged downstairs to the garage, feeling his feet sink impossibly deep into each step, a terrible effort to lift them again.

It was freezing in the garage. Dad must have dropped the heat to save fuel. A strong chemical smell permeated the air, *that can't be good.* Bullets holes through the mudroom door, through the walls. Perforated cans, jugs and glass littered the floor.

How was it he was only hit once? Why was he still alive?

Because once you ran out of bullets you flattened yourself on the floor like a coward. Because you hid until your dad was shot and your sister was raped.

He had tried to break free and help. Malana's brother had jammed the door from the outside. There was no way to budge it.

No way.

The acrid odors came from insecticide, from pools of antifreeze from broken jugs on the floor. Not fuel. Nothing explosive had been hit.

The fumes made him lightheaded, nauseated. He couldn't stay in here long.

By reflex Reed almost hit the button that would roll up the garage door and let clean air rush in. He stopped short.

Malana's brothers' whole gang could be outside.

Reed made his way to the den, took some deep breaths until his head cleared, then came back for the generator.

He was right about it – just an engine, no mysteries there. One thing he would have to learn fast was how to operate Dad's power and monitoring panel back in the studio. He'd have to figure out how to keep the doorway heaters and blowers going, work the shutters and the security cameras. He could bring his own computer down to the mudroom. It wouldn't hurt to have a control point down here.

Reed filled the Ski Doo and Ski Cycle tanks as quickly as he could; clumsy, painful work with one good arm, and his eyes and nose watering from the fumes. He practically flew back into the mudroom. He couldn't shut the door behind him fast enough.

Malana waited in the kitchen.

So much for staying with his father. Was she completely
useless?

What had he done? What had he brought into their home?

There was no way he could have left her in that cave;
no way could he leave her to face one more beating. No
matter how bad the consequences had been, he'd done the
right thing for the right reasons

No you didn't. You did it because she's pretty.

Maxine's words cut through, *"You wanted to fuck me."*

Malana knew exactly what he was thinking. He could
see that. Reed tried not to look her way again as he plastered
duct tape over the holes in wall to keep the garage fumes
from the living quarters.

He kept a wide berth from Malana as he trudged
upstairs to check on his father.

Paco was curled on the floor beside Dad; the chunky
little pit bull lifted his head, wagged his stump of a tail when
Reed walked in. Malana followed a step behind Reed.

Dad's face was still shiny with sweat but he wasn't
moaning now. His lungs no longer gurgled as his chest rose
and fell.

Reed felt his own breath as acutely as his father's
now, falling into the same rhythm, as though his lungs were
coaxing his father's along, supporting them. It would be like

that now. His father's life and Kristi's were Reed's responsibility. Reed had put them all in this position.

With that thought, a feeling of concrete hardening around him, holding him in. A terrible weight.

He fought the urge to run, to escape, instead he sat in his father's chair and went to the task of figuring out how to control the house. A few taps of the wide display brought up a schematic of all the rooms and attached systems. Control sliders and radio buttons beneath each with status bars - green on the functioning systems, yellow and red on the diminished or non-functioning ones. It was like a computer game. No problems there.

A yellow light flashed near the front and garage door icons. He moved the cursor over them. A balloon of text and a new radio button appeared: *Flush System.*

Okay. Okay. That was the water runoff from the heaters, probably plugged with ice farther out.

He hit the *flush* button, pulled up the backyard security cameras and watched a fountain of steaming water spurt across the walkways from the pipes below them.

That can't be good. Not halfway through winter and already a break in the system.

All that steaming water barely made a dent in packed snow and ice out there. In fact a new ledge was forming where it hit. *Great, "instant ice" for the walkways.* That was all they needed.

Jesus, how cold is it out there?

He slid up the temperature displays: fifteen degrees Fahrenheit.

He let enough water go to satisfy the warning sensor then shut the flushing mechanism off.

Another yellow light pulsed over the roof. *Okay, that would be the roof clearing system.* Dad called it *the shaker,* which was pretty much all it did. The tiles up there had their own heating system and a special non-stick surface like Teflon – but even that didn't always stop the snow from building up. The shaker fixed that. Reed clicked the radio button and watched through the roof security cameras as the remaining white frosting cracked, steamed, and slid off the sides.

At least *that* system was working.

This storm couldn't keep up forever. They had food and water. As long as the generator kept running they'd be warm. Kristi would make it through to town and any time now a SWAT and Search and Rescue team would chopper up here to medivac Dad out.

They'd all be okay.

His arm burned. He hadn't been hit squarely. The wall panel in front of him took the shot and only a fragment went through him. That was the good news. The bad news was that bits of the wall had ridden along with that fragment. At some point, those *had* to come out or the infection they started would take his arm. He tried not to think about all those tintypes he'd seen of Civil War infections and amputations. Instead, he moved the roof cameras every way he possibly could.

The snow was still coming too hard to see much out there.

If there's a whole gang coming for us…why did Malana's brother come alone?

"Malana."

She stood and nodded.

"Your brothers' friends? *Compadres*. Gang?" Crap, why didn't he take Spanish?

"Si. Gang. Yes." She nodded, "es gang."

"Where?" *There was a Spanish question he'd heard before…* "Donde esta?" he asked, finally, just remembering to leave off the part about *the bathroom*. He pointed to the floor and raised his palms in question.

"No, aqi. Not here."

"Where are they? Donde?"

"Los Angeles."

So her brothers' gang wasn't with them. But that didn't make sense. What were her brothers doing here – and why hide her in a cave? Who were they hiding her from?

He could tell she understood his questions, but it was slow going, painful. Malana motioned with her hands – jabbed her palm with her finger.

Write. She wants to write.

Reed found a notepad and pen in a drawer beneath the mixing board – she took them quickly, and sketched five quick figures: Four men. A syringe.

"Four drug dealers."

"Si, yes," but she was shaking her head "no" at the same time. There were tears in her eyes.

"Do you mean more? Or worse? They're worse than that? What's worse than drug dealers?"

She began to draw one more stick figure – but only from the shoulders down to his feet. She drew his head separately, a good distance from his shoulders. Then she drew a long, curved knife.

A thumping in Reed's chest pounded all the way through the painful hole in his arm. He'd seen the beheading videos on the Internet.

Now he knew exactly what he had brought into their home.

Chapter 17

With every new storm the landscape, the makeup of the
snow, had changed. Most of the usual landmarks had
changed too, many were simply buried.

But Kristi found what she was looking for.

This stuff is killing you.

Yes. But I need it now. My family needs me, and I need
to be *more*.

Getting to a place in the creek she could break
through had taken some doing; she'd crawled flat on her belly
over her skis to distribute her weight.

When she did find ice thin enough to pierce, the fluid
that looped out was thick, viscous, a green-tinged stream
without bubbles that coated the throats of the bottles she
filled.

No tadpole-mutant fish this time. Thank God for that.

She stowed the bottles away in her jacket, belly-crawled herself back to solid footing, and climbed to the top of the bank.

The snow was falling fast, the wind gusting, flinging it sideways. It made a low roar in the pines.

Enough stalling, you've got to do this. You've got to get moving.

She snapped her boots into their bindings, held one of the bottles up to gray sky, unscrewed the top, and stared at the tops of the marshmallow trees, watched them sway in the wind, all the time fighting to let that goop flow down through her.

Its cold fingers crept along the walls of her plumbing, the oily feel nearly gagging her.

Enough! *That's got to be enough.*

Come on. *Make me feel good. Make me feel strong.*

A sudden flash of heat as the tainted water found that part of her that had grown so ready to accept it, *to need it.*

Ignition.

She pulled her visor down.

The low roar she'd heard deep in the forest was growing louder now, cutting out then in. It wasn't the howl of wind, *a snowmobile!* Her heart jumped. She pumped the air with her fist. The changing wind made the mobile's position hard to place, just somewhere down in that deep white forest below her, and it was coming this way.

Mark! We're saved!

If you'd been a little faster on the draw I wouldn't have had to drink that awful crap.

Mark's snowmobile skidded from the woods. But Mark wasn't driving it.

But it *was* Search and Rescue. The markings were clear. *They were safe now, her dad would be okay.*

Kristi pushed off down the hill to intersect his path, she waved her poles over her head.

The snowmobile slowed, its engine cut off. The man riding it stood straight up, waving his arms the same way she had.

She skidded to a stop and nearly lost it.

The man wasn't wearing Search and Rescue insignia on his jacket. He was just some guy in cheap, black outdoor wear and a black ski mask. What was he doing on a Search and Rescue cycle?

"I am here to help you!"

The words were clear enough – but a feeling came strong and clear with them, *one that had nothing to do with helping anyone.*

Hate.

And now she recognized the voice. He was one of the guys she'd seen on the Morgan's roof – the one who had "welcomed" her for skiing by.

Another feeling now, this one straight from her little power drink.

She felt herself floating again, high above the man masquerading as Search and Rescue, high above the world.

Who is this insect?

And how the hell had she slipped a second ago? Skiing this crap snow was a piece of cake.

"I am here to help you," he said again.

She pushed off hard and low, shot past him straight into the forest. Behind her, the motor revved up once more. Coming after her.

And still, calm spread over her like a soft blanket.

You want to chase me through these trees with that thing, bring it motherfucker.

The trees, the snow-covered rocks that had zipped by her before slowed, the narrow gaps between them widened before her eyes. Where once a dangerous jumble of obstacles had been, a clear path had opened, *a damn runway she could land a 747 on.*

Yes, she was flying all right. She could handle this, anything, anyone.

She cut between trees like they were wispy gate pennants on a slalom course. At the bottom of the icy run laying out before her, a half-dome of snow and ice slowly revealed itself.

Snowfall had turned a deadfall into a grotto, a nativity carved in ice.

But there were no angels, no wise men in this manger scene. Only one kneeling figure. Mark. Scarlet and pink patches of ice and snow around him.

The lightness of flight drained from her. Her heart sank into the frozen earth.

Mark was tilted forward as if deep in thought, deep in the task before him. Until you drifted close enough to see his hands were tied. Until you saw his head wasn't simply covered by the fur of his collar, *it was gone.*

So many feelings at once. Loss, pain, life and future never realized, gone forever.

The roar of the snowmobile, *Mark's snowmobile,* grew louder. Her lips quivered.

Let this go. You're dead if you don't.

The snowmobile careened over the hill above her, fishtailed and bore down on her. The driver had his gun out now – he fired even as the cycle skid out of control beneath him.

Twigs snapping, spinning, snow blasting up all around her, a mechanical burping sound as he continued to fire. He sideswiped a tree, careened off it, the engine cut, started again.

Let's dance.

"You're mother's a pig, asshole!"

She jounced her skis and lifted off, then dropped low, jetted down the slope between the trees, slaloming again. *Flying again.*

"Catch me, pig boy!"

She chose the straightest path down, building as much speed as she could. The engine roared behind her, he was flooring it now.

Four evenly spaced hillocks of snow below her, *way-too-evenly spaced*, nothing but a small rise of clean snow between each of them.

Kristi went straight for the middle hillock, skis together, knees pulled tight to her chest.

She caught serious air; hung in the sky forever; the forest, the valley floor splayed open before her.

Behind her, the snowmobile caught something quite different. She heard it flip over and slide. The engine cut, a sudden, profound silence.

Kristi landed clean, carved upward fast, and skidded to a stop.

The snowmobile slid past her on its side, blazing a scarlet trail across the snow until it came to rest in a snow bank.

Kristi skied down to it, poled her bindings loose and stepped off her skis.

Some fifty yards back, the man hung from his neck like a rabbit in a snare.

She righted the machine, loaded her skis, and wiped the blood off the seat and cowl with her forearm. Then she drove back to the man in the fence.

He'd taken the *easy* path between the buried fence posts. The wire had bitten deep into his neck. Blood fanned across the snow around him. His limbs shook in spasm. His wide red eyes blinked up at her.

"Sucks when it's *your* throat, huh?"

Kristi found the Uzi half-buried in snow. She shouldered it, dug two full clips from the dying man's parka, and drove on.

-=-=-=-=-=-=-=-=-

Reed worked the security controls from his bedroom computer, trying the phones and Internet repeatedly with similar results. FM radio, somewhere on the technology scale near smoke signals to Reed, was his only connection to the outside world now, only went one way, and even that signal was breaking up.

The news from that world wasn't good anyway: this storm was nowhere near over; help wouldn't be here anytime soon. National news was even more ominous: the server outage closing down games like Mythykal had spread across the Internet. Google, Yahoo – even the websites of the news organizations themselves had been affected.

The list was growing fast.

At least their home network was working. He'd connected every computer they had to his dad's console. They now had access to the security and power controls from anywhere in the house.

But they were trapped here. He had to reach out.

Their lifeline was the satellite dish. Maybe Malana's brother had only cut the wires, not destroyed the unit itself. If Reed could get it working again he could reach the Internet and help.

No way to see it from here though. The dish was mounted on the northeast corner of the house, blocked from view even when the cameras were functioning.

He might be able to reach it now. Without all the snow it would have taken their tallest ladder to reach it – but the oak tree on that side of the house towered over the roof, actually scraped the roof in the wind. The snow must be packed tall enough to reach its lowest branches by now. That *had* to be how Malana's brother got to the dish.

He hadn't spotted anyone outside since Kristi had left. It was worth checking out.

Paco looked up expectantly from his comfy perch in Malana's lap as Reed backed his chair from his desk and stood. The two of them had curled up in the corner of Reed's room, the corner where Dog bedded down.

He headed into the studio.

His father motioned for Reed weakly with one hand and Reed knelt beside him.

"Water," his father whispered, his voice like dry leaves rolling in the wind.

Reed opened a bottle, pressed it to his father's lips, and his father drained the contents in seconds.

"Kristi?"

"She's gone for help in Cedar."

Ken closed his eyes.

"Too..." the next words were barely audible, Reed just caught 'dangerous.'

"She's tough, dad. She'll make it."

"Faking it," his father's eyes were yellow; the dark circles around them made gave the impression that they had sunken back into his head.

"...on something, Reed...something bad."

As obvious as that fact was, it hurt Reed to hear his father say it. Kristi was such a straight arrow. Hell, she was an organic food freak, nothing but grass-fed, no GMO for her. But her confidence, her aggressiveness was off the charts these days, and she'd lost any baby fat she'd ever had. It was obvious.

But what could she be *on*? It wasn't the usual sports junk you heard about – not steroids or that growth hormone crap – she was literally getting thinner every day. Whatever it was, where could possibly be getting it up here?

But whatever she was doing, you couldn't deny she was the toughest one in the family, the smartest. Reed conceded that freely now. Juiced or not, Kristi was their best hope, their *only* hope.

His father began to drift. Just before his eyes closed, they squared with Reed's.

"Reed. *Make her stop.*"

=.=.=.=.=.=.=.=.=.=-

Eyes everywhere. Watching her from the forest.

And emotions she couldn't decipher.

She was dealing with gangs and terrorists; the emotions that drove those people were alien, evil.

Not like this. *This is completely different.*

Kristi cut the engine, let the snowmobile drift, listening to the forest, to this new language of emotion.

No, not emotion, at least not the way *she* knew it.

Instinct. Pure, feral, instinct.

Where are you?

But she knew the answer to that question even before this new code was broken, before their language truly became hers.

"Everywhere. We are all around you. But what are you?"

One of you. I'm more like you every day.

The ominous press of eyes left her. Their question answered for now.

Kristi started the engine again, revved it up and picked up speed.

A new message had come through.

-=-=-=-=-=-=-=-=-

His parents' bedroom had become a haunted place for Reed, sealed away like an unused castle chamber. It still held so much of his mother; scented candles, the little statuettes and paintings of Ganesha, the deco jewelry box on her vanity, her jeweled watches lined up before it.

The double sink in the master bathroom was lined with her creams, perfumes and makeup brushes. He carefully placed Kristi's laptop among them, trying not to move any of them too far from their original positions.

When the system woke, he checked the cameras again. The visibility out there was miserable. Malana's brother had come alone. No gang would sit in that crap this long without trying to break in.

But the terrorists Manuel worked for were sure to look for him, and whatever remnants of trail there still was led straight to this house.

And once he was out there they could be on Reed in seconds. Still, he zipped up his jacket and pulled his gloves on. The toolbox and his snow shoes beside him. He called open the bathroom shutter, pushed the window up, snow blowing across the floor.

"No!"

Malana had followed him, an almost constant shadow now. The sacrilege of a strange girl in his parent's bedroom a weird, childhood tinge on top of much more important matters.

She clutched his hand. He pulled it back – but not before she'd ripped off his glove. *God, this isn't a game!*

"Malana. I have to go out there. Now."

Once again, the image of Manuel striking her.

He grabbed the glove and she turned quickly, pulling his hand beneath her sweater. She pressed his palm to the warm softness of her bare breast.

"No...," he said, but his voice broke.

She was like nothing he'd ever felt before. Malana rolled the sweater over her head and pressed her round, warm flesh against the slick of his jacket. She guided his hand over the smooth landscape of her.

She felt him grow against her, his resistance leaving as surely as his passion rose.

And when there was no more resistance in him, she grasped that growing, needful part of him, and guided it purposely and softly as she had his hand.

She was the most beautiful girl in the world.

-=-=-=-=-=-=-=-=-

The toughest strides of a long run are the first and last.

Who was it told Billy that?

Hell that was his father. Couldn't even count how many times his father had said it. *He knew that.* He hadn't forgotten. He wasn't going senile; he wasn't freezing to death.

He was feeling warm now, hot even. He should just take the stupid jacket off.

Billy shook his head, or felt himself do that. It wasn't much of a shake, there wasn't much shake left in him. There was nothing extra left in him. Billy Hick's was setting his sights very low these days, measuring his strength, his progress, in the distance between tree trunks. He rested at each tree, shielding himself from blasts of freezing wind and snow.

When had climbing a hill ever been this hard?

Toughest strides. First and last. But he'd made that first one so long ago.

Come on, Billy. *Say it out loud with feeling.*

"T-t-t'fest," that was all he could do.

"K-kid ss-sister...b-b-baby."

He almost laughed when he heard it come out. The warmth he felt was no joke though. His skin was burning up.

You know what that is, Billy.

That's just your guts saying, "What the hell's goin' on, jackass? Don't you know you're outside in the snow? Don't you know you're dying? Here...here's some blood...some good warm blood...take it and fix the damn problem. Then get inside you damn fool!"

Yep, that's all that warm feeling was. Just his body's last, desperate message to his stupid little lizard brain.

He'd held onto this tree way too long. Billy pushed off, and fell flat.

The gray ghost of the house was right up there. A ski tow line near the garage was nearly buried in snow, it disappeared deep in the forest somewhere far down the mountain behind him. He almost laughed. Crap, I wish I'd come across that a ways back...

The house was shuttered down, mostly dark. But the Carrolls were in that house he knew it. Help waited inside.

They definitely hadn't left the mountain before the storm. Their chimney smoke blew crazily in the wind; surely it came from those damn, super-efficient "odorless" wood pellets, but even through his frozen nostrils it smelled like heaven itself.

The Carrolls could have suffered the same fate as the Morgans. Their home invaded by the same terrorists. It was a very good possibility. Billy could be walking into the same trap all over again.

What the hell difference does it make who answers the door? He was dead if he didn't find shelter.

Billy stumbled over the snow-filled remnants of Kristi's ski tracks. It was a bad sign, a very bad sign.

No one would try to ski out of here in this weather. No one could possibly be that crazy or desperate.

But Billy Hicks was clean out of options.

Malana kissed Reed's forehead, whispered soft, soothing words to him.

Reed didn't understand the words, only that her whispers calmed him, made him feel both like a man and a small boy at once.

He could ignore the burning, the ache in his arm. The ache in his heart, the loneliness that had been his childhood companion, was gone. *How could he have doubted saving her was the right thing to do? How could he have been angry with her before?*

Still, there was something he had to do. Something important.

Only the satellite dish, only their one connection to the outside world.

Something heavy thumped so loud against the back door that Reed jumped and turned so fast he nearly threw Malana into the wall.

The terrorists are here!

He grabbed the pellet pistol – a sure grip this time – and bolted downstairs through the ruin of their house.

A knock, and then one of the best words he would ever hear spoken, came from beyond the back door: "Sheriff."

Just in time, Reed remembered to zip up his pants before he flung the door open. What fell in with a rush of snow and frigid wind scared him half to death.

The Sheriff's face was bloody and nearly blue, a long gash from forehead to ear, ice cracked and fell from his clothing, shattered like little bombs and scattered across the floor. One foot was wrapped only in a frozen sock and a section torn from his jacket.

Sheriff Hicks slammed the door behind him, his hand searching the flat surface madly.

"Bolt this!"

"Voice control. Back door bolt."

Malana looked like a scared rabbit. She clung to Reed as the sheriff's eyes went from her to the duct tape covering the bullet holes in the walls. Reed put the man's arm over his shoulder, eased him into a chair in the kitchen.

"Co'-coffee. Is that coffee I smell?" The Sheriff asked.

"Uh, yeah. We've got some," Reed said.

"I could use a cup."

"Café? Agua?"

"Si, senorita, gracias."

Malana poured him a mug of coffee and a tall glass of water. He gulped them as fast as she could refill them.

"Gracias, gracias. Son, I may scream like the dickens in a minute or two when the blood comes back to my limbs. Don't mind it. What happened here?"

Reed glanced at Malana and looked away.

"Some gangster broke in – we killed him – but he shot me in the arm – my dad's shot in the chest and stomach."

"Gangster? And you killed him?"

"Yes."

"Where's your dad now?"

"Upstairs."

"Conscious?"

"He goes in and out."

The Sheriff winced, *"God damn!"* He shook his head. "Sorry, it's my leg. Help me up there. Is he still bleeding?"

"I think he's bleeding inside."

Billy rose painfully to his feet.

"I'll be honest. We're *all* in pretty bad shape right now."

"My arm's okay, I think."

"We have to get off this mountain fast. The Morgans down the road were attacked like you were. MS-13 working with Islamic terrorists – likely ISIS. What weapons do you have in the house?"

"We took guns off the guy who broke in – AK-47s – not much ammo though."

Reed slipped the big pellet gun out of his jacket.

"He had assault rifles and you killed him with that?"

Reed shook his head as they reached the studio.

"My sister killed him with one of her fencing swords."

"If you need proof of The Almighty, that's surely it," Billy grimaced. "And she skied out of here for help? In a blizzard?"

Reed nodded.

Billy clutched his leg and fell against the wall for support, swearing through clenched teeth.

"What can I do?"

Billy shook his head, "Run cool water in a tub – I'll check on your Dad. Cool water - not even warm."

-=-=-=-=-=-=-=-=-

Jesus H! Sheriff Hicks reached the studio half-blind with hurt.

This wasn't 'pins and needles.' This was that white-hot blast just after the hammer hits your thumbnail – except his entire left leg was the thumbnail. The blood was rushing in all right, but not finding any of those old familiar highways in front of it. No, those highways were gone, that blood had gone straight off-road tearing up everything in its path.

Strength, give me strength. I've come this far.

Deal with it, you baby. It's pain, just pain.

Suck it up and get them out of here.

Ken Carroll appeared awake, but unresponsive. Maroon trails from his nostrils, the corners of his mouth. The fluid in his lung rattled with each shallow breath.

"Mister Carroll, I'm going to do my best not to hurt you."

Ken's eyes wandered aimlessly over the wide monitors as Billy checked the man's wounds. Billy didn't have to look far to gauge the man's chances; he wasn't leaving this house. Duct tape was the only thing holding Ken Carroll together.

"Mister Carroll?"

Ken's eyes never left the monitors. To Billy, those big displays showed nothing but snow.

"We have a bad situation. I have to get your kids off this mountain now. Do you understand me?"

"*Cameras...*" Ken Carroll whispered.

Billy searched the screens – still only snow, gray shadows.

"*Someone's out there...*"

-=.=.=.=.=.=.=.=.=.=-

Mom?

The house in the meadow below Kristi looked dark and empty. Shattered ice and three snowmobile trails fanned out from the garage into the forest.

One of those trails would loop back to exactly where she sat now. Where had the other two gone?

This was the house where all those men had been. A long way from her home, but still the closest. She had planned to avoid it completely, to take a path protected by the forest until she was well past it.

But in the end, she knew she *needed* to come here.

Mom has been in this house all along. Tears came with that awful certainty.

The man on Mark's snowmobile, the same man who'd "welcomed" Kristi for skiing by this house. Had he found her mother in that first snow?

"I am here to help you," was what he'd said.

Is that what he'd said to Mom when she'd been stuck in the snow?

She had to get to Cedar. Her father would die if she didn't make it.

But Mom I know you're in there. You're there and you need me too.

Kristi climbed out of the snowmobile, snapped on her skis and belted her snowshoes and the gun over her shoulder. As deserted as the place looked, she had to assume it wasn't. She quickly inspected her strange new weapon. She pulled out the old clip, snapped in a fresh one.

God help me.

Someone had left in a hurry; a door at the side of the house was open, held in place by a snowdrift.

Two of their men had disappeared, they had to deal with that. She doubted the terrorists cared as much about the men being lost as having them grilled by anyone who found them.

They murdered Mark and they have your mother.

Her stomach growled, she doubled over with pain and nausea. She'd pushed herself too hard this time.

She pulled out a fresh bottle of creek spew, spun off the cap and sucked the nasty, viscous solution into her body. *A flash of images from a horror show, something about a magic monkey's paw that granted you only one wish. A mother had wished her dead son back to life. But the son had already been embalmed. He came back with fire in his veins. She hacked him to pieces to end his pain, but the boy — and all those pieces - could never die again.*

The mother had been granted her wish; it could never be taken back and she had no others.

The creek water was Kristi's magic monkey's paw.

Kristi licked the last, oily drop from the corner of her mouth.

Yes, she had fire in her veins. Yes, she was probably embalming herself. Maybe she was already dead.

I wish my mom were alive.

She pushed off. By the time she reached the door she was flying again.

The house wasn't empty. Not by a long shot. Overwhelming emotions: fear and pain.

She pulled out of her skis and boots, gritted her teeth, and swung the Uzi in front of her. Kristi swept through the door with a gust of wind and snow.

The stench of sickness, of rot, nearly kicked her right back outside. Another odor, sharp and medicinal, cut through it all. She recognized the smell immediately. Whatever poison laced the creek – she'd reached the mother lode. She pulled the turtleneck of her sweats over her nose and mouth. The house was dark, but blasts of static, news and weather reports in English, and Arabic reverberated through the walls.

Unwashed dishes stacked in the sink, on the small kitchen table. Deep stains over the porcelain sink, running onto the floor.

"Ice storm still hammering the Pacific Northwest,"

"…more casualties today, roadside bomb on US highway…fifteen dead…today,"

"…Arctic blast…Columbia River Gorge."

"…more Internet woes…servers everywhere…catastrophic…Homeland Security fears a major…"

And over it all, an Arabic voice; like someone swearing directly in her ear.

She entered a claustrophobically narrow hallway. Hummel Dolls in a glass case, faux wood paneling. A bedroom to her right. Just over the bed, a dust shadow where a large crucifix had been removed from the wall. The bed had been made, but the cover was rumpled and dented. Slept *on,* not in; bedrolls on the floor.

Bathroom. More stains on the tile, and something evil leaking over the side of the tub. This was the source of the awful, stinging medicinal odor.

Her stomach growled.

No. We're not going anywhere near that.

Several shaving kits around the sink, a group of towels carefully folded. No, not towels exactly, more like fine silk napkins. Freshly cut hair in the sink, short curls.

Pubic hair. Uggh.

She moved quickly down the hall.

Half a dozen stuffed animal heads hung in the den. An old-style television here flashed between static and CNN, the screen's bluish glow the only light in the room. The carpet showed a less-dingy square of shag three feet from the television where a big chair must have sat for years; roughly cut squares of the same carpeting marked the spots where its legs had rested, so dented in now they looked like cups of flattened green hair.

She nudged the shade away from the window. Even the snow-choked sunlight was a hundred times brighter than the light here. It nearly blinded her. The garage stood a few feet from the house itself, its access door was closed.

Mom. Are you in there?

An answer, weak and unformed, closer to the feral messages from the forest, scrambled by the pain and fear in this house, the shouts of hate from the radio.

At the back of the den, a strangely thin door with a crystal doorknob, those voices were blasting from somewhere beyond it.

She held her breath, and pulled the door open.

A short wooden stairway down to a cellar. Three radios screamed from a roughhewn worktable below. The missing den chair, a Lazy-Boy, sat in a shaft of cold, blue-gray light from the cellar window. Its over-upholstered arms wrapped with silver layers of duct tape.

Eye-watering odors of sickness and rot sat like a cloud of autumn fog in here, and a coldness the likes of which she'd never felt – nothing to do with the outside temperature. *Cold terror that bit deep through her bones, straight into her soul.*

This is where evil lives.

Woven into the duct tape, deep in its silvery layers, tufts of human hair, skin, and blood.

Nausea and horror blasted through her harder and louder and clearer than the Arab man shouting in her ear, the weather reports, the casualties of terror, and tales of a collapsing America.

"Mom! Where are you? Mom!" She shouted, no more time for fear.

A large square of heavy plywood leaned against the wall. Bits of rock and earth lay at its feet. Kristi tugged the panel, it fell flat to the floor; a rough cut, narrow tunnel in the dirt behind it.

NO TIME FOR FEAR.

She ran headlong into it, leaning low, holding the Uzi in front of her.

"Mom!"

The tunnel curved away ahead. Two makeshift doors, one lined with a sickly greenish glow. She kicked that one open.

A veritable cavern, a cannabis forest under grow lights. The smell of pot and more of that harsh, medicinal smell too. A bench and basin glittering with glass beakers and flasks.

But no one inside.

She kicked open the other door.

The sickness, the rot came from this room was overpowering.

The pot farm grow lights showed a bare, shattered bulb dangling from a wire that ran up the wall and disappeared. Heaped at the far end of the room, two broken bodies, a large man, a tiny woman, their hands bound, their heads misshapen, blown apart. The Morgans.

Mom was in the garage. *She had to be.*

Kristi dashed back through the tunnel only to see a wedge of blackness moving across the entrance. *The plywood panel was being pushed back in place.*

I'm being buried alive! Buried with those bodies!

Something small but heavy flew toward her through the opening. It struck the earthen floor with a metallic ring, bounced and rolled.

A moment of decision. Fight or flight.

She grabbed it, underhanded the grenade back before the panel shut. The concussion was like a hammer strike to the temple, more felt than heard. Her entire body seemed to compress from the force. Her ears rang.

Flames leapt over her, she'd been knocked all the way back into the pot farm. The plants had caught fire.

Kristi stumbled to her feet, forced herself through the smoke back into the tunnel well-lit now, the opening nearly twice as wide as before. Dust and smoke swirled into the cellar with her. The cellar window, likely every window in the house, had blown out with the explosion.

A dark, bloodied man convulsed in the rubble outside the tunnel.

"Good move, asshole."

She fired a burst into his body, as much to check the Uzi as to finish the man, any care for his pain well past her now.

Smoke and flame poured from the tunnel behind her. The open window pulling the flames toward it. A face appeared in the doorway above her. He was slight, bookish; his thick glasses, pushed sideways from the blast.

She let loose another blast, comfortable with the weapon now.

He screamed, darted back into the den as she fired another burst. A glass ball arced over her head as she pounded up the stairs, it shattered against the concrete floor with a blast of yellow-green smoke. That acrid medicinal odor swirled up the stairs with her. She choked, coughed, and tasted blood. Kristi tugged her sweats over her nose, firing through the wall where she knew he'd be running on the other side.

Another door slammed as she reached the den.

Her head ached. She slipped as the floor shifted beneath her, rose and fell, her feet desperately trying to find it; she stumbled, fell flat. The gun blasted holes through the door and walls, through the floor. She slipped her finger off the trigger, got to her knees and threw up.

Better. Better now.

The room stretched, then shrank suddenly, crushing in from all sides. Her feet baked from the heat building in the cellar. Choking smoke billowed from the floorboards.

Get out! Get out now!

The front door was just ahead. Her movements toward it were painful and slow. *Another wall.* The door she thought she'd seen was gone.

This isn't a room. This is a coffin. She could feel the satin pressing her face...

No. This is a room in a house. There's a way in. There's a way out.

Smoke belched from every direction; thick, black clouds full of the skunky stench of burning pot and harsh chemicals.

Outside, an engine turned, caught and revved. She knew just what that engine belonged to, had heard it so often in the past few years it was trapped in her DNA now.

The Denali! Our car!

She hurled herself toward the sound with all her might. Her thigh collided with a low wall, sending her end-over-end into a bank of snow, glass from the shattered window tore her jacket, cut into her gloves – but she was outside! *Free!*

The garage, the house, the sky, they twirled around her, settled. Then it all stretched taffy-like, toward unknown horizons. Nausea welled inside her.

The squeal of a badly maintained and frozen garage door struggling to open, and their big SUV rolled onto the iced-over driveway, snow chains rattling from its tires. She focused, willed the world to stand in place.

Through the tinted window – her mother's face.

"Mom!"

No. Not Mom; not anymore. Vacant eyes disregarded the girl struggling to her feet in the snow, focused on the path ahead. The truck lumbered down the long drive to the open road, the slight man sat in the passenger's seat, barking orders to a woman who used to be Kristi's mom.

No. No!

Kristi stumbled away from the house, from the smoke churning through the broken windows, one side of her baking, the other freezing, her temples pounded.

It was a battle to get her boots on, an excruciatingly long journey back to the snowmobile, and once she was there, another major effort just to turn the key. The snowmobile lurched beneath her, almost left her. Kristi found her balance, picked up speed, braced by the frigid wind in her face.

She held a bottle to her lips; the contents thick but not solid.

It can't freeze. What does that tell you, Kristi? The phrase, *not for internal use,* came to mind. *You're drinking the same crap he threw at you.*

No…not exactly - a mix of that poison with every other drug they were making. *You're drinking a whole damn cocktail of crap.*

But you need it now.

The raw pain in her throat, snaked its way through all of her the plumbing, brought tears to her eyes.

She throttled up, lurched sideways and nearly wiped out. She corrected, eased it down; went full throttle again.

Now you've got it. Now you're moving!

The main road bowed out and away from the Morgan property, followed the cliffs from here all the way down to Cedar. Kristi cut through the forest. Trees swam by, then slowed, parted, that sense of a clear path opening before her once again. Then it all stretched away from her again, shrank quickly back. She teetered on the snowmobile.

Come on, come on!

Mom. Mom are you there at all?

No answer.

A flash of heat in her skull. It was awful, so painful her vision doubled, she fought to keep her bearings, keep powering forward.

Mom!

A vision: *The man waving his arms, smiling as he broke from the forest.*

"I can help you! I am here to help you."

Mom's hands checking the door locks. Relief mixed with a new apprehension. She didn't trust him. Where had he come from?

Silver-eyed shadows, wolves, slipping from the forest behind the man.

Mom unlocking the door.

No! No, Mom!

It's too late, he's inside. Wolves snarling, leaping at the window. The man has a gun.

Darkness and pain.

Men dressed like soldiers. American soldiers. Children blown to bits. Prisoners, naked, humiliated. The American flag burning.

Talk of brave freedom fighters. So many brave freedom fighters.

Darkness and pain.

The president of the United States, "There is no terrorist threat...ISIS is the JV team."

An American diplomat, head swathed in a scarf, grinning like a happy child, as she meets with the Syrian president.

Friends...yes, we can all be friends.

"There is no terrorist threat."

There are no Islamic extremists.

"...the JV team."

"We are not at war with Islam."

We are your friends.

We are here to help you.

We are here to help you.

But the pain. The fire under her skin, in her head.

Modifications. Making modifications.

Why is there fire?

There is fire so we can cool you. We can make you feel cool and
refreshed.

We are here to help you.

Sadness...and then *nothing.* The connection was gone.

The path before her was wide open all the way to the far wall of the canyon. Kristi was firmly in control.

The black Denali passed beyond the trees much faster than it should.

Mom. Slow down. Fight them. Please slow down.

Nothing.

Mom, I know you're there. Talk to me.

Nothing.

A snowy break between two trees. Kristi tucked down behind the cowl and floored it.

The skids hit pure ice as she bounced onto the road just behind the Denali, sliding all the way across. A thunderous crack as the roadside gave way; a ledge of ice and snow dropping away.

Jump!

Instead, she poured it on, the treads bit, whipping her back onto the solid road. Snow and ice thundered into the canyon below.

The Denali swung into a curve and the passenger door opened. Kristi steered away, pulled to her mother's side. Muzzle flashes lit the cab. The burping blasts of an Uzi.

The Denali sped away and the man nearly fell out trying to line up another shot. The big car slid.

Her mom corrected, pulled it back online then sped up again.

Mom! Slow down!

Tears of frustration broke. If she hit the Denali's tires at this speed her Mom was dead.

The distance between the snowmobile and the car was growing. The little man with his little gun had finished his James Bond moment, pulling himself safely back inside the cab now as the road straightened before the next big turn.

Kristi expected him to break out the back window for a clear shot at her like they did in the movies. He didn't do it.

He doesn't want the car marked. He doesn't want the attention once they hit the main road.

Getting away.

Kristi stopped fast. She cradled the Uzi against the snowmobile's cowl and took a bead on the passenger side taillights.

"I love you, Mom."

She squeezed off a long burst, plastic and glass exploded from the car. She continued firing up the hatch until her barrel touched dark gray sky.

The Denali moved on, dark glass littering the snow behind it. The right taillight was completely gone – so was a major part of the back hatch.

I think you'll get noticed now, asshole.

The passenger side door popped open again. Kristi throttled up, swung quickly across the road to the forest.

The Denali turned into the first long curve of the switchbacks, when it came back into view, she saw the man lean out. His torso dropped to the running board, he hung there like a rag doll from his shoulder harness. Then the snow caught his dragging hands and yanked him out. The last Kristi saw of him was his head being pounded deep into the icy road by one of the Denali's back tires.

The car disappeared behind the mountain.

-=.-=.-=.-=.-=.-=.-=.-=.-

Billy saw two men in the forest armed with automatic weapons. There were likely more out there.

The household arsenal consisted of two AK-47s, two 30-bullet clips, a .22 rifle, and an air pistol with all the pellets you could ever ask for. Available transportation: two Ski Doos, one working Ski Bike to carry them five miles through gunfire and blizzard conditions to Cedar.

They'd been able to raise Ken Carroll to the level of his studio console on a bed of cushions, and blankets. Trying to move him out of here at this point would kill him outright.

Billy scanned the forest through the clouded eyes of the security cameras like a submarine captain tracking the inevitable approach of destroyers through a faulty periscope. A submariner with no torpedoes waiting for a hail of depth charges.

The Ski Doos were gassed up and ready. All they had to do now was roll that garage door up and pray their ski-jackets and woolens were bulletproof. The D-Day scene from the movie, *Saving Private Ryan,* came to mind; the landing craft ratcheting open to machine guns and artillery; the trapped soldiers raked with gunfire, exploding like fish in a barrel.

It hadn't taken long to get to the real story behind the attack that had left one man dead and another dying here. A boy Reed's age couldn't keep a story like that inside. If they lived, Billy supposed he and the law would have to deal with it at some point. With what they were up against, it probably wouldn't matter in the long run.

"Maybe they don't know he came here," Reed offered, hopefully. "Maybe they're just looking for him."

"I wouldn't count on it. They have a good trail to follow."

"What are they waiting for?"

"They're looking for the easiest way to take us out. Soon as they've got that figured they'll move fast. They don't want to be out in that storm long."

"Maybe we should just floor it out of here on the snow cycles before they're ready. Surprise them."

"Son, that's not exactly a surprise. By the time that door cranks open high enough to get those bikes through there'll be so many bullets in the air you'll think you swatted a hornet's nest."

"We can't just wait here."

"Sure we can."

"What if they're planning something big, like *911*? What if they do that and we're just sitting here?"

"Can't do anything if we're dead. Right now we're safe and warm with food in our bellies and they're freezing to death. The colder they get, the better even a stupid idea's going to sound brilliant to them."

"You're waiting for them to do something stupid?"

"I'm counting on it."

Malana sat next to the bikes with her eyes closed tight, not sleeping but praying, Billy knew.

Billy looked from foggy view to foggy view. Something glinted in the dying sunlight.

"Can you zoom that camera?"

Reed spun the mouse wheel. The dark shapes grew.

"That look like a pair of binoculars to you?"

Reed spun the tracking wheel, squinting at one more dark shape amongst many other dark shapes. It could be – yes.

"What's he looking at? What's over that way?"

"The satellite dish - a big oak tree close to it. I was going to climb up to it myself before you came."

"Give us a view."

Reed switched to the roof camera – only to see another man drop from a branch to the roof. He fell to his knees on the slippery tile, inched himself toward the chimney.

The man pulled himself to his feet.

Reed found the shaker control and hit it. Locked! The control had been overridden.

"He's got a bomb!"

"Voice control. Roof clear."

The woman's voice, "Fault."

A soft purring began overhead. The camera showed a thin layer of snow sheeting off the roof. The man's legs flew out with the snow; his chin cracked hard against the brickwork chimney before he dropped out of view.

A loud thump outside the mudroom door.

"Dad! Dad got him!"

But Billy had already shouldered his way out the door, yanking the man down into the ice pit at their entrance. A whine of bullets flying through the air, and the eave shattered over his head. Billy wrested the gun and the tangled backpack from the man's shoulders – he swung the pack out into the night and fell back into the house with a brand new Uzi.

The entry camera showed the bloodied man rising slowly to his knees. He pulled a handgun from his jacket. Beneath the floor, pipes rattled and hammered, a geyser of water and ice knocked the man to the ice, soaking him. He shrieked.

Billy dropped next to Reed in the garage. Bullets ripped through the walls.

"Where are they now?"

"Same place – just standing and shooting."

"Just the two?"

"Yeah."

Bullets plinked through the garage door, shattering bottles, throwing cans off the shelves high above them.

Billy had never held an Uzi before, let alone fired one. His injured left hand ached almost as badly as his leg. He wasn't sure he could fire it if he had to.

"They say they hate Jews; I guess they don't mind using their guns."

"I can work that," Reed said. "First person shooter games…" he added.

Billy handed it over. When he and his buddies played army as a kid, sticks stood in for rifles. The world had changed.

"There a way out near that tree?"

"Yeah, the window in my parent's bathroom. The shutter's locked down, but there's a voice override."

A single gunshot rang in the enclosed space just outside the mudroom door. The sound rang in their ears like a hammer strike. Malana wrapped her arms over her head and screamed.

Billy checked the laptop display, "Our frozen bomber just went to collect his virgins."

Reed dashed out the front door. He returned with a 9MM Glock, two boxes of bullets and another clip for the Uzi. He handed the Glock to Billy.

"This is just like the video games," he said.

"No it isn't. You only get one chance here," Billy said checking the monitor, "One of them is on the move." He checked the action on the Glock. "We'll send out a decoy. Give me thirty seconds to get upstairs, then tape down the throttle on one of those snow bikes, crank that door open and let it fly empty."

God help us.

Billy mounted the stairway bent as close to the ground as possible as bullets randomly peppered the nearby walls. One whined through the drywall just over his head. A frame crashed to the floor; a Carroll family portrait; bullet hole dead center.

He hazarded a quick look into the studio. Ken had dropped back onto the cushions, mouth open, lifeless eyes staring blankly at the ceiling.

Looking straight into our future.

No time to close those eyes.

Billy opened the shutters onto the same frigid nightmare that had nearly killed him today. His entire body withdrew from it, went nearly rigid. He forced himself outside, dropping the short distance to the snow. Ice crystals slapping his face in the wind. Those men were insane to be out there, but that was what all of this was about wasn't it? *Insanity.*

He pressed himself low against the wall, then dropped behind the tree. From here he could see one of the men crawling toward the house; the other man visible only from muzzle flashes as he covered him. Only a few yards from the crawling man, two dark ribbons in the snow - *the shoulder straps from the backpack.*

Going for the bomb? Oh you are one dumb son of a bitch.

Billy gripped the pistol with both hands, picking his target, steeling himself against the frigid, buffeting wind.

There was an ugly metallic squeal over the wind, and then the growl of an engine. Billy waited as the bike lunged through.

The man with the assault rifle rose to his knees as the bike roared into the night – but gunfire from the garage sent him diving back to the snow before Billy could pull off a shot.

Damn it! Pinning him down was the last thing he wanted Reed to do.

Billy took a bead on the crawling man, then to the package in the snow just beyond his reach. He squeezed off a shot as the wind gusted, snow kicked up five feet past the man.

Ice and wood chips clipped him. Billy held firm, and squeezed off two more shots; one hit home.

The blast sent a column of flame into the air that took the man with it. He soared into a nearby tree like the Human

Torch and fell to the snow below. The tree exploded in flame.

The shooter bolted and Billy fired twice more before the man disappeared down the hill. Billy threw himself forward, forced himself through the snow, lungs and throat burning from the effort, from the frigid air they were pulling in. The Torch stumbled to his knees shrieking like a Banshee, he slammed into another tree and that one went up to.

Reed and Malana rode off into the darkness past the flames.

Out of site at the bottom of the hill, another engine started up.

God damn it! Had he missed with both shots?

His skin baked from the conflagration before him. The stench of fuel and the cloying scent of burnt hair and flesh heavy in his nostrils.

He'd seen a plane crash victim who'd looked as bad as the charred man in the snow. But that man had died instantly. This one should have.

One side of his face had melted away to the bone, his throat was open down to the shiny grill of his trachea, yet he was still breathing, still alive. One eye fluttered, staring up at Billy.

There was only one humane thing to do. Billy took a bead on the man's forehead.

"F-fuck America," the man spat, his voice like wet gravel.

"Then you have yourself a nice day."

Billy shoved the gun in his jacket, and dropped down the hill to the man's waiting snowmobile.

"Fucker of mothers, don't leave me like this!"

Billy throttled up the bike as cinders swirled around him, drilling fiery holes through his jacket. He set off down the shooter's trail, praying to God he wasn't too late.

-=-=-=-=-=-=-=-=-

Each bounce of the snowmobile was a knife stab to Reed's wounded arm as he sped through the dark forest.

Flare-ups from the fire threw shadows, created false dips and hills in the flats. He steered one-armed, over-steered and teetered. With each rise frigid wind and snow blasted them sideways. Malana's added weight dug the back treads in fine, but that lifted the skids. The bike turned on a thought.

Slow down.

Each time he let up on the throttle the roar behind him closed more distance. The gunman chasing them had less weight, better balance, and a packed trail to follow.

No, he couldn't slow down. Not now.

Malana screamed.

The buck crashed through the branches across their trail like an oncoming train. Silver eyes glowed, nostrils flaring as it leapt, Reed barely had time to cover his face.

The skids wrenched sideways, they flipped and rolled. Branches clubbed him, his arm collapsed and white-hot pain split his shoulder.

Beneath him, the forest floor dropped away with a rush of powder. The bike spun away into nothing.

-=.-=.-=.-=.-=.-=.-=.-=.-=.

Billy Hicks throttled down, listened. The wind was playing tricks. It was at his back now, its howl the only sound he heard.

Where did they go?

He hit the gas turned back to the cover of trees just as the burp of machine gun sounded. A fire started under his collarbone, fanned quickly to his back.

You stupid old man!

He fell beneath a group of trees pressed tight as old friends against the snow, and dragged himself behind their snow-covered branches.

He could feel his warmth, his life's blood, draining away. His body tried hard to hold that blood in, painfully hugged each drop one last time before it left him. He gripped the gun with hands that no longer seemed keen on taking orders from an old fool like him and watched for the next flash in the darkness, certain it would be the last thing he'd ever see.

-=-.=-.=-.=-.=-.=-.=-.=-.=-

Smoke swirled from the trees ahead of her. She was too late.

But their house was standing, Kristi could see that much as she sped over the hilly, snow-covered meadow of their backyard. Snowmobile tracks everywhere – two had come from the Morgan house. Two more trails from the garage back into the forest. The rolling door was wide open to the storm, the snow already claiming the inside of their garage.

Her father was in that cold, dark house.

Not your father, his body. There's no one alive inside.

Beneath the trees where a steaming battle of the elements still waged on, a man lay in the snow

Not one of yours.

Still, she wasn't prepared for the sight of the hideous burnt thing half-buried in snow and ice.

God!

She throttled quickly away from it, as if speed would leave the image behind her. But it wouldn't. She would always see it.

But you will see worse.

Yes.

Kristi whipped the snowmobile around to follow the tracks from the garage. One Ski Doo had made a shallow, slowly curving trail into the forest. *He sent one out empty. A diversion.* The other's treads had bit deep, changed direction sharply, with purpose.

Kristi throttled up and followed that trail. Reed had made it out on one of the snow cycles. But out to what?

-=-=-=-=-=-=-=-=-

Billy heard it now, the rumble of an engine carried along the wind somewhere behind him; his addled old head, his old ears, really playing tricks on him now.

That's okay. I've got you covered wherever you are. You just come close. Give me one clear shot.

He cradled the gun in his bloody hands.

One shot.

The roar was louder now. The terrorist was coming straight for him, no matter what the wind said.

One shot.

Shadows shifted. His eyes clouded. A form appeared. He nearly took the shot.

Not a snowmobile. Not a man either. *Something.*

Silver stars twinkled in the shadows.   Billy's weak heart beat faster.

Wolves.

And they smell blood.

They fanned out around him now, surrounded him.

The engine sound was practically on top of them all now.

You have to hear that. Run away.

The snowmobile passed behind a group of trees to Billy's right. The engine cut. He followed the sound with the gun as the snowmobile slid into the clearing below him. A *Search and Rescue* snowmobile, but it wasn't one of the terrorists driving, it was the Carroll girl.

"*Wuh…*"

His dry throat and tongue couldn't form the warning he tried to shout, less a cry than a dry rattle that went nowhere in the snow and wind.

She cocked her head, and looked straight to his hiding place.

"Wolves!" he croaked.

I know. Hide the gun or die.

Where had that come from? Slowly, he slid the Glock back into the folds of his jacket.

She throttled up the snowmobile and powered up the hill to him, unafraid of the gray shadows in the forest.

The shadows vaporized. Maybe they were never there.

Yes, he was old. Yes he was addled and crazy. But he was glad as hell to see Kristi Carroll.

Until she came close, until he saw the skull her face had become, the fiery eyes that burned inside. Those eyes were hungry and too bright by half. She had an Uzi strapped to her shoulder and she was high as a kite.

But she was all he had; if he could just get the words out.

"Terrorist is tracking your brother."

"I'll find him. My Mom…my Mom's one of them now. She's driving down the mountain in our car. *She's driving a bomb.*"

"The radio on the Search and Rescue bike. We'll call it in."

"It doesn't work. Nothing does. They've shut it all down. *We're all there is.*"

She yanked her skis from the Search and Rescue snowmobile. Moving, it seemed to Billy, at light speed. His pain was receding; his vision blurred and this time it didn't come back right away. It was if the whole world was ebbing away, and maybe it didn't matter anymore.

He stumbled toward the tipped snow cycle he'd come on, but Kristi had other plans. She stomped her boots firmly into the bindings.

"Take the Search and Rescue. If the radio clears use it. She's in a black Yukon Denali. You have to kill her. I couldn't do it."

He barely felt the grips in his hands. Barely feeling anything, now. His right arm was nearly useless. Running out of moving parts. But he had to keep going.

"How many with her?"

"She's alone. There was one, I killed him. I shot out the right taillight and the back window. If she makes it to the highway she'll be easy to spot."

The skeleton that had been an Olympic hopeful pushed off down the hill. In a blink, she was gone.

Billy aimed the snowmobile for the road, rolling in its hull like a big dead tuna.

What had he just seen and heard? *You have to kill her. I couldn't do it.* She was upset that she couldn't complete that last little part of her chore. Killing her mother.

What are we raising? What are we teaching our kids?

We got cocky and left the gates open. We let the wolves in and wolves are what we're leaving behind.

Move! The Carroll woman had too much of a head start. He'd never catch her with the snowmobile.

But Mary Ann could catch her. If Billy's heart beat long enough to get her into the air, Mary Ann could.

-=-=-=-=-=-=-=-=-=-

Wake up, DeerSlayr. It's time to spawn back to life.

Ice water. Drip, drip, dripping. A far off howl.

Open your eyes, and choose your weapon.

Open your eyes and drink deep of The Pyrian Spring.

Reed's eyelids fluttered. *So cold.* He floated above the world.

No he wasn't floating, he was suspended, hanging over the creek. A burst of wind gave the treetop a little shove. That shove found its creaking way down the trunk, little more than a nudge by the time it found his level, a nudge that lifted him higher for a moment, dragging his boots behind him through the snow. His boots struck a small boulder that gave just a little and slid forward.

His jacket wrapped him like a baby in swaddling, pinning his arms and leaving his face to the cold needles, whip-like branches, and an icy rain. The branches swayed, taking Reed with them, the boulder moved again.

So tired. Go back to sleep.

A hand dangled in front of his face; it wore his glove. *My hand.*

But it was wrong, not where it should be and twisted in the wrong direction. He commanded it to do something. *Clench hand.*

It did nothing.

Maybe he needed to type in the command.

Ice water dripping onto his neck, running down his face.

He couldn't stop it.

He was awake. He wasn't dreaming this.

Malana.

The trees hadn't snatched her from the air. She had flown all the way through. She lay face up beside the frozen creek, motionless.

All my fault. I did this.

A man walked along the bank. He kicked Malana's limp body.

A cough, a moan. *She was alive.*

The man gazed into the trees, shielding his face from the sleet with his forearm. He smiled when he saw Reed.

"Hello, my friend!"

He stepped onto the ice behind Malana and drew his foot back, lining up her head like a soccer ball. Reed's entire body tightened painfully.

The man stopped his kick short, enjoying Reed's reaction.

"You are a lucky boy." He called up to him. "A very lucky infidel boy. Before you die you will bear witness to a Holy event, the birth of the new Caliphate. A great, great honor for someone so unclean and unworthy."

He knelt beside Malana.

"Is she clean and worthy, my friend?"

The man withdrew a long curved knife from his jacket.

The branches shook around Reed, signals firing inside him without direction or purpose, only his legs able to respond. He managed to push himself forward, but the branches pushed him back. The boulder shifted.

The man crouched, lifted her head, and exposed her throat. She moaned in pain. He touched the cold blade to her throat.

"Witness the power of Allah."

"Freeze asshole!"

Reed was only sorry he couldn't turn his head, that he couldn't see his sister, her cold, dead aim on the man below.

"Before your bullets strike me, her throat will open. I am prepared to meet the Almighty One. Are you prepared to choose her moment of death?"

The man smiled up at her.

"Shall I let you decide?"

Reed hooked the boulder with his boot. He clenched his stomach, crunched in with all his might. The boulder slid, and then it was gone.

He heard it crack against other boulders beneath it like a solid billiards break; those rocks struck others and then a cascade of them spun out over the creek. By the time the man had thrown his forearm to his face the ice beneath him snapped like a string of firecrackers.

The man was up to his neck in the frigid slush, head bobbing as he fought a current intent on pulling him under thicker ice downstream.

The man let out a scream louder and more brittle than the snapping ice. Something dark swept toward him beneath the surface.

Reed saw the silvery flash its huge eye, as it rolled over, taking the man's screams with it beneath the ice.

"Say hello to my little friend..." Reed whispered.

Chapter 18

"I can't go back in there."

"It's our house."

She'd stayed inside just long enough to cover her father with a blanket, to cry, but it wasn't her house, not anymore.

"We'll freeze out here."

"It's yours. I can't go back in there."

Reed couldn't fight her, couldn't reason with her. Popping his dislocated shoulder back in place had been the most excruciating, exhausting act in his life - much worse than being shot. And Kristi had done even that, stretched his stricken arm out like a wad of taffy and dropped it like an easy eight ball in the corner. No big deal for Kristi. If it had been left to Reed, he'd have just as soon died.

But Malana had clearly gotten the worst of it. Broken leg, broken wrist, her cheekbone was shattered, it had swelled to the size of a grapefruit. They'd carried her into the house, made her as comfortable as they could, but she would need medical attention soon, and lots of it.

As soon as the phones were back, they'd get help. *As soon as the world was normal.*

Normal.

Their father's body lay in that house.

No, nothing would ever be normal again.

The sky was finally resting. No snow, no freezing rain.

"We need to go up the hill."

.=.=.=.=.=.=.=.=.

They drove full throttle up the mountain toward their favorite viewpoint, where the glow of Portland city life provided a sense of calm and familiarity in a strange place, the sense that civilization as they knew it, was not so far away.

But the clouds lit up, and thunder rolled.

Great, all they needed was another storm.

An uneasy sense of weightlessness.

A white line broke from the flats ahead, a bar of snow, no - *a rolling white wave of snow.*

"AVALANCHE!"

Treetops, swayed, slapped high-fives over their heads. Trunks snapped with the force of canon fire, sent broken limbs whickering into the night. A storm of snow and debris.

The bikes lifted and dropped beneath them in the tide; tossed them from their mounts. The twins tumbled and rolled as the wave swept on, louder, more powerful the farther it traveled, picking up snow, picking up trees, *picking up speed.*

They pulled themselves from the snow without words.

And still it rumbled on, building as it went.

They drove on through a new landscape, an eerie glow lighting their way as if the moon had somehow risen beneath the clouds, the remaining trees still swaying, the "clack-clack" of branches sounding a jungle war beat. The shattered trunks of the others pointed accusingly to the skies.

By the time they reached their vantage point, the snow was falling again. Reed brushed it from his jacket.

Kristi dropped to her knees in the snow beside him, her hands clasped to her face.

The flakes smeared beneath Reed's fingers, a sickly sweet odor rising from them.

Far down the gorge, a reddish shaft of steam and smoke, the new glow of Portland. *Where Portland had been.*

"It's not snow. *It's ashes.*"

She nodded.

"He couldn't stop Mom."

"She couldn't have made it to Portland this fast. There must have been another terror cell, maybe a lot of others."

The thick blanket of snow over the ground had already grown dingy and gray, the cloying odor unbearable. They pulled their sweats up beneath their visors.

"They'll come to help us," Reed said, his voice gravelly, throat raw from the smothering ash. "The *Feds* will come in and get us. They'll come in with helicopters and food and stuff. You'll see."

The woman who faced him was a total stranger, her visor smeared with ashes, the eyes behind them silver in the false moonlight.

"No one's coming."

"They'll take us somewhere." Reed could barely speak, barely swallow, his tongue was dry and swollen. He choked, "The Feds will come."

Kristi shook her head.

"We *are* the Feds."

THE END

Titles by Steve Zell

Running Cold by Steve Zell
Pub: Tales From Zell, Inc. ™

An ancient gift turns deadly in the hands of a young boy. It's
the mid-1960s, and Brit Helm, mourning the recent loss of
her husband and eldest son, struggles to make a new life with
her youngest boy, Michael, in a southern California beach
town. But lingering suspicions about the horrific "accident"
that took her eldest begin to rise, and soon Brit realizes she
must control Michael's anger at all costs. A pretty surfer
threatens to break her tenuous hold...

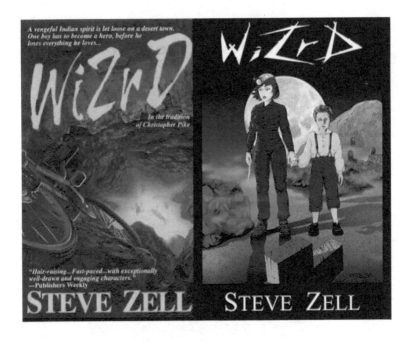

WiZrD by Steve Zell
Pub: Macmillan, St. Martin's Press, Hodder|Headline

Caught in a centuries-old cycle of boom and bust, the
northern Arizona ghost town, Pinon Rim, is booming once
more, but ominous signs are beginning to emerge. It's up to
newcomer Bryce Willems and his stepsister Megan to end
that lethal cycle…or not.

LIMIT
STEVE ZELL
They are already inside...

Urban Limit by Steve Zell
Pub: Tales From Zell, Inc. ™

Members of an Oregon family move to the mountains hoping to escape city life, only to find themselves fighting for their own lives and, possibly, for civilization itself.

Twins Kristi and Reed Carroll could not be more different. While Kristi trains for her shot at Olympic glory in the winter games, Reed spends his days in the cyber world of video games. But something sinister has found its way into both worlds that will soon bring them together, or tear them apart forever.

About the Author:

Steve Zell is a former animator and digital animation tools instructor for the Los Angeles area feature film animation and effects studios, and a session vocalist. While at the University of Arizona, he developed a love for sabre and foil fencing, which he studied along with Studio Art and Chemistry, eventually becoming UA's first interdisciplinary studies graduate. Recently retired from a fifteen-year stint with an international microprocessor manufacturer, Steve now lives with his wife, Nina, and daughter, Victoria, in Portland, Oregon.

Please visit: www.talesfromzell.com

Made in United States
Troutdale, OR
12/17/2024

26748727R00229